All the Lies
We Tell:
Heaven and Hell Series
Book 2

All the Lies We Tell:

Heaven and Hell Series

Book 2

M. Skye

www.urbanbooks.net

Urban Books, LLC
300 Farmingdale Road, NY-Route 109
Farmingdale, NY 11735

All the Lies We Tell: Heaven and Hell Series Book 2

ISBN 13: 978-1-64556-047-0
ISBN 10: 1-64556-047-3

First Mass Market Printing May 2020
First Trade Paperback Printing January 2019
Printed in the United States of America

10 9 8 7 6 5 4 3 2 1

This is a work of fiction. Any references or similarities to actual events, real people, living or dead, or to real locales are intended to give the novel a sense of reality. Any similarity in other names, characters, places, and incidents is entirely coincidental.

Distributed by Kensington Publishing Corp.
Submit Orders to:
Customer Service
400 Hahn Road
Westminster, MD 21157-4627
Phone: 1-800-733-3000
Fax: 1-800-659-2436

All the Lies

We Tell:

Heaven and Hell Series

Book 2

M. Skye

Chapter One

"Come on, babe," Mia called out from the back door of their home. When she got no response, she called out again. "Tyree Johnston, I know you hear me."

Looking up from his basketball game with Kyan, Tyree gave her a smile, and a blush appeared on her flawless cheeks. They had been trying for another baby, and it was time for another round. They had been at it for over six months, and it was getting frustrating, but he still loved when she called out for him to try. It was the fun they had trying that kept him sane.

Tyree had made good on his promise and bought a new house for them three years prior and finally convinced her to marry him again a year later. After two years apart, their reunion had been solidified. They had been surprisingly happy, being remarried after a tumultuous divorce and two-year separation. The only thing that would make matters better would be if

Tyree and Mia could have the baby they both craved. His father, John, and their biggest obstacle, his ex-fiancé, Renee, were both dead, and the only threat to their happiness was Mia's psychotic father, Richmond. He'd been dodging the authorities for three years.

While Mia and Tyree gazed at each other, Tyree broke his gaze in time to see Kyan roll his eyes. Their game was a thing of the past. "Mama, can I go to Aunt Asha's?" Kyan asked.

Mia nodded and answered Kyan. "Yeah, baby. Get your stuff and Dad will take you over."

"Mama," he hissed, "I'm not a baby. I'm ten years old. I can get the car to take me."

Mia opened her mouth to respond but was cut off by Tyree's angry voice. "First of all, don't roll your eyes at your mother. Secondly, you don't give orders to our driver. We do. I will let Abel know to drive you over, but you better apologize to your mother first."

Kyan looked at Mia and rushed into her arms. "I'm sorry, Mama."

"It's okay, baby. I just forget you're so grown up now. I just love you so much."

"I love you too, Mama." He turned to look at Tyree. "You too, Dad. I'm sorry I forgot what you said."

"It's okay, son, as long as you never forget again."

"I won't." He ran into the house.

Once Kyan was gone, Mia turned to Tyree and crossed her arms over her chest. "What was it that he forgot?"

"That no matter how old he gets he is still your baby, and even if he doesn't like to hear it, he is to suck it up because you do so much for him. He can at least give you that."

"Thank you, husband, but I'm never going to get used to this." She leaned her head on his shoulder.

"Get used to what?"

"Him wanting to do things without me. He used to always invite me wherever he went."

"Mia, he is ten now. You have to let go sometime. There are going to be things he wants to do with just the kids, and now that Terence and Asha have Jonathan, he is going to want to spend time there. He loves his little cousin." Tyree kissed her forehead.

"That's why we need a new baby." She smirked. "We need a new baby to get our old baby back." She laughed as they turned to walk inside the house, but he saw through the fake smile. Mia always put on a brave face, but Tyree knew she was sad because of their baby troubles. Asha and Terence had a child two years ago without even trying, and Tyree and Mia loved him, but Mia said it sometimes made her feel like she was failing him, failing them. He assured her she was wrong, but he knew it still got to her.

While Tyree sat contemplating their situation, Mia sent Kyan off with Abel, leaving them all alone in their home. He had kicked back on the couch when she entered the house.

"Well, Mrs. Johnston, what shall we do now that we have the house to ourselves?" He pulled her into his lap as she approached him in the house.

"Well, I thought maybe we could play a little game." She began to unbutton his shirt.

"That sounds interesting. What kind of game?" He pulled her into a kiss, momentarily stopping her response. For a few moments, he felt her succumb to his zealous kisses and thought he had it made until she pulled away.

"I have to get up from here." She attempted to move from his lap.

"Kitten, I want you now." He was urgent in his request.

"Be patient, and you will have me and so much more." She pried herself from his lap and retreated to the stairs.

"This woman is going to be the death of me," he hissed as she made her way to her destination. He took off toward the stairs, following the scent of her perfume. They had been doing these little song-and-dance routines to keep everything interesting between them. Mia was so good at these games that it made him more aroused than he had ever been. He was grateful for that.

"Johnston, you get up these stairs right this moment," Mia yelled down from the bathroom.

"What are you up to, kitten? You told me to wait downstairs." Tyree began to undress on his way to the bathroom. As he approached the door, he heard the water running in the shower and got excited.

"Tyree, I'm getting cold in here all by myself," she pouted as he sat outside to savor the sight of the candlelight flickering off her naked body.

"I'm right here." He saw that he startled her when she jumped. "So what's the game?"

"The object of the game was to see how long it would take for me to get you naked, and from the looks of it, you caught on very quickly." She walked over and ran her fingers down his chest. Feeling her fingers on his skin excited him. He took her into his arms, began to plant kisses all over her neck, and worked his way down to her shoulders until she halted him.

"Not so fast, mister. You're still a little over-dressed for this game. Now, all we need to do is lose these." She ripped his boxers down to his ankles in one swift motion.

"I like it when you take charge."

"You haven't seen anything yet." She pulled him into the shower with her. Once inside, she pressed her body against his and reached her hand down to claim her prize. She took him in her hands and began to massage him. He moaned into the steamy shower as she squeezed gently.

When he began to squirm under her touch, she bent down, teasing him with her tongue. First, she just licked the tip, and then she proceeded to take him in and out of her mouth. As she slowly moved her head back and forth, his moans intensified. She listened to the sheer pleasure she was inflicting on him. Tyree was amazed when she began to move faster and reached to grab him from behind to take more of him into her eager mouth.

"Oh, God, Mia," he screamed out as he began to reach a state of euphoria. As much as he loved what she was doing to him, he had to have her, all of her. "Baby, come up here." He grabbed her arm and pulled her to him. "I love you." He pulled her into a scorching kiss before dropping to the floor of the shower. Once on the floor, he slid her back against the shower wall and pulled her legs over his shoulders.

He pulled her warm center to his mouth, and with just a few flicks, he felt her moisture on his tongue. "Kitten, you taste so good." He plunged his tongue deep inside her.

Her body began to shake, and he knew she was excited. Her uncontrollable movements forced him to speed up his pace and dive deeper with each flick. "Tyree, I want you. I need you now," she said breathlessly after a few minutes of sweet torture. He continued his flicks, and she jerked.

Her words brought a huge grin to Tyree's face as he moved her legs aside to stand. He slid her back against the shower wall and molded into her slippery body. When he began to plant kisses all down her neck, she jumped up and wrapped her legs around his waist.

"Now, Tyree." She held a penetrating look in her eyes.

As much as he wanted to draw out this heated experience with his wife, he could never deny her anything, especially under the circumstances. Slowly sliding her backward, he positioned himself to enter her. "I love you. I love you. I love you," Mia chanted as he introduced himself to her warm center. It was all he could do not to lose control when she locked her legs tighter around his waist and took him deeper inside her. Feeling her so close to him ignited a fire within his body that caused him to thrust faster and harder.

I love this woman, he thought as he moved fiercely within her slippery walls, pinning her body between him and the shower wall. The warm shower water that descended upon their bodies only heightened the sexual experience as he rammed her so hard he felt like he could break her. Pushing himself further and further, he drowned her in his intense feelings, pouring himself into her completely. While he continued, her screams soon began to float through the whole house, signaling that she was near her breaking point. As pleased as she was with their lovemaking, he was just as thrilled as he fought his climax, wishing this experience would last forever. He slowed his pace to gather himself, but the feel of her was just too much. He still found himself buried inside her to the hilt. He realized then, no matter what the pace was, he was cumming soon. Nothing could curb the storm brewing within him.

Her body was sliding up and down the shower wall with each deep thrust. When she began to move her hips to match his rhythm, he exploded with a passion that forced several hard thrusts that sent her body into two of the most intense orgasms he had ever seen her experience. The first one came hard and fast, but the second one left her speechless with her body jerking and a look of sheer pleasure on her face. As her body spasmed against his, he finally lost control and filled her with his sticky nectar. After the climax, without disconnecting their bodies, he slid down to the shower floor with her resting on his lap.

"That was some game." Mia leaned in to kiss a very exhausted Tyree.

"Yes, it was, but maybe we should get out of here. The water is cold now." He leaned his head against hers.

"Yes, we should." She stood up from his lap, and he chased her.

"Hey, not so fast." He grabbed a towel to wrap around her. "You let me dry you off, kitten." He rubbed her down, and she ran her hand over his head. After drying her body off, he wrapped a towel around himself and picked her up, walking her out to the room.

"You take such good care of me." She turned to kiss his lips.

"I always will."

As they walked into their bedroom, Tyree noticed that Mia had a single baby shoe sitting on the bed. "What's this about?" He held up the shoe for her to see. When she realized what he was holding she looked surprised, and he flooded her with questions. "Are you . . . are we . . . You're pregnant?" He finally stuttered with excitement in his voice. "How do you feel? Are you okay? Do you need anything?"

"I'm fine, Tyree, calm down." She looked like she was holding back tears.

"I'm sorry I was so rough with you just now in the shower. How is your back?"

Mia seemed so overwhelmed, and Tyree could tell she was trying to hold everything together but failed, falling into a heap on the bed. "I'm all right, and don't ever apologize for giving me such an amazing experience."

Tyree watched her struggle with the tears drenching her cheeks and took a place beside her. "You're not fine. Tell me what's wrong, kitten." He swept the hair from her neck and bent down to kiss it gently, and she shivered. "You can tell me anything."

"We're not pregnant, and we might not ever be. I had some tests run at my last appointment, and they said I have scar tissue that could make it hard if not impossible for us to conceive the natural way again. Even if we were to luck out and get pregnant, my body could reject the pregnancy."

"How long have you known about this?"

"A few days. I was just trying to find the right way to tell you."

"It's okay, baby. We can find other ways, and there are so many options out there. You should have told me as soon as you found out. You shouldn't have had to go through this alone."

"It's my fault. If I hadn't—"

He cut her off. "Stop it. You can't control situations like this, but why torture yourself with the baby things?"

"I was just reminiscing about when Kyan was this little. It was a very good time in our lives."

"It was great." He felt a goofy grin tugging at his lips, and he ran his hand down her cheek. "I loved taking care of our boy when he was that young, but we are happy now too, kitten. I know things aren't going exactly the way we wanted, but we are still very blessed in spite of that."

"Yeah," she sighed. "I just don't want you to miss out on things because you're stuck with me."

"I'm not stuck with you. I chose you. I will always choose you. Without you, none of it matters. Those two years without you were the hardest, and now that I have you back, I just want to focus on what we have. We can't stress about what we don't. It will happen if it's meant to, and if not, we still have an amazing son to give our love to."

"You're right, Ty." She finally smiled, and he kissed her forehead.

"I know I am. Here, lie back and let's get you comfortable. If we're going to get something cooking in there"—he ran his hand over her flat stomach—"we need you completely relaxed."

"You think there is a chance?"

"I know there is," he whispered against her bare back before laying her down face-first on the bed. "You know, you're lucky, kitten. No other woman gets this kind of treatment from me."

"I know how lucky I am. More than you know," she agreed.

Chapter Two

"Whitney is getting married," Rick sighed into the air. It had been a month since Rick found out Whitney and Jude were getting married, and he still couldn't wrap his mind around the fact that his only daughter was going to be someone's wife. He had grown to care for her fiancé over the years and was excited, but he still had the sick feeling he was losing his little girl.

He and Whitney had always been close, and now Jude could be taking her affections away from him. For so long, he had been the only constant man in her life, besides Tyree. She and Tyree were always indescribably connected. Him being married to Rick's sister, her aunt Mia, seemed to be just a formality. He was more like her blood uncle than only being joined by marriage. They had an unbreakable bond.

While things were going well, Rick was happy to be where he was now. With the help of Tyree and Mia, he had taken a step back, and Mia was running most of the Livingston side of the media conglomerate that had merged with Tyree Johnston's hotel conglomerate with the support of their associate, Felipe, in Paris. Rick was only consulted when there was something too big for them to handle or when he was needed to schmooze with some of the clients who dealt more with him.

He and his wife, Cassandra, had been traveling around the world for the last year. He was incredibly grateful to Mia and Tyree for giving them the opportunity to follow a dream they had for a while. Mia and Tyree had become a true power couple and loved the opportunity to spend time together at home and work. It was a win for all parties.

Things were finally looking up, and he was looking forward to the future. His family was stronger than ever, and with his daughter home, he felt like he was able to breathe again after all the murder scandal their father had burdened them with. Richmond Livingston, family murderer or tycoon, had been splattered for the past few years over every news station and magazine they didn't own. With Mia and Tyree taking most of the major responsibility with the company, he felt like a weight was lifted from his shoulders, at least in business.

He looked up to see Cassandra watching him fret before she walked over, placing her hand on his shoulder. "You okay?"

"Yeah, I'm fine," he replied, pulling her hand to his lips, placing a gentle kiss on it. "Just thinking about everything."

"Everything like what?" He saw her looking at the papers on his desk before she swept her hand over her face. "Are you regretting taking a step back? I know running the company with Mia and . . ." She paused, instantly regretting, he knew, what she almost said.

He caressed her hand and looked up, offering her a relaxed smile. "It's okay. We can't tip-toe around the fact that Janelle is dead, and yes, I wanted to run the company with both of my little sisters, but things just changed. My father took Janelle and my mom away from me, but I don't regret what I did. Stepping back was best for us, just as merging the companies was best for everyone else. With me not being able to dedicate my whole heart to it, Mia needed people who could. You know no other family knows more about our business than the Johnstons, and I know they would never let anything happen to Mia."

"That's all true, but do you miss it?"

"I miss it sometimes, but I think I miss Janelle more. It's hard focusing on that place knowing it's the reason she's gone."

"The business isn't the reason. Richmond is."

"Where do you think his greed came from? I almost feel like every dime we make from there is blood money. I just couldn't do what needed to be done. It would be too much for me, but Mia can handle this. She has a heart of gold, and I feel that she is the one who can transform it back into what our grandfather would have wanted it to be."

"Yeah, she and Whitney." Whitney had come home from school and announced that she wanted to work for the company. Rick was opposed to the idea at first, but Mia assured him she and Tyree would look out for her, and he caved. He felt better knowing that she had Jude close, as well. He was going to be working nearby with Tyree's best friend and brother-in-law, Terence, at his law firm.

"Babe, you know I love Whit, but I don't think she is going to be in this for the long haul. I gave her the chance to prove me wrong, but I just have a feeling this isn't for her."

"I'll admit, I was shocked when she announced she wanted to work for the company, but maybe she will surprise us."

The last two and a half years had been a struggle with Whitney. She had taken the situation with Richmond hard. Being home the past six months had done wonders, but her parents were still worried. Mia and Tyree tried to do all they could, and it seemed to be helping. Whitney always responded to whatever Tyree had to say.

Cassandra walked out of the study. Rick was combing over a few papers when Marta, their housekeeper, entered.

"Mr. Livingston, there is a call for you." She handed him the phone.

"Thank you, Marta. I'll take it in the library."

After promptly reaching his chair in the library, Rick pushed the speakerphone button on the receiver. "Hello, this is Rick Livingston."

"Rick, how's the family?" an all-too-familiar voice said into the phone.

"You bastard. You have a lot of nerve calling here." Rick was practically screaming at the speaker.

"I have every right. This is my family too."

"It's been three years. I'd hoped you were smart enough to just disappear. You have no family, and soon you will have no freedom."

"Now, Rick, is that any way to speak to the man who gave you life? Is that any way to talk to your father?"

"My father is dead. Well, at least his heart is."

"My son, I have so much in store for you, your sister, and those brats you let into our company," Richmond said gleefully.

"You listen to me. You are never to come near Mia, or I will kill you."

"No, you listen to me, son. I will do exactly what I set out to do, and there is nothing you can do about it." Richmond laughed and disconnected the call.

Rick may have stood tough on the call, but inside he knew this was all far from over. It was just the beginning. Tomorrow he would have to deal with breaking the news to Tyree and Mia that Richmond Livingston was suddenly back in their lives.

Chapter Three

As daylight broke into the living room, Asha woke up before everyone. Well, almost everyone. She was in the kitchen when she heard Jonathan's booming little voice. "Mommy, I help you?"

"Yes, Mommy's big helper, I would love that." She swung him up to her hip. Asha was close with both of her children, but Jonathan, the youngest, really made her smile.

"Wut you make?" he asked as she sat him on a stool next to the countertop.

"How about pancakes, eggs, and bacon? How does that sound?"

"Gud, Mommy."

"Here, come help me stir." She held the bowl out to him. After getting all the lumps out of the batter, she let him help pour some into the skillet.

"Wow, it make a noise." He looked amazed at the pancakes forming. It took them twenty minutes to get the rest of the food ready, and after everything was prepared, they began to make plates for everyone.

Most of the plates were prepared when the phone began to ring. It only took her a second to realize it was Tyree calling to check on Kyan. They joked a little about his night and spent a few minutes talking about everything until she ultimately invited him and Mia to breakfast, and he accepted.

After concluding the call, Asha went back to setting the table, only to find herself wrapped in Terence's strong embrace. "This smells great." He glanced over her hard work.

"Thank you, honey."

"Who are the two extra plates for?"

"Mia and Tyree are coming by."

"Cool, sounds like a good time."

"Could you get the kids up? I don't want them to come in with all the sleeping bags lying around."

"Yeah, I got it." Terence walked into the living room, and once the children were all up and dressed and the living room was spotless, he sent the children into the kitchen one by one. They all took their seats around the huge table. As they filled in, Asha told them to leave the two end spots open.

They were all around the table laughing when they heard Tyree's voice, calling out from the front door. "We're in here," Asha announced.

"How are you, sweetheart?" Mia took the seat next to Kyan.

"I'm good, Mom. How are you? Did you have a good night?"

"We had a magnificent night."

Kyan chuckled, and Mia drew in a deep breath before brushing the hair back from her face. "I'm glad." Kyan leaned over and kissed her cheek before turning to look at Tyree. "Dad, thank you for making Mama's night fun."

Tyree nodded and placed his hand on Kyan's shoulder. "You know me. I do what I can."

"Well, I don't know about you guys, but I'm starving," Asha said, interrupting the sweet family moment.

"We are too." Mia picked up her fork and began stuffing her mouth. The table overflowed with laughter, watching her devour the food, and as they all began to dig into their plates, and the room fell silent.

Smiles were ever present, and Jonathan was the first to comment on the delicious breakfast. "Tis be good, Mommy. I cook."

"You sure did, sweetie." Asha patted him on the head. He went back to his plate, proud of himself, while she smiled down at her precious little boy.

After they finished up breakfast, Asha sent the kids to the playroom while the adults enjoyed hot tea in the living room. While Terence and Tyree discussed sports, Asha and Mia chatted about the business. In the middle of the conversation, Mia smiled and looked over to Tyree, who was reaching for his ringing cell phone. When he answered, he looked over at her and winked. She blushed, noticing how his eyes traveled up and down her body in lustful gazes. He studied her intently until something on the phone call distracted him. She noticed when his expression turned sour.

"Rick, slow down, what's going on?" Tyree snapped. Rick said something, and Tyree began to speak again. "We're at Terence and Asha's." He paused again and then huffed, "Well, meet us here. We'll wait for you."

Tyree hung up the phone and then turned to face Mia, who had made her way over to him. "That was strange."

"Who was that?" Mia asked after seeing the puzzled look on Tyree's face.

"Rick. He said he needs to talk to all of us."

"What could possibly concern all of us?" Terence asked as they all sat waiting for the urgent news.

The doorbell finally rang, and Rick and Cassandra made their way into the living room with tense looks on their faces.

Mia was the first to speak. "What's wrong?"

"It's Richmond. He contacted me last night." Rick sat down next to her.

Hearing the news, Mia dropped her glass and spilled her drink all over the floor.

Tyree quickly rushed to her side as Rick rubbed her back. "What did he say?"

"Not much, just his usual gloating."

"What does this mean?" Asha asked, looking shocked.

"This means the old bastard is up to his tricks again," Tyree said furiously. "He can try, but we will end him if he returns here. It's time we called and got Rock involved."

Mia smiled half-heartedly and laid her head on Tyree's shoulder.

"Look at me," he said. Tyree held his hand to her chin and forced her to look into his eyes. "I will never let anything happen to you."

Seeing his love and determination made her smile, and she was relieved for the moment.

Shortly afterward, Rick informed them that he alerted everyone from the local police to the FBI. "I have been feeling like something was going to happen for the last few weeks," Tyree admitted.

"Things have been going too well. Something was bound to happen. It is never this perfect for us," Rick sighed.

"What should we do?" Terence asked.

"Whatever we have to do." Rick scanned the room, and Mia smiled as his eyes landed on her. "We are more than capable. If he wants a fight, then he will get one."

Tyree nodded in agreement, and Terence did as well. Without saying a word, they dispersed and went to their separate corners of the room, making the necessary phone calls.

While they were inside trying to figure out a course of action, Richmond sat outside in a black car, watching their house. "Now, how did I know my little Boy Scout was going to run over to their house and tell them all about big, bad Richmond?"

"Maybe you should just stop this whole thing. Calling him was a stupid move. You like to draw too much attention to yourself."

"I will do what I want, Lenae," he barked at the woman who had been his confidant for the past few years. "I've been hiding in plain sight for the past few months, and nothing has happened. Stop your worrying. You just need to focus on your beautiful little girl and how to give her the things she deserves."

"Why now? After all the time we have been eluding the law, what makes now so special?"

"Our little friends overseas are making moves that will shake the Livingston/Johnston empire to its core. I have to stop the destruction. I will get back all that I lost and all that is sure to be lost in the future."

"Not everything," she sighed, looking out the window.

"No, I will never have everything, but this will get me damn close. These kids have no clue what they're up against, but we do."

"We're not here to start a war. Maybe it's time to cut our losses and accept things the way they are. I would love to have the life I once had, but I don't see it as an option. Too much has happened. Besides, you don't have any solid proof that something is coming. We have been in the shadows for too long, and I feel it's no longer worth it."

"This is worth everything," he growled before ordering the driver to flee the scene.

Chapter Four

Whitney held out her left hand, admiring the huge diamond that rested there. She was sitting in her living room when Jude came in, breaking her thoughts with a huge grin on his face. "I take it I did well."

"Huh?"

"Your ring." He pulled her hand up to his lips. "You love it, don't you?"

"Oh, that. Yeah, it's great." She knew her nonchalant answer threw him off as he crossed his arms, observing her.

"Why do you not sound more excited about this? I thought this is what you wanted."

Whitney sighed and moved from her place on the couch to stand in front of the window, gazing out. She hadn't wanted to get into this with him, and she hadn't really thought about what she would say when she had to. All she knew was that the past four years with him had been remarkable, but she wasn't sure they were on a status to be thinking about forever.

The truth was, she wasn't even sure she could be a wife. She had seen in her lifetime so many reasons not to get married. Almost everyone in her family and close circle had problems. Her parents were the only people she knew whose love seemed to outlast everything. Well, theirs and Tyree and Mia's.

Tyree and Mia had their share of problems but never once, even when they were apart, did she doubt the love between them. Even when it wasn't obvious to the delusional two, everyone around them could tell Mia and Tyree were each other's destiny. When given the extra push, they finally found their way back to each other. It was great to Whitney, seeing them together, but just knowing what they went through gave her pause in believing in happy endings.

She was still looking out the window until she felt Jude's strong hands on her shoulders. Turning to look at him, she saw a genuine smile and his dazzling eyes sparkling in the bright room. Jude had dropped the glasses he once wore, electing to have laser surgery on his eyes. He still had his slim figure but was more endowed. His arms had grown in size from working out, his chest was broad, and his stomach was flat with ripples so strong you could bounce quarters off them. He had transformed his image, and everyone noticed, including other women.

Whitney never considered herself the jealous type, but she saw how women looked at Jude and damn if she didn't want to rip them apart. She saw how he brushed them off for her. She could tell in his eyes there were only two women's opinions that meant anything: hers and Mia's.

Jude and Mia had grown close, and even though she loved that her family accepted Jude, she had to admit she was jealous. Not jealous because she thought something was going on between them, but jealous in the sense that Jude seemed to be closer to her aunt than she was. Her whole life, she wanted to be closer to Mia.

When she was younger, and Janelle was around, it was always the two of them, their cousin Milan, and Asha. Now, Milan had moved, and Asha had her own family, and Janelle was dead. Whitney thought it would be the two of them gaining the closeness she always wanted, but Jude seemed to be the one she connected with.

Mia was nice to her, and they always had a blast together, but she also saw how different it was with Jude. It just looked so natural between them, like they had known each other forever.

That was why she valued Tyree so much. With Tyree, she felt free to be herself, and he never judged her for anything she ever told him, which was a lot.

No one in her family ever knew how she felt about her life. She always kept her true feelings suppressed and put on the façade of the perfect daughter and tried her best to please her parents. Only Tyree knew it was all an act and that she secretly felt like she was always the odd man out.

Growing up, Whitney was always sent to the best schools and given the best of everything, but she never felt like she had the loving family they were portrayed to be. She knew her parents cared, she was their pride and joy, but she needed them to actually be there, and they weren't. She was always sent abroad for school and would return on holidays. Every time she returned home, she wished they would let her stay, but it never failed that at the end of every break, she was packed up and shipped back to school.

Never finding the courage to admit her resentment to her parents, she confided in Tyree. She told him all about her feelings of abandonment and how she felt like they didn't really know how to talk to her or be real parents. Tyree always explained that they felt being away from their toxic situation was best for her, but she never let go of the pain. She always carried it around with her.

"Whit." Jude drew her attention away from the window. "What's wrong with you? Why are you so out of it?"

"You know why." She tried to step out of his reach. When she did so, he tightened around her and pulled her lips to his. She attempted to fight her way out, but he only pressed harder, making her cave to his will. Once he released her lips, she stepped back, and he gripped her hand. "That only works during sex." She chuckled.

"Well, we can make that happen, too, but not before you tell me what's on your mind. You got a little weird when I came in."

"I was just thinking, maybe we rushed into this whole thing."

"What whole thing? Getting engaged?"

"Maybe," she admitted, and he ran his hand over his face.

"I don't get it. We live together, we've been together for four years. What did you think was next for us? I needed something more for us."

"Are you sure your need for more isn't because of what happened?"

Jude sank down on the couch, and Whitney knew he was thinking about what she was referring to. A year before they graduated, Whitney had attended a party where things had gotten a little out of hand. She was extremely drunk and did some things she couldn't honestly explain. She tried to block it out, and the next night, she slept with Jude for the first time. They both knew something was off and that if she was truly still a virgin like they thought, the experience would have been different. It was then that Jude assumed she had been sexually assaulted.

After hearing Jude's interpretation of the party, Whitney went off the deep end for a while. Her grades began to slip, and she took up a habit of wild partying that Jude couldn't understand. He stood by her through all the craziness and promised to keep everything a secret. After graduation, they both decided going back to Atlanta was best for the time being. He felt like being close to her family would balance her out, and he was right. Being there had helped, and he thought they should be back to where they were before any of this happened, but in her mind, Whitney knew she was still stuck there.

"Actually, it is the reason I want to move forward. We were on track to getting here before all that, and I felt like we needed to get back. We shouldn't let it shape our future," Jude advised.

"How could it not?" she screamed out in frustration. "You know every time you're with me you think about it. You think about the fact that someone else ruined me. I don't even know who the hell he was."

Jude reached out and pulled her into his lap. "You're not ruined. True, I wanted to be your first, I wanted that for both of us, and we've had that. That other time didn't matter because it wasn't your choice. As far as I'm concerned, I'm the only man you've ever been with, and I want you to think of it that way too."

"How can I? Him touching me will always be in my head. I can't remember the rest, but I will never forget his hands on me."

"Remember this." He captured her lips. "You wouldn't let me tell your family or try to bring the guy up on charges. Hell, you wouldn't even tell me who he was, so forget him and only think of me."

"I try that, but I don't know, maybe I was wrong to just let him go free."

"You give me a name, and I'll do whatever it takes to nail his ass."

"I can't."

"Why are you protecting this guy?" he snapped. "Tell me his name."

"I can't! I don't know it. I couldn't tell you his name then because I didn't know it. He was some guy who gave me a drink. I remember taking a drink and then him sliding his hand into my pants. Everything else is a blur."

"Well, I don't know then." Jude sighed in defeat. "We will figure something out."

"Why don't you just admit it?"

"Admit what?"

"You think I got what I deserved. You told me we needed to study that night, and you were smart enough to stay home. I know you're wondering why I'm such a fuckup and why you're stuck cleaning up my messes."

For the first time in the conversation, Jude let out a chuckle and stared into her eyes. "You listen to me, little Miss I Know Everything, I am only interested in helping you feel better. I knew what happened to you was wrong, and I understood your need to unwind. We were in the middle of midterms, and we had been cramming, and I needed a break too. I actually thought that if I had listened to you we would have been there together and nothing would have gone wrong."

"You can't blame yourself. I chose to go there."

"Yes, you did, but you didn't want to get taken advantage of." He looked away suddenly, but she never took her eyes away from him. "Enough of this talk. I wanted to discuss an engagement party."

"You still want to marry me? Even with all my doubts?"

He ran his hand down her face and cupped her chin. "I asked, didn't I?" She nodded, and he grinned at her. "I knew all of this when I asked you and I didn't care. You're it for me, and I want you. Plus, we need to stop all this shacking up. I'm a Christian boy, and my mama wouldn't like it that I'm taking you all over this house and we're not married."

As in true Livingston fashion, they had a house built for them as a gift. It was outside of the compound, which did not sit well with Rick, but Cassandra stressed the need for them to have privacy. Rick had no choice but to cave with both his wife and daughter pleading the case.

Whitney laughed hysterically and leaned her head against Jude's neck. "Well, we wouldn't want to ruin her image of her perfect little boy, although I can attest to the fact that he is not so little." She ran her hand down and rested it on his growing bulge. "Definitely not a little boy."

"All right," he sighed and stood up, throwing her over his shoulder.

"Where are you taking me, caveman?"

"To that incredibly comfortable bed upstairs and then to Aunt Mia's to get her help with our party. Is that okay?"

Whitney tried not to let her true feelings show and plastered on a big smile. "It sounds great. You know she plans the best events." Jude had apparently missed the decline in her mood and proceeded up the stairs. It wasn't that she didn't want Mia's help, she was just a little upset that she was the first person he thought of for anything. It just made her point more valid: he was her aunt's favorite, not her.

Chapter Five

"You ready?" Terence called out into the office. As he walked farther inside, Tyree looked up, not bothering to hide his scowl. "What happened now?"

Terence took a seat in one of the vacant chairs. Tyree bounced his shoulders nervously, and Terence raised an eyebrow. "What's got you so jumpy, Ty?"

Tyree had been going back and forth about how to feel about Richmond and everything going on regarding the baby mess. He had never felt so helpless in all his life. He had promised Mia things would be okay, but he wasn't sure he could keep that promise. As much as he wanted to believe in his own words, he was beginning to lose hope, and worse, faith in himself. He only hoped Mia still had faith, because without it and with Richmond being back, things could quickly fall apart for them.

Mia had been so understanding through everything, and it made him feel worse. She was blaming herself for their issues, and he just couldn't bring himself to believe he wasn't the reason they weren't able to conceive. He knew what the tests said, but he blamed himself. Maybe there was something he did while making love to her. Maybe he was too rough at times. He could never be too sure. Even with all that, the one thing that kept replaying in his mind was the constant avoidance from everyone regarding what happened to Mia.

It had been five years, and he still hadn't figured out exactly what occurred in this so-called accident of hers. He was gone off looking for Kyan during the time it took place, and the only thing he could think of was that he had caused it before he left and no one wanted to make him feel guilty by sharing what it was. All he knew was that it was bad, and that made his guilt even worse. His sister seemed to be the one who knew the most about it. She was always so protective of Mia, and when he would bring it up, she would go into defense mode. Asha would clam up, and it would ultimately turn into a fight between them. Mia was no better.

The one time the subject of the accident was brought up, Mia started crying and got so hysterical he had to spend hours calming her down. By the time he was done comforting her, he had dropped the conversation, and he never brought it up again. He decided it was better to have her calm rather than to know whatever deep, dark secret she was holding. He was certain that if it was harmful to their family, his sister would have shared.

Tyree stood and walked over, pulling the door closed before starting his statement. "Every time Richmond shows his face or calls in with some bullshit, things get crazy for Mia and me. I just don't need this, not right now."

"What do you mean by not right now? Has something happened?"

Reclaiming his seat, Tyree crossed his arms over his chest. "Don't think I'm a complete female for this . . ."

Feeling this way reminded Tyree of the first time he admitted he was a virgin. Considering that Terence had already lost his virginity to his little sister's best friend, Deanna, he was the most experienced in the group. Deanna was a girl that Terence and Miguel, Tyree's younger brother, both had a thing for, but Terence was the one who got the prize. His caramel skin, deep brown eyes, and blindingly innocent smile gained him access to the pleasure they had both dreamed about since they were kids. Tyree was every bit as attractive as Terence, but he just saw his first time going differently. He always thought Mia would be it for him. While Tyree was still holding his ground, waiting for the chance to make his first time meaningful, Miguel slept with Deanna, just to even the score. They were always competitive that way, at least until Terence started dating Asha.

Tyree was more accepting of their relationship, giving them his blessing after a while, but Miguel was way overprotective. He challenged their relationship at every turn until he finally saw the way Terence looked at her. There was no lust, no undressing her with his eyes like he usually did with women. All he saw was love. Pure, deep, and innocent love. He had never seen Terence like that with anyone and was convinced, giving them his blessing.

Terence laughed at the look on his face, drawing Tyree's mind back to the present dilemma. "Do I really want to know what you're thinking? I swear sometimes the stuff that comes out of your mouth surprises even me, and I've known you my entire life."

"It's not like that," Tyree sighed. "I just wanted to say, well, I'm just jealous. There I said it. I'm jealous of you."

"Jealous of me, why? I mean, you have a great company, a beautiful wife, and a son who loves you both. You have every . . ." Terence paused, undoubtedly realizing what was going on. "The baby thing? You're upset that you guys haven't been able to conceive?"

Hating admitting his shortcomings, Tyree just nodded and ran his hand over his face. "I hate feeling this way, and you know I love my nephew. I just wish it could have been us. I know you love him too, but you weren't trying, and Mia wants this so bad. I just feel like I keep letting her down."

"She loves you, and I'm sure she doesn't blame you. It will happen, I'm sure. When you had Ky, you weren't trying, so maybe you just need to take the pressure off and have fun with it."

"It's always fun, you know that, but maybe you're right. I should just stop obsessing."

"Yeah. Now, can we get to lunch? I'm starving."

"Yes. Let's just go over to Mia's office and let her know we're leaving." They had a deep conversation on the way to the elevator, only stopping when they reached the door.

Walking into the office, the guys found both of their women laughing loudly at something on Mia's computer. When they saw the two men entering, they tried to hush it up but were too late. Terence was already on alert. "What's funny, ladies?"

Mia pushed the laptop back and walked around the desk, throwing her arms around a confused Tyree. Although Mia was draped around him, Tyree still found a way to break free and made his way to the computer. When he saw what had them laughing, he almost fell over, and the room was filled with laughter. Terence still looked puzzled and walked over to see what was so funny for himself.

"Really, guys?" he questioned with a playful grin present on his face. While he tried to keep up an angry front, they all continued to snicker. "Is it really that funny?"

"Of course it is," Mia voiced, taking a break from her laughing spell. They were watching a video of Terence singing to Asha at their wedding. He wasn't the best singer, but his hand gestures made the performance more memorable.

"Oh, you're just mad because you never got it. It's not my fault Tyree wasn't original enough to serenade you at either of your weddings. As a matter of fact, you should feel cheated."

Tyree turned and glared at Terence, no longer finding the situation funny. "T, you ready for lunch or what?"

"Oh, changing the subject, are we? What's wrong, Ty? Can't take the heat?"

"I just don't feel like you pointing out that Mia was lucky enough to marry a smooth brother like myself, twice, is fair when Asha only got to marry your corny ass."

Terence's eyes bucked, and he stepped forward, ready to fire off another cheap shot, when Asha stepped between them, ending the conversation. "All right, boys, where were you headed before all this?"

Tyree chuckled at their silliness and raised his hand in surrender. "We were about to tell you ladies we were headed out for lunch, but my baby is looking so good right now, I want to know if she's free to join us." Asha cleared her throat and waved her hand in frustration. "Oh, yeah, you too, sis."

"Well, thanks for that gracious invite," Asha hissed.

"It's all love, sweetie, I swear." Tyree walked over and pulled her into his arms. "You know I got mad love for you, sis, but that's baby right there. She distracts me so easily."

"Okay, let's get something to eat. Are you free, baby?" Terence ran his hand through Asha's curly tresses, and she offered him a giddy smile.

"Yes, I'm free and starving. Gina's?"

"No!" Mia and Tyree yelled at the same time.

"What's wrong with Gina's?" Terence questioned.

"That gape-mouthed wench always flirts with Ty," Mia snarled. "I don't have the stomach to watch her fawning all over my husband today."

"Come on, guys, Gina has the best fried chicken," Asha whined.

"Fine," Mia conceded. "But if she touches his ass, I'm kicking that prosthetic hip of hers."

"That's elderly abuse, Mimi," Asha chuckled. "You know Gina is on the other side of sixty."

"Well, she had better behave herself then."

Terence and Asha walked out ahead of Mia and Tyree, and Tyree held Mia back. "We need to eat fast and get out of there. I set up an appointment with a new ob-gyn. Maybe we might get some different answers."

"Tyree," Mia sighed, "we've been through this."

"I know we have, but you did it alone. I'm going with you this time."

"What if the answers are the same, Tyree?"

"Then we will start asking different questions. I'm here for you."

Tyree grabbed her hand and led her to the elevator where his sister and best friend were waiting, and she leaned her head on his shoulder. He felt relaxed because he felt as if he had reassured her.

Chapter Six

Returning from lunch and her appointment, Mia found herself submerged in work. She had the files on a project in Montenegro lying in front of her when she looked up to find Rick leaning in her doorway. He offered her a lazy smile, and she waved him over. "Hey, big brother. What are you doing here?"

"I just wanted to check in on you."

"I'm all right." She smiled. "You're my favorite brother, you know that, right?"

He ran his hand over the top of her head, and she huffed at him, adjusting the hair he moved out of place. "I'm your only brother."

"Don't let Miguel hear you say that," she laughed. "Sit down. Tell me how semiretired life is. We never got to discuss how your latest trip to Paris was."

"It was incredible. We saw so much more than we were able to when we were visiting you."

"I know. All the times I tried to convince you to stay longer, you always had the excuse about the business. I told you it was unbelievable. Tell me, how did you enjoy my villa?"

"I didn't know you had done so much to the place. We really enjoyed ourselves. Thanks for letting us use it."

"I was happy to. There is no telling when I will be able to go back, and it just doesn't seem right taking Tyree there when Jake and I shared most of our relationship in that house. It would just seem like a slap in the face if you ask me." At the mention of her ex, Jake, Rick's eyes drifted downward, and Mia noticed instantly. "What is it?"

Leaning back in his seat, Rick cleared his throat and locked eyes with her. "Cassie and I saw Jake."

She swallowed hard. She wasn't sure if she should ask about him or ignore the comment. She and Tyree just didn't discuss him. They pretended like he didn't exist, but she still thought about him. He had been her friend and lover when Tyree was gone. He had protected her and made her feel loved. She wondered if his life was as happy as hers. She wanted that for him. "How was he?"

"He seemed happy."

"That's good." She smiled, feeling relieved. She had always worried if she had ruined him for other women by leaving him for Tyree.

"He asked about you and wished you well."

"You don't know how happy that makes me. Was he alone?" Rick's eyes bucked, and she rushed to clarify herself. "No, it's not like that. I just want him happy. I hoped he would find someone there."

"He wasn't alone. He was with a guy: tall, skinny, with dark hair and blue eyes. You know him?"

"His brother, Vincent. He's a little off."

"How so?"

"He kind of creeped me out. I always got a bad feeling about him, but Jake always made excuses. He said he was always a magnet for trouble, but he was trying to turn his life around. He was embarrassed because of the way Vincent was."

"Well, it's good you no longer have to see him. Anyways, how is my nephew?"

"He is great, getting smarter every day, and he misses his uncle Rick and crazy aunt Cassie."

They went on with their conversation for over thirty minutes, and at the end of it, Rick prompted her to get everyone together for dinner later in the evening. She made the necessary

phone calls, gaining acceptances from everyone
except Miguel, while Rick headed home to in-
form Cassandra of their plans. She left Miguel
a message she was sure he would receive, and
then she decided to head home to prepare for
the evening.

No one knew what was going on with Miguel,
but he hadn't been his usual exuberant, fun self.
It was as if everything over the years was hitting
him all at once, especially what happened to
Janelle. No one knew as well as Mia how much
Miguel really loved her sister.

Mia hadn't told a soul, but just before Janelle
died, she could tell something was off with her.
She wasn't acting like herself and had been
speaking vaguely about life and death. It was
weird to Mia. She had never known Janelle to be
anything but carefree and fun. The girl she saw
in Janelle's last days was nothing like the baby
sister she had grown to know.

Neither Miguel nor Janelle knew that Mia
was present when they were talking, and she
didn't mean to eavesdrop, but they were in the
foyer, and the conversation was clearly audi-
ble. Mia heard when Janelle admitted her love
for Miguel, and she saw when he froze just before Janelle ran away. Janelle had offered him
a nervous smile before retreating up the stairs

and into her room. Just as Mia was about to follow, she heard Miguel speak. It was low at first, and she wasn't even sure she heard him right until he repeated it. He had mumbled that he loved her too. The next day she was gone.

Mia saw how composed he tried to remain after getting the news of her death, but she also witnessed the breakdown he thought was private until he looked up and saw her standing behind him. At that point, he cried on her shoulder and confided in her his true feelings. They grew closer but soon lost that comfort when Mia left Tyree. Miguel took her leaving hard and practically refused to accept her calls when she was in Paris. He was never good at letting someone in, and to have her leave put a strain on their relationship. They had gotten back to friendship, but he wasn't near as open as he once was. Mia knew she only had herself to blame. Next to Tyree, he had become one of her best friends, and she lost that.

Arriving home, Mia was greeted by the sight of her son on the couch, doing his homework. She had finished her day, but the appointment still rang fresh in her head. It had only given her more questions, and she had been put through more tests. They had been told she would get a call when most results came in, but she was anxious.

He dropped his book and raced over to hug her when he saw her. "Mama, you're early. Where is Dad?"

"He has some things to wrap up, and he will be home after that. How was school?"

"Okay. I'm just glad it's Friday."

"I'm glad your day was good. What would you like for dinner? Dad and I are going out."

"You don't have to cook for me, Mama. I can just eat out. I know you are probably tired."

Mia smiled and ran her hand over his cheek. "You know I don't mind cooking for my favorite guy." Kyan had always been a fan of her cooking and wasn't used to eating out. No matter how busy she got in her life, she tried to keep things pretty routine for him. She made sure he had a set time for bed on school nights and a regular study session, and she always cooked when she got home from work. She knew both Tyree and Kyan loved this about her, so she did her best to spoil her boys.

"I love you, Mama, and I love your cooking, but please just this one time order me a pizza." He flashed her a goofy grin, and she nodded in agreement. "Thanks! Who's coming over to watch me tonight?"

"Amy is coming, and she is going to watch you, Meelah, and Jonathan."

"Cool. I'm gonna go finish my homework and then play video games until they get here. Is that okay?"

"Sure."

"Thanks."

Entering her room and stripping off her clothing, she was in a trance, running her fingers through her long, dark locks when she heard a whistle. She turned to find Tyree standing in the doorway, gazing at her. She fought back the blush appearing on her cheeks and was amazed that he could still make her giddy like a schoolgirl. His golden-brown skin and intoxicating brown eyes always gave her shivers. He still took her breath away.

She watched his movements as he made his way to her. His eyes told her everything she needed to know, and ever so slowly, she slid her hand down his neck, past his chest, and down to the ever-present bulge in his pants. He swelled tremendously under her touch, and just when his lips met hers, she pulled away.

"Not right now, babe. We have to get ready."

Tyree sighed in obvious frustration and gripped her wrists tightly. "Why would you start something knowing you couldn't finish? That was cruel."

"Whatever you say." She smirked. "I'm getting in the shower and locking the door. Don't try anything funny."

She swayed away from him, making sure to start up a rhythm with her hips that would drive him crazy. "The only thing funny will be when you come to me wanting it later tonight and I don't put out," he yelled just before the bathroom door closed.

Hearing his comment, Mia pulled the door open and flashed him a sneaky grin. "Oh, is that so?"

"Yeah, kitten. Try all you want, but you won't break me down. No sex for you tonight."

She made her way to him and bit down on her lip gently. "Really, now?" She dropped her remaining article of clothing, pressing her body against his. She could feel his heart beating rapidly and saw a slight tremor in his hands. "So you're telling me"—she ran her tongue down the side of his neck, and he drew in a deep breath—"that if I wanted you right now, I couldn't have you?" Tyree's breath hitched when her tongue began circular rhythms, and her hand found its way back to his zipper. He shook his head. She could tell he wanted to speak but thought better of it.

"What's that, baby?" She pulled his zipper down and put her hand inside his boxers. An involuntary moan escaped his lips, and she could tell he was cursing himself for it. "It's okay to admit you can't deny me. I swear I won't hold it against you," she whispered in his ear, stroking his hardened flesh.

She could tell something flickered in him, and he stepped back, removing her hand from his pants. "Nice try, kitten, but I think I'll take my shower in the other bathroom now. You really should get started with yours. Wouldn't want to keep everyone waiting now, would we?"

Mia stood amazed as he walked out of the room, closing the door behind him. He had never been able to stop her during a sexual advance. The moment he walked out, she knew he was playing a game he had no intention of losing. She knew he was ready for war. Now, the only question was, when would he make his move?

Chapter Seven

Just as Tyree expected, Mia taunted him on the way to the restaurant. She had really tried, and he had to admit he almost caved. When they were at a stoplight, she unzipped his pants and pushed her hand inside, stroking him slowly. He assumed that when the light changed, she would stop, but to his surprise, she kept going, almost causing a wreck on his behalf when his foot slipped off the brake in a traffic jam. He could tell how amused she was by his lack of restraint, and he focused back on the road, fighting the moans that almost escaped his lips.

After a few minutes of no response on his behalf, she withdrew her hand and flopped back in frustration. Tyree laughed to himself and counted it as a round in his favor. He had every intention of getting to her first and couldn't allow her to get one up on him.

Tossing his keys to the valet as they pulled up, Tyree made his way over to her door and opened it, reaching his hand out for her. Mia accepted his gesture and fell into his chest while exiting the car. Tyree chuckled and stabilized her, sliding his hands down to grip her waist. "A little clumsy there, aren't we, sweetheart?"

She rolled her eyes and tried her hardest to pull out of his embrace. "Asshole," she mumbled playfully.

"That hurt," he whispered, allowing his cool breath to travel down her neck. He allowed his lips to linger next to her milk-chocolate skin, and he felt her trembling. He still had her pressed against him until a couple walking up distracted him, giving her the opportunity to break free and dart into the building. "Dammit." He followed her and saw the hostess leading the way to the main seating room. Once in the room, he discovered they were the first of the party to arrive.

"Come on." She smirked, walking swiftly behind the skinny girl leading them to their table.

Tyree shook his head and sprinted up and caught them just as they reached the table. Mia reached for her seat, but he grabbed her arm and pulled her away from the chair. "I got that."

"Such a gentleman." She kissed him, and he ran his hand down her back. After taking his seat, he reached across the table and grabbed her hand. "Looks like everyone is on CP time tonight." She scanned the room while he continued to hold her hand. She was still looking around when he placed his lips on her skin. He saw the flustered reaction her hazel eyes held, and he continued his torture. "Stop," she hissed, and it only fueled him further.

Doing as she requested and dropping her hand, he slid closer to her and placed his hand on her exposed thigh. He leaned in and swore he could hear her heart beating in her chest. The amusement he felt was present in his eyes, and she huffed. Instead of pulling back, he moved in farther. With slow, lingering glides, his fingertips took on more of her exposed skin, and he felt her breathing hitch.

"What are you doing?"

"Nothing," he whispered, finding a stopping point at her throbbing center. "Nothing at all." He had been focusing so hard on not caving, he had forgotten it had been an entire day since he made love to his wife. The teasing was exhilarating and slowly turning him on. As agitated as she was, he found himself swelling, and his slacks felt tight. Caressing her covered center with his fingertips, he took a deep breath before pushing past the barrier. Pushing in one finger at first, he felt her tense, and her eyes flew open.

"Ty," she hissed quietly, "you can't do this here."

"Shh," he warned, and she bit down on her bottom lip as he pushed in another finger. "You got to have your way with me. Now I'm just having fun."

"We're in public, Ty. Your mom is on the way, and so is my brother."

"Well, just keep it down then." Watching her grip the tablecloth, he moved his fingers in and out and took pleasure in the low, short moans escaping her. He knew he shouldn't be doing this, not out in the open in a roomful of people with their family on the way, but he couldn't control himself. As good as it was making her feel, it made him feel so much better. He loved watching her writhe around because of him. He loved having that unspoken power over her body.

Tyree continued to stroke her flesh until he felt the quakes of her orgasm vibrating against his fingers. Just as she was approaching the ultimate release, he withdrew, and her eyes fluttered. Her breathing slowed down, and he slid his fingers into his mouth. "Mmm, you taste good, baby."

"You're an ass," she whispered.

"And you're easy, kitten. If I wanted to, I could have stripped you and taken you right on this table."

"Easy? I'll show you easy."

Tyree stood and leaned over, kissing her cheek gently. "I'll be waiting." With that, he turned and walked toward the restroom, and her eyes followed him. He could feel her watching as he disappeared behind the large door. He found himself in front of the sink. He quickly washed his hands and studied himself in the mirror. He was well past worked up and needed a release only his wife could give. How he had gotten to this point, he would never know. Wanting her so badly was taking over all his senses.

Finding his way back to the table, he saw she was still alone and took the chance to feed his desires by claiming her mouth in a kiss. He found his hands drifting from around her face back to her thighs. He began to explore her body once more until he heard a throat cleared behind him.

He saw Mia's eyes widen when she looked up and saw his mother, Karen, grandmother, Kiyoko, and stepfather, Rock, standing behind him. Karen smiled, and Rock gave Tyree a nod before he stood to hug his mother and grandmother. Mia stood and gave Karen a hug and Rock gave Tyree a firm handshake, pulling him close enough to whisper in his ear.

"Good to see you two haven't gotten bored with each other."

Karen had moved back to Hong Kong after everything with John came to a head, and surprisingly to everyone, Rock joined her. After two years of claiming to only be friends, they announced that they were dating, and things escalated from there. After spending nearly two and a half years in Hong Kong, they came back home married, bringing Kiyoko back to live with them. It was an exciting change for Tyree and his siblings because they hadn't seen her in years. They had a lot of catching up to do.

"Never," Tyree chuckled. "I'll be old and gray still finding out new things about this one." He wrapped an arm around Mia's waist, and she leaned into him just as Asha and Terence entered with the rest of the group trailing behind them. Tyree studied the people trickling in and noticed one guest was missing: his little brother, Miguel.

"Babe, did you call Miguel?"

"Yeah, I called. He didn't answer, but I assumed he would just show up like he normally does."

"I don't know," Tyree sighed and ran his hand over his head. "He has been off lately. I haven't been able to reel him in, and I just think he is going through a lot more than he lets us in on. I just wish I knew how to help him."

Mia nodded, and Tyree saw something flicker in her eyes. He wanted to investigate it further, but the rest of the group greeting them threw him off. He made a mental note to ask her about it later and went on to converse with the table. Once they were all seated, the waiter came over and began taking their drink orders.

The evening progressed with laughter and plenty of embarrassing stories. Whitney and Jude had an especially funny story about catching Mia and Tyree having sex in her office after Karen and Rock revealed what they walked in on. To even the scores, and to get back at Asha and Terence for laughing, Mia shared a story about them in the copy room after business hours. Karen held a shocked expression, stating that she never knew her children were so out in the open, while the rest of the table rumbled with laughter.

The night was shaping up to be one of the best they had shared together in a long time, but Tyree couldn't help but think something was missing. He missed his brother, and not just tonight. Besides Terence, Miguel was one of his best friends as well as his brother, and he felt like he had no clue what was going on with him. They had always shared so much of their lives, and now it was like his little brother was a stranger to him. That just didn't sit well.

While Tyree tried to stay focused on the dinner and the people present, he felt his thoughts keep drifting back to Miguel. He laughed at their jokes and even attempted to share a few of his own, but he knew his heart wasn't there. He figured he had nearly everyone fooled, everyone except the person who knew him better than anyone at the table. Mia had been watching him the whole time, and he knew she recognized that fake laugh and smile of his anywhere. She squeezed his leg, which he knew was to let him know she was there, and he loved her more at that moment. She always seemed to know exactly what he needed at all times.

Deciding to push everything but the here and now out of his mind, Tyree looked around the table happily. Despite everything they had all been through, they were still able to sit and enjoy their time together. He felt like even with all the bad, they were blessed to have each other.

Even though Tyree knew Richmond could make an appearance at some point, he chose not to let it affect his thoughts that they would all be okay in the end. He knew that whenever he decided to show his face, they would be ready, and now that Rock was around full-time with his mother, he didn't worry as much.

Just as everyone was finishing up their food, Tyree heard a familiar song come on and a smile formed on his face. It was the same song he and Mia danced to at their second wedding. When he reached for her hand, she was halfway out of her chair as if she had read his mind. He pulled her out to the dance floor without saying a word, and she rested her head on his shoulder. He loved the closeness of their bodies.

"You know, you look gorgeous tonight, kitten. I mean, you look great every day, but tonight you look so damn amazing."

She blushed and kissed the part of his neck closest to her lips. "Thanks for the compliment, baby. Any other night, I would be dragging you out of here to our bed, but I haven't forgotten. You played a dirty trick on me, and it won't go unpunished."

"You're harsh, baby. You're sitting here with all this skin on display, smelling like you rolled around in a cloud of vanilla, looking so damn good every man in this place has their eyes on you, and you're seriously telling me I can't have you tonight?"

"I'm telling you that you won't. You have to learn your lesson."

Tyree chuckled and gripped her waist tighter. "I'll have you in our bed screaming my name by the end of the night. Trust me."

Just as Mia was about to protest, the song ended, and they were back at the table. The group was in a light chatter, and Asha stood, clearing her throat. "You guys, this has all been great, and we should do it again soon. Terence and I would like to cover the bill tonight as a thank-you to everyone for all your help with the business and our personal issues."

Just as she was taking her seat, Rick grabbed the check from her hand, objecting to her gesture. "I won't hear of it. We invited you all, and it's only fair that we pay."

Asha was about to protest when the waiter walked over, making his presence known. "I didn't mean to eavesdrop, but the bill has already been paid. A nice gentleman in the corner over there paid and left a generous tip." They looked to the corner, and the person he was referring to had a menu up to his face, blocking their view.

"Who is he?" Mia asked.

"He didn't give a name." He paused and shrugged his shoulders. "If you don't need anything, I'm going to take these dishes to the back."

"Thanks." Mia nodded and leaned over, trying to see who the guy was. After a few moments of looking back, Terence stood and told them he was going over to thank him. Everyone watched as he approached the table and saw his expression drop. He had his hand extended, but when he saw who was behind the menu, he withdrew it and turned to hurry back to the table. Sitting down, he was greeted by all their confused stares.

"Who was it?" Asha asked with everyone waiting for his answer.

"It doesn't matter. Actually, we need to go."

"Go? Why?" Tyree asked, knowing something was extremely off.

"We just do. Trust me, okay?"

"No," Mia said. "Tell me who it was. Was it my father? Is he here?"

"Let's go," Terence barked loudly. They were all stunned because Terence never raised his voice. He was usually always the levelheaded one. When he snapped, Tyree stood, pulling Mia by the arm.

"Come on, kitten, this isn't the place. We just need to get in the car."

"Dammit, stop treating me and everyone else here like we're stupid and tell us who the hell it was. We deserve to know!" Tyree could tell Mia's blood was boiling, but he got such a bad feeling about whoever it was.

"It's time to go." Tyree pulled her arm a little rougher than he meant to and she stumbled into him. He felt horrible witnessing the look on her face. He had never handled her like that, and he knew he was wrong. He just wanted to get her out of there before something dangerous popped off. He knew Terence, and for him to react the way he did meant there was something crazy about to happen.

Mia gave up her argument and followed Tyree toward the entrance, but he could tell the damage was already done. He knew he was going to have to do a hell of a lot to get back into her good graces after this. He didn't know what came over him. All he knew was the thought of something happening that he couldn't protect her from made him a little crazy.

When they got to the entrance that led to the lobby, he stopped and took her chin in his hand. "Listen, I'm sorry. I never meant to jerk you like that, and I would never hurt you. I just got a little excited, but it's no excuse." She remained quiet, and he searched her eyes for a reaction and got nothing. All she held was a blank stare. "Baby? You okay?"

She opened her mouth and closed it, and he was confused. He felt her hands shaking before she swallowed hard. He tried to coach her into saying whatever was on her mind, but she shook her head, leaving him even more puzzled. Looking into her eyes, he noticed that she was staring at something behind him. When he turned around, he felt his anger boil over. Jake was there, tossing an envelope on the table he vacated, heading in their direction.

"Dimples." Jake smiled, approaching Mia and Tyree.

Mia said his name quietly, and Tyree stood in front of her, blocking Jake's access. "Mia, go to the car," he snarled, and she shook behind him. He knew his attitude tonight was probably making her nervous, but he couldn't pull back. His emotions were running too high. When she didn't make a move, his voice got louder. "Mia, go."

She shuffled her feet, and by this time Terence and Asha were right behind them. "Asha, Mia, go to the car please," Terence requested quietly, and Asha grabbed Mia's hand. When Jake began to laugh, the tension hit an all-time high. Terence stopped trying to usher the girls out and turned to his enraged friend.

As the rest of the group approached, Rock placed himself between Tyree and Jake, trying to diffuse the situation. Wrapping his arms around Tyree and whispering to him was proving to be helpful. Tyree felt himself growing relaxed listening to Rock's soothing voice. He seemed to know exactly what to say to bring him back to a calm state.

While Tyree tried to keep his focus on Rock, he couldn't help but notice a man sneaking away from Jake's table with the envelope he'd dropped there. It was as if he was waiting to slip over until he'd vacated the table. He found himself wondering if talking to them was all just a ruse. He somehow felt like Jake's presence meant more than whatever bullshit he was spouting right now. He felt like there was a deeper meaning. He figured it had something to do with getting Mia back, but he felt like there was so much more below the surface. There had to be for him to come back after all these years.

Jake was still laughing, pretty much taunting Tyree, but he managed to present with a confident smile. Turning to Mia and grabbing her hand, he pulled her to his side. "Baby, let's go home. We're done here." Asha rushed out and told the valets to get their cars immediately. With the way things were escalating, they all knew having the cars there would be the best option.

Mia, who had remained quiet through the whole ordeal, squeezed his hand and leaned into his side. He felt relieved by her gesture and headed past Jake. They were almost out the door with everyone trailing behind him when Jake uttered a statement that had Tyree right in his face.

"Dimples, it was good seeing you. Maybe you could stop by the room later, and we can catch up. I missed you, girl."

Before anyone could grasp the situation, Tyree had Jake by the collar. "Don't address my wife ever again."

"What's wrong? Afraid she'll see through your violent ass and come back to the only man who ever put her needs first? She was my top priority. What was she to you, option one for now?"

Mia put her hands on Tyree's shoulders and tried to talk him down. "Let's just go. He's wrong. You know he's just saying this to get to you."

"Oh, really, Dimples? How can you leave with this man knowing you can't even be yourself around him?" Mia didn't have the chance to respond before Tyree punched Jake and drew back a bloody hand. Jake's body was sprawled over a table, and all Tyree saw was red. He took note of the broken dishes and the table that split in half when Jake fell, and he got the sudden urge to hit him again. Just as he rushed back toward him, the guys pulled Tyree out of the restaurant while Mia held her hand over her mouth.

Rock tossed Tyree into his car, and Mia got into the car with Asha and Terence. The rides were impeccably quiet between Mia, Asha, and Terence while Rock, on the other hand, had a lot to say in the car with Tyree. Tyree was rolling his eyes while Karen looked on disappointedly.

"What in the hell were you thinking? We can't have you losing your head like that. You know the press is just looking for the next big story on this family," Rock fumed while everyone else just sat quietly.

"He pissed me off." Looking out the window instead of at Rock, Tyree tried to dial down his anger. "He shouldn't be here."

"Yes, and you shouldn't have let him get to you. You have the woman. He is just trying to get in your head, and you let him."

"I know. I'm just . . . dammit . . . I just fucked up."

"Look, I know I'm not your father but—"

"You're right. You're not him. You are so much better than him."

"I just want you to know you can talk to me. Next time, I want you to come to me before you lose your head."

"I know. I was wrong, and I should have never pulled on Mia like that. I never want her to be afraid of me, and tonight I think I scared her. I'll never forget the look on her face."

"You just get passionate about things. She knows you love her, and I'm sure she's not afraid of you. She may be pissed, but she's not afraid. That girl of yours is resilient. You're probably in for one hell of a night, but you guys will be okay."

The car had grown silent until Kiyoko voiced her opinion. "Well, son, I think it was just amazing when you slugged that son of a bitch. He deserved it for hitting on your wife."

Tyree had never known his grandmother to speak so candidly, but he had to admit it made him smile. She placed her hand on his leg and patted it. This made him feel like everything would be okay.

Tyree chuckled and addressed both Rock's and Kiyoko's statements, and began to believe things would be fine. "You're probably right. I'm not looking forward to the kissing up I'm about to have to do, Rock, and yes, Grandmother, he deserved it and worse for all he did." Tyree looked out the window as they pulled into the back entrance to their house. They noticed a slew of reporters on the front lawn and Tyree huffed. Stepping out of the car, he noticed that Mia was already home, and he sighed loudly. He knew as soon as he walked in the door he would be in for it.

Chapter Eight

Tyree walked into the house, and it was like the Twilight Zone. Asha and Terence were sitting on the couch, talking, while Mia was quiet with the same blank stare he witnessed at the restaurant. Making his way over to her, he prayed she would understand and not hold his actions against him. He bent down and reached for her hand, which she promptly withdrew.

He got on his knees in front of her. He placed his hands on her face and forced her to look at him. "I'm sorry. I don't know why—"

She stood, making him fall back, and he looked up at her, confused. "Shut up. You're not sorry. You meant to hit him. You intended to cause a scene and embarrass the hell out of us. I'm not about to talk about this right now. Don't follow me, and don't wake our son. He's sleeping and doesn't need this bullshit tonight." Her outburst helped to clear the room, and everyone disappeared as she rushed past Tyree and up the stairs. When the door to the bedroom slammed, Tyree made his way up, pausing before twisting the knob.

Inside the room, there was nothing but darkness with the moonlight streaming in. He could make out her figure sitting on the edge of the bed, and he reached out to touch her after undressing himself to nothing but his boxers. When she recoiled from his touch, he dropped his head in frustration. "Dammit, Mia, can we talk? Will you just yell at me and get it over with? I'm tired, and it's been a long day. I just want to shower and lie next to you."

He ran his hand down her back, and she snapped. "Don't touch me. You manhandled me in public and made an ass of yourself. Are you seriously expecting me to just lie next to you? You're out of your mind."

"I told you I didn't mean it, baby. I just . . . I let him get to me."

"Why?" she screamed, and he could feel his past anger boiling out. He knew he should be over it, but he had just learned how to hide it over the past few years. The rejection he felt when it came to Jake would always be with him.

"Because of you!"

"You're blaming me? How in the hell is this my fault?"

"You left! I try to act like I'm okay with it, and for the most part, I am, but that doesn't change the fact that you left me for him."

"Not this shit again," she yelled. "At some point, you need to get over that. I messed up! We both screwed up, but it's been years, and you said you forgave me."

"I did."

"You couldn't have. You keep bringing it up, and I'm tired of feeling like you blame me for everything."

"I don't. I'm just stupid. Come on, baby, we have been doing so well. Let's just forget all this and get back to where we were before we ran into him." He ran his hand down her cheek, and she closed her eyes before pulling away. He hated how insecure he allowed himself to become.

"Stop. Stop drawing me back in. I'm pissed, and this isn't going to happen tonight."

"Just give me a chance." He leaned in, kissing her forcefully, and she responded with an intensity that shocked him. He allowed himself to get comfortable, and he pushed her back on the bed. It took her only a second to realize what was happening, and she pushed him away, wielding a pillow.

"Get out."

"What? What do you mean get out?"

"Get out of my room, Tyree. I want you out of here now."

Tyree threw his hand over his face and rolled back on the bed. "Fine. I'll give you a little time, but I'll be back in a few minutes. We will finish this tonight."

"You're not coming back. I want you to sleep down the hall." She jumped up and reached for the door. Just as she was about to pull it open, he grabbed her arm.

"Now, you wait just one minute."

"Let me go."

"You're not putting me out of our room. I'm going to sit here, and we are going to end this now."

She pulled away and stumbled into the door. He reached out to catch her, and they both ended up pinned against it. Her breathing was heavy, and he could sense the uncertainty in her as he leaned in and claimed her lips once again.

She pushed at him, but he didn't relent, forcing his lips harder against hers. No matter how hard he pushed, she wouldn't kiss him back, and he drew his lips away in frustration. Looking into her eyes, he saw the confusion and anger, and he decided not to stop there. Finding his way to her neck, he kissed the spot that always made her cave. When she still didn't react, he knew he had to take things a step further.

"I know you want to be mad, and I know I deserve that, but I need you. I need to know that we're okay. Please?"

"Just stop," she hissed. "I just want—"

He kissed her neck, interrupting her statement.

"I want . . ."

He dropped to his knees and swung her legs over his shoulders. He ripped her panties in one movement, and as his breath tickled her center, she tried to speak again.

"I want . . . Shit." She bit down on her lip when his tongue invaded her most private area. "Fuck, that feels . . . uh . . ."

Tyree smirked against her flesh, knowing she was giving in. "I'm sorry, baby. Say we're okay."

"I . . . I can't," she uttered quietly. "You can't just use sex to make me forget. I'm still angry."

Not taking no for an answer, Tyree pulled her legs down and stood before her. He saw the passion twinkle in her eyes, and he knew he was on the right track. Pushing his boxers down, he stood pressed against her and snatched her legs up around his waist. Before she could put up a fight, he buried himself inside her and stilled her heavy breathing.

Thrusting himself in and out of her, he felt her body relaxing, and he let loose. He was slamming her into the door, and he heard it rattling loudly. She wasn't herself, but he had a plan to change that. Pulling her away from the door, he sat her on top of the dresser and pushed himself as deep as he could possibly go. Running a hand through her hair, he tugged hard, causing a loud moan to escape her lips.

"You done being angry?" He threw his hips forward and held her tighter. She was panting, unable to form a word, and he rolled his hips harder into her, their bodies molding each other. He could feel her uneven breathing on his cheek, and he forced her lips apart. Plunging his tongue into her mouth, he massaged hers and tasted the screams threatening to escape.

Even with all that, she still wasn't as responsive as he wanted. Running out of options, he bent down, capturing her breast between his lips. Taking her hardened bud and twirling it around with his tongue seemed to do the trick, because by that time, she dug her nails into his back and wrapped her legs tighter around his waist. She also allowed his hands to glide down and grip her from behind. He felt her throbbing around him and was slowly losing what little resolve he had left. He wanted to move freely, but the part of him that needed them on the same level held back. He needed more cooperation on her part.

Pulling her in and out, and rubbing himself roughly against her, he heard what he had been waiting to hear all night. She leaned in and nibbled on his ear, whispering what he thought was the best thing he could ever hear in his life. He would never grow tired of hearing her say she loved him while he was inside her. It made his night, and he took her from the dresser to the bed. Pulling her legs tighter around him, he delighted in the pulsations emitted by both of their eager bodies. Never had he been so happy to find the bed as he was at that moment.

"I love you too, kitten." He kissed her neck, taking a seat on the bed, allowing her to be on top. She wrapped her arms around his neck, and she pushed him back, sliding her hands up his chest. Tyree closed his eyes and got lost in the sensation tingling through him. His hands found a place around her hips, and he swore he felt her push harder.

He always loved when she took charge and rode him, but this was different. He could feel her palms trembling on his chest and her body quivering with each thrust, but she never slowed down. Each time, she pushed her body down and filled herself with him completely and slid back up. Feeling his climax approaching, he grabbed her neck, pulling her down to meet his lips. Her breasts crushed into his chest as she continued moving against him, and he kept his hand planted on her body, running up and down her smooth skin.

Holding her body like she would get up and run away, he forced her to come down harder against him. When he felt her breasts graze over his lips, he took the chance to pleasure her with his mouth. She moaned, and he could tell she was holding back, so he took more of her into his mouth. She stilled her movement only for a second to gather herself and he could tell she was getting closer. He loved it when she was almost at her breaking point. It made everything so much more intense. He saw her head swinging from side to side, and he reached for her hair. Pulling her hair was something she loved, and he made sure to take advantage of it.

With each thrust, Tyree felt himself drawing closer and closer, and he stopped her to catch his breath. Holding her in place, he ran his hands up and down her back. She smiled at him, and he felt his heart melt. She was so beautiful in that moment, and he couldn't help but smile back.

"Thank you."

"For what?" she asked, looking puzzled.

"For being here. For loving me like you do."

"It's not hard when you love me back just as much." She ran a hand over his cheek, and he kissed the inside of her shoulder just above the breast. Slowly, she began to move, causing loud exclamations to roll off his tongue.

"Shh, you'll wake Ky."

"I can't help it, baby." He kissed her neck, and she dug her nails deep into his chest. He began to thrust upward, and she raked her nails over him, leaving red trails. "You feel so good." Moving together, he felt his climax building back up. Pulling her hair roughly, he pushed into her harder. He could hear their skin smacking together, and just as he was about ready to erupt, she screamed and shuddered above him. Feeling the quakes of her body gave him the most glorious sensation, and he erupted inside her.

Collapsing on his chest, Mia ran her hands up and down his arms. He let her breathing regulate and decided they needed to talk about things before either of them fell asleep. He knew he was wrong about most of it, but the comment Jake made was eating away at him. He needed clarification on some things.

"Kitten, can we talk?"

"Baby, I'm sleepy. Can it just wait?"

Kissing the top of her head, he tilted her chin to look him in the eye. "You know it can't. I can't say it enough, but I'm sorry for acting the way I did. I was wrong for grabbing you and for raising my voice. It will never happen again."

"None of that matters. I know it wasn't intentional, and I was really never mad about that."

"You don't have to pretend for me. I know I scared you tonight."

"I was a little caught off guard, but I wasn't afraid."

"I saw the look in your eyes. I never meant to—"

"You didn't. I've been with you over fifteen years, and I've done some crazy things that should have made you snap, but you have never raised your hand to me. Hell, you never even spanked our son. I will never be afraid of you. I just had to make you work for it."

"Work for it? This was all a game? You were never mad?"

"Oh, I was, but not for the reason you think. You better not ever call me easy again. Got it?"

"You made me do all that because I called you easy?" Mia laughed, and he laughed with her. "Okay, you got me. I won't do it again. There is something else I wanted to ask you, though."

"Yeah?"

"I almost feel crazy asking this while lying here naked with you in my arms, but I have to know."

"What's up?"

Tyree sighed and sat up against the headboard, bringing her with him. "You know I trust you, but why did he say you can't be yourself with me? I mean, we've known each other our whole lives, and I like to think there is no one alive who knows you better than me. Am I wrong? Is there something you're not telling me?"

He saw the fear dance in her eyes, and a nervous feeling he had never experienced built up in his chest. As he awaited her answer, his mind raced with the most awful thoughts. He only hoped he could handle whatever she was about to say, and he focused his eyes on hers, studying her intently.

"Jake, well . . . When you were gone, we talked a lot, and I told him stuff. I was pissed at you, so it wasn't positive. I said a lot of things I didn't mean, and I'm sorry. I didn't know the full story back then, and I was wrong."

Tyree ran his hand through her hair and placed a kiss on her forehead. "It's okay. I understand, and we both said things we didn't mean. I just . . . Promise me you won't see him again. I trust you, and I know you won't do anything to jeopardize us, but I don't like him being around you."

"I know, and I get that, but I need to see him at least one last time. There are some things I need to say."

"Mia, I don't—"

"Ty, one time, please? I need to let him know that his little act tonight did nothing but push me further away. He needs to know he can't disrespect our marriage."

"I don't like it. I don't think he deserves anything more from you."

"Maybe not, but he is going to hear it anyway. I need to do this for me."

Tyree just stared at her. After a few moments, he turned his back to her, leaving the answer in limbo. After almost a full minute, he responded, "Fine."

"Thank you for understanding. I know he gets to you, but he shouldn't. I never left you for him. My decision to leave had nothing to do with him. He just happened to be there after the decision was made. He was someone to fill the void I had from losing you. No one has ever gotten me like you do. Always know that."

"I just don't like him. I never will. I can't help that."

"I know, but you can't go around hitting people when things don't go your way. We are not children anymore, and there are consequences to our actions now."

"Even so, it felt damn good to finally take a swing at that bastard."

"You're such a guy."

"An exhausted guy. Conversation over. Sleep now."

"Sleep sounds good."

"Yeah, as long as you're sleeping next to me."

"There is no place else I would ever be."

"Good."

He closed his eyes, and she snuggled closer to him, pressing her cheek to his chest. Once he felt her settle down and drift into a deep sleep, his eyes fluttered open. Something was still bothering him about the whole Jake situation. Something about her answer didn't satisfy him. He knew there was more, but he couldn't put his finger on it. There was something deeper between them, and until he knew what, it was going to fester in his mind. He had to know the truth.

Chapter Nine

Mia held her breath as she knocked on the door. She knew she probably shouldn't be there, but she couldn't resist. She needed to see this through. It was important to her.

After a few knocks had gone unanswered, she fished out her cell phone. Just as she was about to dial the number, the door flew open, and she was face-to-face with a curvy, petite girl with light brown eyes. The girl wasn't someone she recognized, but her attitude was unmistakably bad. The girl rolled her eyes at Mia and looked as if she was about to shut the door, but Mia threw her hand out, forcing her way in. The girl huffed and reached out as if to grab Mia's arm, but before she made contact, Mia walked up, pressing her against the wall.

"Don't you try me, bitch. Today is not the day. I suggest you get him out here and save yourself the ass-whooping you are about to receive if you lay one hand on me."

"I'm not scared, and he doesn't want to see you. He doesn't want to see anyone."

"Well, how about you let him tell me," Mia snapped, and the girl went into the bedroom. After a few minutes and a series of loud exclamations from the back, Mia saw the girl walking through, fully dressed, with her purse in hand. She looked like she had been crying, and she rushed out the front door.

Mia sat anxiously, anticipating the conversation she knew would be incredibly awkward. She was nervous, but she knew this couldn't wait. The sooner she handled this, the better. As soon as she saw his shadow nearing, her breath caught in her chest. She swallowed the dry lump in her throat and stood to receive him. As soon as he approached, she could smell the liquor on him, and tears glistened in her eyes.

"What happened to you? You used to be so much better than this."

He sighed and sat down on the couch, prompting her to follow his lead. "Mia, it's early. What's going on? Why are you here?"

"Why are you? Miguel, you're supposed to be at work, and it's not early. It's past noon."

"I lost track of time, that's all. Just go back to work. I'll be in once I freshen up." He stood and raked his hand over his head, and she pulled him back down.

"Come on, we can talk about whatever is wrong. We used to talk all the time."

Miguel looked at her, and she could see that he was struggling with something heavy. "Look, I get that you're worried about me, but you don't have to be. Just save your energy for Tyree. He is the one you should be looking after."

"I can handle you both. I want you to have someone to talk to as well. You shouldn't keep it bottled up." She watched as he weighed things in his head anxiously. She wanted him to say anything that could help. She needed him to let her in.

"You really want to help me?"

"You know I do. What can I do?" Mia was beginning to feel hopeful, like she was finally getting through to him, but that hope vanished as soon as she saw his demeanor change. "What?"

"Rewind the last few years of our lives. Rewind it to before Janelle, before your mom died, before you left Tyree. Just give me back those years. Can you do that?"

Mia felt the tears pouring down her face and tried to blink them away. "You know I can't. I wish we could have all that time back. There are so many things I would have done differently."

"Like what? Like not leaving?"

She had been waiting for this. Although years had passed, they had never discussed her moving. It was as if they had just pushed it to the back of their minds when dealing with each other, but she knew it was still with him. It was still wearing away at his mind.

"I'm sorry. I never told you that, but I am. I know what I did when I left, and I'm not saying it was right, but it was what I needed at the time. If I would have stayed, there is no telling what would have happened to me."

"You think I'm mad about that? I'm not. It was never about you leaving, although it was completely out of left field. I understand why you left. Things here were a mess, and if you needed a clean break, I get that. I just wish Ty didn't have to suffer while you were gone. I'm mad because you felt like you couldn't come to me before you did what you did. I told you everything. I came to you when Janelle died, but you couldn't do the same with me. I thought we were better than that. I thought we knew each other better."

Mia's eyes widened. She would have never guessed in a million years that he knew what happened. "Miguel, why . . . why didn't you say something? If I had known—"

"I wanted you to talk to me. You should have told me before. I shouldn't have found out the way I did. No one should have found out that way."

Mia was lost. She tried to replay in her mind the night he was talking about, but she came up short. She remembered Jake and the hospital and nothing more. She didn't remember seeing Miguel after the first week Tyree left, and she wasn't sure what he was hinting at.

"Miguel, what exactly do you know?"

"I know about the pills, Mia. Why did you do it?"

Sniffling, she reached for his hand. "Did you tell Tyree?"

"No."

"Why?"

"Because he would only blame himself and I didn't want that. What you did was selfish."

"I know." She dropped her head. "I . . . I just needed to feel nothing. With everything going on, I was feeling so many things at once, and I needed to feel nothing at all. Now, I just feel like I should tell him everything."

"Why mess up a good thing? You guys are doing great now. Why stir up old feelings?"

"Because I'm not the only one who knows. I know I can count on you guys, but I can't say the same about Jake. He is so pissed at me, and he hates Ty. He might just blurt everything out to be spiteful. I don't want him knowing that way."

"What does Jake have to do with anything? He is thousands of miles away."

"He was thousands of miles away. He is here now."

"Why?"

"I have no idea. I messed up, Miguel."

"Why did you feel like you had no other way? You had a husband, a child, us to think about. It wasn't all about you. What is going through your mind?"

"I wasn't thinking." She placed her hands on her head, and her shoulders began to shake. "I just needed to be free of it all. I couldn't look at myself in the mirror anymore."

"What was so bad that you needed that kind of escape? If you had died, it would have broken me. You're more than just my sister-in-law. You're my friend, and I love you. Don't you get it? We all love you."

"I love you too. You were the one person whc understood everything I was going through when Janelle died. I never knew—"

"I found you. I thought you were sleeping." His voice cracked, and for the first time since Janelle died, she saw tears in his eyes. "I let you lie there. I almost let you die because I thought you were sleeping." He looked at her, and she saw him breaking before her eyes. "Did you hear me? I almost let you die! You should hate me. I hate me. I couldn't save her, and I almost let the closest person to her die." Mia reached out and pulled him to her. His body was trembling, and he sobbed loudly. "I just want to go back. I need things like they were. If I had said it back or kept her with me that night, then maybe she would still be here."

"You can't think like that." She hated that he blamed himself, and she hated her father more at that moment than she ever had before. "Richmond killed Janelle and Mom. He tried to ruin our lives, but we made it. We made it in spite of him. Yeah, we lost her, but she wouldn't want you like this. She would want you to move on and be happy. This"—she waved her hand around the room—"is not making you happy. You can be happy."

Mia could see his internal struggle and wanted to appeal to him as the friend he needed. "I know there has to be more to all of this. You didn't just wake up one morning and feel like everything was your fault. What happened?"

Trying to hold back tears, Miguel looked her in the eye, and she saw his heart breaking. "I wish it were all about her. The truth is, everything is finally hitting me. I guess I just tried to ignore it until I couldn't anymore. These past few months, the memories have just been wearing me down, and I haven't been dealing with it well. I know I blew it with Janelle and I'll never get that back. That was all my fault, but my dad, what did I ever do to deserve what he did? What did any of us do?"

Miguel stood, pacing the floor, and she saw his hands swing up in the air. "This bastard's birthday is coming up, and I actually felt sad. I forgot, and I went out and bought him a damn gift. I forgot. How did I forget?"

"It happens. Just because he did what he did doesn't mean you didn't love him."

"I want to hate him. I really do, but I can't." Tears rolled down his cheeks. "He tried to kill me, he kidnapped my nephew and screwed with all of us, but I can't hate him. What the hell kind of man am I?"

"A good one." She smiled, and he locked eyes with her. "You are a great man. Yes, you have your flaws, and you're a bit of a whore," she chuckled quietly. "But you're one of the men I've come to count on. We all love you, and the kids adore you. I just want you happy. I need it."

"I want to be. You have no idea how much I want what you guys have. I want someone who loves me despite my flaws. Someone who I love enough to give my child to. I want a person I can grow old with. When I look at you and Ty and Ash and Terence, I feel like I'm missing out. Being around that all the time is starting to get to me. I need to find something real."

"You will." She smiled. "I'll help in any way I can." He let out a silly smirk, and she tilted her head to the side. "What?"

"I suppose I should thank you."

"For?"

"Getting that girl out of here. If you hadn't shown up, I would have had to learn her damn name. Thanks, sis."

Mia laughed and threw her arms around his neck. "It's good to have you back." She patted him on the back and settled in on the couch.

"You know, I was avoiding you."

"Why?"

"Because as much as I hate to admit it, you know me pretty well. You see through my bull-shit and make me own up to it just like she used to. You're so much like her, and it makes me miss what I can't have."

Mia laughed and ran her hand down his back. "Well, I must admit, my sister and I were two of a kind, but I kind of like talking to you. You help me remember the good times together, when it wasn't always so serious for us."

"Y'all were bad kids," he chuckled.

"You were the worst. You and Janelle used to keep us on our toes. Poor Milan was always the timid one and was always afraid we were going to get caught."

"Amateur."

The more they talked, the more comfortable Mia got. She kicked her shoes off and crossed her legs just as she often did on her own couch. It was just like old times between them, and she felt like just maybe they would all be okay.

When she noticed him looking at her funny, she stopped in midsentence and allowed him to ask his question. "Hey, you going back to work?"

"No. Let's just hang like we used to. You down for that?"

"I'm game. Just call my bro and let him know where you are. I wouldn't want him getting his panties in a bunch when he realizes you aren't at the office." Just as he spoke the words, her cell phone went off. She held it up, and they both began to laugh.

"Tyree," they both said in unison just as Mia answered the phone.

Chapter Ten

"Baby." Tyree smiled as he addressed his favorite girl. "Where are you? I came down here to take my very sexy wife to lunch, and she is nowhere to be found. I need some time alone." He heard her sultry laugh and wanted her that much more. "Are you coming back soon?"

He heard a pause in her laughter and then a deep sigh. "I'm going to be a while. I'm sorry. Can I make it up to you tonight?"

"Yeah, it's cool, but where are you?" He heard her shuffle around a bit and held his breath, hoping he wasn't about to hear that she was with Jake. He knew she told him she wanted closure, but he still didn't want to think about them being alone together. Her hesitancy was making him nervous, and he found himself growing impatient. "Kitten, you still there?"

"Yeah, sorry, I'm still here. I didn't want to say anything before I left because I knew you would try to talk me out of it, but I really needed to come. I'm sorry I left without telling you."

"It's cool. I mean you said you wanted to, and I know this is something you need to do. I just wish you would have told me first."

"I knew you wanted to talk to him, but I felt like I could do more. I'm fine, and things are okay. I'm going to spend the rest day here if you don't need me back."

Tyree was trying to remain calm, but hearing that made him hit a breaking point. "Why would you want to stay there? What more could you have to say to him after clearing the air? Babe, he is not your man. I am."

He could hear her laughing, and he almost snapped until he heard her voice coming through. "Well, of course I know that, sweetie. He only jokes about us being more, but you know I'd never let him touch me. It would be too gross. He's my brother, silly."

Now Tyree was confused. He knew she wasn't where she said she was. "You're not with Rick. I know this because he came here to see you. If you're with him, you can tell me. I won't get mad. I trust you."

"Apparently not enough," she sighed. "I'm with Miguel, and if you don't mind, I'd rather we didn't continue this conversation. I'm not in the mood to get accused again."

"Baby—"

"No, Tyree. I don't want to do this. Just one last thing."

"Anything, kitten. Just ask."

"Why can't you just trust that I love you? Are we always going to take two steps forward only to be knocked back five?"

"I'm sorry."

"You've been saying that a lot lately. It's starting to lose its effect."

With that, she hung up, and Tyree felt an emptiness inside. He didn't know why he let Jake rattle him so much, but he knew he had to get over it. Ever since he showed his face again, his marriage hadn't been the same. This time, he could only blame himself for letting it become a problem. The suspicions he had were driving him insane, and he knew that to move past it, he needed to answer whatever questions he had left.

Placing his phone down on her desk, he sank into her chair. How he had allowed his temper to flare again where she was concerned was baffling to him. They had been wonderful since reconciling, and he couldn't have been happier. He knew he needed her. Maybe that was driving him to be such an ass. The person he should have been mad at was here in town, so why was he using his wife as target practice?

He sat in her chair with his eyes closed for over thirty minutes and felt himself drifting into a nap when he felt hands on his shoulders. His mood drastically improved as he felt the small hands moving back and forth, giving him a light massage. He allowed himself to enjoy the peaceful movements for a few minutes and then reached to pull her into his lap. After the most recent argument, he needed her to know how important she was to him.

Once the small woman was in his lap, he jumped in shock to see that it was Whitney and not Mia. Ushering her out of his lap, he stood, not really knowing what to do next. "I'm sorry. I thought you were your aunt. We just had a moment, and I thought she was coming to make up."

Whitney blushed and let out a soft giggle. "It's okay, Uncle Ty. I came looking for her and saw you here. You looked stressed, and I wanted to help. I should have announced myself."

Tyree took note of the nervous look on her face and ran his hand down her cheek. "It was an honest mistake, honey. It wasn't like you did anything wrong. I was just caught off guard a little because I was expecting to see her. It's no big deal. But anyways, what are you doing? You fitting into the office okay?"

He saw her bright smile bursting through and found himself smiling as well. "Yeah. Everyone here is nice to me."

"That's one of the perks when your family owns the company." He chuckled, but he could see she was less than amused. Seeing her smile falter, he pulled her into an empty chair and took the one beside it. "Hey, what's wrong?" She was shaking her head telling him nothing, but the look in her eyes said otherwise. Tyree felt bad, like maybe he had said the wrong thing. He was pissing off all the women in his life on the same day. "Come on, Whit, talk."

"Sometimes I wonder if the only reason people are nice to me is because of you guys or because they think Grandpa is going to kill them. I just feel like no matter how hard I work to prove myself, none of it matters. Being in this family dictates the way people treat me, no matter what."

Tyree knew she always felt like she was in the shadows of everyone else, but he also knew how smart she was. "Baby girl, you know I understand better than anyone what it's like to prove yourself in a family like ours. It's hard. Before my dad was outed as what he was, he was a big deal, and it was tough getting people to see me as an equal."

"How did you do it?"

"I worked hard. I put in late hours, I gained the trust of the major players, and I proved I wasn't just another handsome face. You're smart, and you're capable. Just find your voice in this company and use it. They won't ignore you. Your brain will be your biggest asset. I've seen what you can do. Just show them."

"I will never be as good as Aunt Mia. She came into this, and they loved her without any doubts. She always wins people over the first time they meet her. She's perfect."

Tyree never noticed it before now. He always thought Whitney was in awe of Mia. Now, he saw she was intimidated. "She's just outgoing. She takes risks, and most of the time she is right. People love her because they see her. She makes herself seen. I'm sure once you get comfortable, they will love you too. You have so much of her and Cassie in you."

"You think so?"

"I know so. I know you've always felt like you weren't as much a part of the family as her, but she loves you and would do anything to see you succeed. If you need help or pointers, she's the one who can help."

"Really? She isn't too busy?"

"For you, never. Mia will make the time."

When she leaned over to hug him, he felt her relax and knew he had gotten through. He was all set to get up and go back to his office when she tugged at his shirt. "Okay, now that we have my episode out of the way, let's talk about what has you upset."

"I'm fine," he lied.

"I remember you saying you guys had a fight. What was it about?"

"Nothing major. You know us. We'll be fine by the end of the night."

"Don't tell me you're fighting about Jake being here. You know she's done with him, right?"

"You're too smart. In my head, I know this, but I guess I get antsy when he's around. She left me before, and he was the one she ran to. I just don't want it to happen again."

Whitney sighed and crossed her arms over her chest.

"I don't trust him."

"But you trust her, right?"

He was silent, and for the first time he admitted it out loud. "I don't know. I want to believe her, because me saying that I don't means I think she will leave again, but damn, I never thought she would leave the first time. Is that bad or what?"

"It's okay to have doubts, but it's not right to keep telling her it's fine when it isn't. If you feel like it's going to be a problem, you should say something."

"I love her."

"I know."

"Her laugh, it makes me crazy. The way she smiles when she talks to Kyan is amazing, and the way she throws herself into my arms when she's excited just makes me melt. I don't want to lose any of that."

"Just talk to her. Tell her what you're feeling."

"I feel like we've had this conversation too many times before. I should be over it. She has been back for over three years, but—"

"Uncle Ty, before Jake came back here, did you have any doubts?"

"None," he answered quickly.

"Then it's not her. It's him. Your problem is with him, and until you confront it, you're going to doubt her."

Tyree raised his hands, conceding, and he nodded at her. "You know, to be so young, you're very insightful."

"I've been told I'm smart beyond my years." She smirked, and he draped his arm over her shoulder.

"You know, kid, I don't know what I would do without you. I'm glad you're staying in town. You keep me sane."

She smiled up at him and kissed his cheek. "I don't know what I would do either. I love you, Uncle Ty."

"I love you too, baby girl. You free for lunch? It's on me."

"Sure, and I know just the place. Just let me text Jude and let him know where I'll be."

Tyree stepped out of the office, pulling her out by her arm. He loved the time they spent together. Besides the conversations with Mia, some of the best he had were with Whitney. Whitney always knew what to say to him, and she valued his opinion so much. He wasn't lying when he said she reminded him of Mia. Even if she didn't know it yet, he was aware that she possessed the same special something Mia did that captivated a room. She just had to unlock her potential.

They got into his car, and he smiled, watching her. How the little girl he once comforted when she cried about having to go back to her boarding school had transformed into the beautiful young woman before him was baffling. He always knew she would be special and that she would change some young man's world. He was just grateful that the young man who stole her heart was as deserving as Jude. He knew Jude would be the perfect addition to their family, and he couldn't wait to make it official.

After pulling up to the restaurant, Tyree got out and walked over to open the door for Whitney before letting the valet park his car. He reached for her hand and helped her out as she leaned into his shoulder. He had always been close to his niece, but he never knew how much he had missed her until she was home for good. Now, he was excited. He felt like he could really be a part of her life. He wanted to watch her get married and start a family of her own that he could love as much as he had loved her. To him, as long as he settled things with Mia once and for all, things would be perfect.

Tyree completely spaced out, allowing his thoughts to envelop him. He hadn't registered anything around him until he looked up and they were being seated at a table. He looked over to his niece and felt himself being transported back into the present. He could tell she was excited, and in a way it made him feel guilty. He hadn't realized how much he had been neglecting her since she had been back. True, they were all busy, but that was no excuse. Here she was taking time out of her day to have lunch with him, and he was sure she had other things she could be doing. After all, she was newly engaged, and he knew exactly what that entailed: spontaneous lovemaking for no reason at all. He and Mia were there once, so many years ago.

Once they took their seats, he reached across the table and pulled her hand to his. "Thanks, kid. This is exactly what I needed."

"What, Uncle Ty, lunch?" she chuckled.

"No, a day to spend with you. It's been so long since we did this. I miss it."

"I miss it too."

He cleared his throat. "So, how is everything going? How is the wedding planning?"

"Great."

He loved the smile that graced her face, and he waved the waiter over for their drinks. The timid boy came over to take their order and stood shuffling in his apron. He seemed nervous to be serving them, but there was something more to his behavior. The way he was looking across the room gave Tyree pause. Just as Tyree began to scan the room, the skinny boy disappeared to the back, and Whitney looked confused.

"What's up?" she asked. "Why are you looking like you just saw a ghost?"

"Did you see that? That boy, the way he ran off . . . And who the hell was he staring at?"

"People act like this when they're around you. You make them nervous."

"Me?" he laughed. "Why?"

"You're Tyree Johnston, one of the richest men in town, and they know about Grandpa and Uncle John."

"I'm not them."

"People who don't know you think you're always so serious. They don't know the man we do, the crazy, fun uncle who loves his family to no end."

"How'd you get so smart, kid? I swear you put everything in perspective for your old uncle."

"You're not that old, and I'm not that smart."

"You're brilliant, and Jude is a lucky guy."

"You keep saying that, but I don't know, maybe I'm the lucky one. Having someone accept me the way he does is more than I could ask for. He's the only one who . . . He just knows stuff."

He saw a tear roll down her cheek and was confused. "Whit, what's going on? You can tell me."

"It's nothing," she rushed to answer, and he felt his suspicions grow. "I don't want to ruin our lunch with my melodrama. What we need to be thinking about is how you're going to get back in Aunt Mia's good graces."

Ignoring the noticeable change of subject, Tyree questioned her further. "Did something happen to you?"

He could tell she wished he would just drop it, and when the waiter appeared again with their drinks and appetizers, she was able to evade his questions. She chewed her food nervously and sipped her drink in silence. He was watching her intently, waiting for her to give him a response, but she just kept on eating.

They sat quietly enjoying the drinks and appetizers until the main entrees arrived. When Whitney bit into her food, her eyes lit up, and she flung her fork across the table right into Tyree's face. "You have to try this, Uncle Ty. It's magnificent."

He smiled his first real smile since the uncomfortable moment, and he allowed her to share the dish with him. Surprisingly, he loved it, and the awkward moment was gone. The rest of the lunch went by as if nothing had happened, and they fell back into the fun banter they were accustomed to. They just enjoyed each other and spent time catching up, never once noticing the person watching them from across the room.

Chapter Eleven

Stripping her shoes off, she heard a sweet little voice and smiled. "Mommy, wur you been? I miss you."

Asha bent down, scooped her sweet little boy up in her arms, and littered his cheek with kisses. "I missed you too, sweetie. Mommy was at work, but I'm home now."

"Gud. Daddy cook."

She loved how his eyes lit up at the mention of his dad and food. She only assumed Terence had let him help out in the kitchen and he was aching to show her what they had pulled off. She loved coming home to this, her husband and children all home and waiting for her. It made her feel special.

Walking into the kitchen, she found Meelah sitting on a stool and Terence behind the counter. He was listening to a story she was telling about school, and she watched how he paid close attention to each detail she relayed.

He was oblivious to her in the room, and she just watched them for a minute until Jonathan announced their presence. "Daddy, Mommy here."

Terence looked up, and she felt her skin tingle as his eyes roamed her body. "That she is. Hey, Mommy." He smirked.

Jonathan looked at him in confusion and then back at Asha. "She not yer mommy, she mine and Meeha's."

Terence chuckled, and Asha giggled, kissing his chubby cheek. "Thank you for correcting him, baby. Your daddy is just silly sometimes."

"Wat silly?"

She looked to Terence for help, and he turned out his hands and shrugged, telling her she was on her own. When she turned back to find her inquisitive little boy waiting for an answer, she bounced him on her hip and ran her hand over his cheek. "Silly is a little thing your daddy does that makes us laugh." She tickled his little stomach, and he started to giggle.

"That's the best you got, Mommy?" Terence laughed, and Jonathan stopped what they were doing and begged to be put down.

Jonathan walked over to Terence, tugged at his pants leg, and with the most serious expression he crossed his arms over his chest. "She not yer mommy, Daddy. She mine, silly."

Terence picked him up and looked over at Asha. "Now you got the boy calling me silly. Is it ever gonna end?"

"Nope. They all think you're silly, and quite frankly, so do I." The kids' heads flew to the door, and in an instant, they were running toward the source of the comment.

"Uncle Miguel!" Meelah yelled and threw her arms around his legs. Jonathan was still making his way over when Miguel scooped Meelah up, kissing her cheek.

When Jonathan finally reached him, he tugged at his pants, throwing his hands up. "Uncle Gel, me up too."

"You got it, little man." He bent down and swung Jonathan up, making him squeal. "How're Uncle's babies?"

"I not a baby. I two. I big boy," Jonathan pouted.

"You sure are, and you're already taller than your daddy."

They all laughed, and Miguel played with the kids until their attention was stolen away by the second person walking through the door. Jonathan's loud shriek alerted them that he was there. "Kyem! You came to pay wift me!"

They watched Jonathan jump down and run over to Kyan with open arms. Kyan picked him up, and Jonathan wanted his airplane as soon as he was settled in Kyan's arms. Terence told the boys to take it in the living room, and Meelah followed them, offering her uncle a kiss on the cheek on the way out.

"So," Terence said, catching Miguel's attention, "what brings you and Kyan over? It's been a while since we've seen you out and in this type of mood. What gives?"

Miguel turned and looked around, making sure the kids were out of hearing range. "I needed to bring him because his parents need a night. Things were a little rocky earlier, and I owe Mia for what she did."

"Rocky? What happened?"

"Let's just say Jake being back in town is putting a strain on things. Mia was over earlier, and they got into a heated discussion over the phone. From what I heard, this isn't the first argument they've had since he's been back."

"I would assume not," Asha piped in. "I think we all know what happened the other night after Ty punched him."

"Whoa, Ty did what?" Miguel asked in amazement. "Why haven't I heard any of this? What the hell has been going on?"

Asha walked over and placed her hand on his. "Look, I'm sorry we didn't tell you, but honestly, you had your own things going on. We didn't want you to worry when you were already dealing with something."

Miguel developed a look, and Asha could tell he felt guilty. "I'm sorry. I know I haven't been there for any of you lately, and the fact that you felt like you couldn't come to me sucks. I know I was in a bad way, but I'm always here. That's another reason why I came tonight. I need your help, but I also wanted to apologize for how I've been. Mia made me realize how my actions were affecting all of you."

"It's okay. We've had to deal with more over the past few years than most people face in a lifetime. You're entitled to go off the grid for a little while."

"What about you, sis? You never unravel, and you've been through just as much."

"I would love to unravel, and I've had my moments, but unlike you, I have three people who need me at my best. As much as it all hurts, they need me, and it makes me stronger than I could have ever been otherwise."

Miguel nodded, and Terence stepped in, offering his support. "What was it you needed help with?"

"I need to know why Jake is here and what he wants. I told Mia I would stay out of it, but I need to know if he is just here to stir up trouble for Ty."

"I'm already ahead of you. I have eyes on him, and I'm looking into the last three years. Soon, I should know everything he has been up to and everyone he has been in contact with."

"Damn, that's a good start. Well, you will let me know what you find out, right?"

"Of course."

He looked around the kitchen, taking in the smell coming from the stove. "Well, what's for dinner? You have enough for us? I was going to take him and the kids out for pizza, but this smells way better."

"Yeah, we have enough, and he can stay here tonight if you have something up later," Terence supplied.

"It's good, man. I want him to spend the night at my place. I've been slacking in my uncle duties, and I need to do better. Get the other two ready, and I'll take everyone."

"You want all of them?" Asha laughed. "They are going to run you crazy, and Jonathan won't sleep in the guest room alone. When he isn't home, he needs to sleep next to someone."

Miguel smiled, and Asha saw a glimmer of the brother she used to have so much fun with. "I'm okay with the kid sleeping in my bed. We will all be fine as long as he's potty trained. I don't want to wake up wet."

"My baby has been potty trained for months now. He is an old pro at going to the restroom."

"Good. Well then, I'll take them all."

"Good luck," Terence laughed. "Meelah is going to have you playing dress-up, and Jonathan is going to have you doing the airplane so much your arms might fall off."

"I don't need luck, and it's exactly what I need to spend my night doing. I missed them, and it's time I grew up. Family is what's important."

"I agree." Asha hugged him, and he melted into her embrace. She felt like for the first time in months her brother was going to be just fine. "Let's get the kids packed, and then we will all sit down to dinner. We have so much to discuss, you and me."

"That we do." He pulled her up and swung his arm around her shoulder. They walked out of the room while Terence stayed behind to put the finishing touches on dinner. They chatted their way through the living room, past the children, and up the stairs, and Asha felt like things were finally going back to normal for them. The strain was finally gone.

Chapter Twelve

Mia felt the walls closing in on her as soon as she closed the door. Sure her house was decorated with rose petals and darkened, with only the candlelight flickering against the wall, but she felt anything but loved at the moment. It wasn't because of the latest fight with Tyree. It was because she knew it was only a matter of time before she had to come clean. She wanted to at least feel the comfort of him before she did.

Mia knew he was probably feeling guilty about questioning her, but if she were completely honest, she would admit she didn't blame him. His insecurities were all her doing, and she knew they would only get worse after she told him everything there was to know about her and Jake. She couldn't begin to figure out what she was going to say, but she knew it had to be done. She was tired of the secrets, tired of trying to cover them.

She was moving through the house, removing articles of clothing with each step. To feel the gentle caresses from her husband was what her body ached for. She made it as far as the stairs when she felt herself being lifted into his strong arms. She felt as his lips made contact with her skin, and she felt herself sinking into his kiss.

He carried her to their room and pushed the door shut with his foot. As soon as he dropped her to the bed, he attacked her lips with his and ran his hands up her sides. She swore her skin was on fire. She had never wanted him as much as she did now. When they finally broke from the kiss, she could tell he wanted to talk, but she didn't want to ruin the moment. He sat up on the bed, and she pulled him back down.

"Don't." She pulled his lips back to hers, and he caved into the kiss before catching himself and pulling back again.

"No, wait. I need to—"

She moved to his neck, and she could tell she was affecting him, clouding his judgment. "I don't want to talk about it, Ty. Not right now."

"But we need to clear the air. I need to tell you how wrong I was."

The guilt swelled and almost suffocated her. She looked into his eyes and saw the pain and knew she needed to say something, anything to make this better. "It's not your fault. I haven't been honest with you. I haven't told you everything I should have. I just didn't want you to look at me that way."

"What way?"

"Like I wasn't the woman you fell in love with. I've done so many things I'm not proud of, and I just don't want you to hate me."

He kissed the tear rolling down her cheek, and she shuddered. "I could never hate you, and truth be told, there are a lot of things you don't know about when we weren't together. None of it is important. I'm willing to let it go if you will. I want you to focus on what we are right now."

"Why would you do that? You just wanted to talk."

"Because you're upset and it's making you question my love for you. I never want you to do that, and if it's that hard to remember, then I don't need to know. I know I've been pushing for it, and I'm sorry. If it makes you this uncomfortable, then forget it. I don't want us having any more days like today."

There it was, her chance to bury everything and start fresh, but something about it felt off. She didn't want to continue with the lies that had clouded them for so long. She knew that whatever he had done in no way topped what she had

been afraid to reveal. Now was the time to come
clean and pray they could recover.

"I have to be honest with you. I wish I could
just forget everything, but it's not that simple."

He covered her body and began to plant kisses
on every exposed area. He danced his fingers
down her stomach and across the band of her
panties. He hooked his fingers on both sides
and slid them down, and she felt more exposed
than ever. Her body was on display and her
very soul bared to him. She had never felt more
vulnerable than she did at that very moment.
"Make it that simple. Forgive yourself and let me
help you forget."

"No. . . ." She tried to object, to make him
listen, but when his fingers invaded her body,
her back arched and her mouth clamped shut.
She had no control over herself. He had taken
all her power with one single twirl of his fingers.
If only he knew the authority he had over her. If
only he knew the things he could make her do.

She felt him doing his signature move down
her body, and she knew exactly where he was
headed. His mouth was one of his best assets
when it came to making love. The way he flicked
his tongue over her sensitive pleasure points
always made her scream. It was almost as good
as when he pushed inside her and made her

body his in every way. This was the release she needed, the release she wanted, but she needed even more for him to feel it first.

She pushed him over, stopping his journey to his favorite place between her legs. He landed on his back, and she took advantage of his position. This was the one place they never had trouble. She always knew what he wanted and vice versa. She knew he wanted to plant himself between her thighs and taste her, but she wanted to take charge of this. She wanted to feel like she had the same power over him.

Unbuttoning his shirt and opening it to reveal his chest, she made her way to his nipples and nipped at them gently with her teeth. He loved this, she could tell by the way he wove his fingers through her hair. His light rubbing on her scalp pushed her further, and she started a sucking motion only to follow up with a light nibble. She repeated it on the other nipple. She was sure he was more than ready to have her when he grabbed her hips and forced her hard against him. Even with his pants still on, she could feel the hard mass pressing between her legs.

Feeling his desire for her pushed the moment from lustful to purely primal. She yanked his zipper down and tugged at his pants legs until they lay at the foot of the bed. Tyree sat up and gripped her hips, but she pushed him down, holding a palm to his chest as her other hand found its way to the object of her desire in his boxers. He let out a deep growl when she pushed the boxers away, allowing him to spring free. She didn't permit him to take them off fully before her tongue poked out, bathing his tip with her warm caresses. His hands found their way back to her hair and tightened. Pushing her head farther, she took all of him in and allowed her tongue to ravish his hardened member.

The bucking of his hips excited her more than she ever thought possible, and she sped up her movements. She started off with her hands, stroking wherever her mouth couldn't reach, and began to dance her fingertips from his base. She could feel the throbbing under her finger pads and delighted at the thought that she made him this way.

She had never enjoyed this before, but with him it was different. Every time his fingers dug deeper into her scalp, she felt a new level of passion. Every time his hips propelled, she felt stronger, like she could do anything. That was the effect he had on her. He made her feel like she had power she never knew she possessed.

Treating his erection like her own plaything, she pulled him all the way from her mouth just to dance her tongue down the side. When his head flew from the pillow, she pushed him back with one hand. Dancing her tongue down the other side, she felt his hands fist her hair. The pain mixed with pleasure drove her to take him as far as she could. Her sucking intensified and her tongue danced around in her closed mouth until she felt the trickling sensation of his climax.

As his body drained, he emptied himself into her mouth. This time, she didn't make him pull out or release in a towel. This time, she swallowed every bit of what he had to offer and then lay on her back. She needed to catch her breath. She needed to slow down her pulse, but he didn't give her that chance. Before she could prepare herself, he was back between her thighs and pressed against her. He didn't enter her just yet. Instead, he grabbed his erection and brushed it over her wet, sensitive folds.

He was teasing her, tracing her entrance with his tip, and she needed to feel him. He had to know what he was doing. She looked up at him. The look he held told her it was going to be amazing. Capturing her lips, he fell into her, and the initial feeling sent tiny bolts passing through her. He hovered over her for a while before he began to move and pushed the hair from her face. She swore she had only once before felt the tenderness he was giving her: the first time they made love. They were children, things were so new to them, but he was everything she could have wished for. They were both nervous, but he made her comfortable with every touch.

The way he was looking at her now reminded her, and when he took her mouth and thrust forward, she felt her patience shatter. She could tell he wanted slow and steady, but she wanted something else. Placing her hands on his ass, she pushed him deeper, and he picked up on her need. Sliding his hands up to her waist, he buried himself completely, and she gasped. Wrapping her legs around his waist, she locked her ankles together, holding him close, and he threw himself hard against her.

Tyree grabbed her hands, locking their fingers together before sliding her arms up above her head. She loved the way he shifted his body up and propelled himself into a frenzy of thrusts that took her breath away. She tried to scream out his name, but it presented as a series of light whispers. She tickled his neck with her breath, and he dropped his head to rest in the hollow of her neck and pushed himself harder, still gripping her hands. She turned her head to him and tasted the ecstasy radiating off his tongue.

She had no idea it could be like this between them. When he secured his hand around her waist, flipping them and allowing her to take her rightful place on top of him, she brought herself down, taking in every rock-hard inch of his erection. Reaching under them to toy with his sack, she took joy in the moans that escaped his lips. Curling his arm around her waist and sliding his other hand into her hair, he gripped her tight and forced her body up and down. She placed her arms on his shoulders and dug her nails in deep just as he met her neck with his tongue.

He licked her neck, and she sped up, rolling her hips forward, and then she teased him by swaying from side to side. With each sway of her hips, he sucked on her neck harder and harder. She was sure she would have a hickey, but she didn't care. It felt too good to make him stop, and she was too far gone to put up a fight. When he moved to the other side of her neck, she threw her head to the side, and he slid his hand to the small of her back and pushed her harder against him.

Their sweat intermingled and Mia swore her body was floating off the bed. Locking her legs behind him, she crossed her arms around his neck and placed her hand on the back of his head. Lacing her fingers together, she pulled his mouth to hers and swore they shared the same breath. When she exhaled so did he, when she gasped he did as well, and as soon as his lips parted, she pushed her tongue inside, tasting him for what felt like the millionth time that night. His kisses were intoxicating, his lips were addictive, and everything he was doing to her body was exhilarating.

He was still on her neck, one hand in her hair and the other on her back, when she felt it coming. She felt her legs shaking and her insides fluttering when he took her mouth in one last kiss. As soon as their lips met, she felt the quakes take over, and she heard his grunts, letting her know he was there too. Nothing felt better, and she basked in the moment. He kissed his way from her mouth up to her earlobe and whispered to her.

"You forget yet?"

She sighed when he pulled away and looked her in the eyes. She swore she saw nothing but love and understanding, and it made her heart hurt. She knew he said to drop it, but she somehow felt she didn't deserve what he was giving her. She didn't deserve a clean slate, not until he knew everything that clouded the old one. She opened her mouth, but he put his finger on her lips. "If the answer is anything but yes, then don't say it. I want you happy, and you won't be as long as you feel like anything that happened between us was your fault. We all did things, we said horrible things, but we're here, and that's all that matters. Trust me."

"I tried to overdose." Like verbal diarrhea, the words came spilling out of her mouth before she could stop them. His eyes widened, and she felt his body tense. He was still inside her, and she felt him twitch. The look in his eyes was blank. She put her hand to his cheek, and he felt cold. His skin was covered in goosebumps, and she was frightened by the dejected look in his eyes. He gently lifted her body from his and moved to stand in front of the dresser. Grabbing the sheet, wrapping it around herself, she moved behind him, and he shivered at her touch. "Baby—"

"Just stop," he said, cutting her off. "I can't . . . I just . . . Why? Why would you do that to me? To us? I can't think about . . ." He was shaking, and he recoiled from her touch. He was walking backward, and she saw him withdrawing from her emotionally, too. She wanted to say anything he needed to hear to make this better, but when she went to speak, he held up his hand. She looked at him with pleading eyes, and he rushed for his boxers and robe.

"No." She reached her hand out, and he pulled back like she burned him. She walked up, placing her hands on his face. "Come on. Talk to me. Tell me we're okay. I promise it wasn't you."

He shook himself free of her hands and moved toward the door as she just stood, watching. "I need to get out of here. I need a walk."

"Just talk to me."

"I'll be back." He fled the room and she crumbled to the floor. Suddenly, she felt like she should have just kept her mouth shut and listened to what he said. Finding her robe and her way to the stairs, she watched as he slowly pulled the door open. He looked so helpless, and she knew she only had herself to blame. She was the reason for his pain and wanted to fix it. She was still running behind him but slowed her stride when she heard the door close.

She just stared at the door as she felt her heart sink. So many things were racing through her mind, and she cursed herself for opening her mouth. At that point, she knew she had to get to Jake and shut him up. If hearing that caused the despair she saw in his eyes, she could only imagine what the rest would do. Now, her main focus was going to be keeping the past hidden by all means necessary.

***

"What in the hell is going on around here?" Richmond yelled. "You were supposed to handle this shit before it got too far. A fight in a restaurant is not what I meant by handling it."

Lenae huffed and threw down the stack of papers she was holding. "I've been doing that, but what I won't do is sacrifice my daughter's future. Your plan for revenge is putting her in danger, and I won't stand for it. You get yourself together or leave us alone."

Richmond looked at her, and before she knew what was happening, he slammed his hand down on the table in front of her. "You would have nothing if it weren't for me, you remember that. I built that empire, and I'll be damned if it goes up in smoke because they're being careless."

"You're overreacting as usual. Why do you have to be so damned dramatic?"

"Because you don't worry enough. We have a plan, and we have to stick to it if we're going to get back what's ours."

Lenae huffed and threw her hands over her face. "What if it's not possible? I mean, we've been outsmarted so many times, and every time you get your hands on a sliver of that company, we get the rug snatched from under us. I just can't be hopeful for it any longer. I wanted it only because you made me believe it was possible. I don't want to keep living in dreamland. You are delusional if you think you will ever be able to walk free again. You will forever be in hiding, and so will Jenna and I for going along with this ridiculous plan. You're taunting them, and they're never going to take you seriously that way."

Richmond had been on the run for the better part of three years, for the murders of his wife and daughter, and every time he thought he had an inch of leverage, Mia or Rick snatched it from him. He had been kicked out of Livingston by his own children and had to sit and watch them merge his life's work with the Johnston family's business.

"You're wrong! I will have my vengeance, and you'll see. You all will see how wrong you were about Richmond Livingston. I know more than their ungrateful asses. Just you wait and see."

Richmond stormed out of the room, and his companion Lenae stood, staring off into space until she heard Jenna's quiet, frightened voice come into play. "Mommy, why were you and Papa screaming?" Lenae looked down to her little dimple-faced sweetheart and picked her up, smoothing the stray tears from her eyes. "Were you screaming because you miss the old house?"

Jenna looked away and dropped her head. "I miss the old house too. Why do we always have to move, Mommy?"

Running her hands through Jenna's curly hair, she kissed her on the cheek. "We have to move because Mommy messed up. She talked to someone she shouldn't have and could have gotten us into a lot of trouble. I'm sorry, baby."

"Why can't you talk to people?"

"Because some not-so-nice people want to hurt us. Mommy's sorry she messed up. Are you upset with me?"

"No."

"You're Mommy's best friend, do you know that?"

"Yes. You're my best friend too."

She sat Jenna down, and she ran back to what would be her room for the next few days before they took off again. She really hated having to shuffle her daughter around so much, but honestly, she had no alternative. As much as she threatened Richmond, she knew that without him they were as good as dead. They could never survive without him.

Chapter Thirteen

He kicked his shoes off and lowered his robe to the floor. Never in his life had Tyree felt so exhausted. Never in his life had he felt so out of it. Walking over to their bed, he paused. He was confused and lost. Should he just get in the bed and pretend the past few hours hadn't happened, or did he hold on to the sour feeling that was taking over his every thought?

He was standing, afraid to get into his own bed. Every time he made a move to pull the covers back, he froze, deathly afraid he would wake the sleeping woman lying before him. With one hand on the comforter and one hand on the bedpost, he stood there silently, watching her toss around.

He knew she must be having a bad dream because she only tossed that way when she was distressed. He knew that about her. He knew so many things about her, so much that he swore he could even read her mind at certain points.

He knew all this, but what he couldn't wrap his mind around was how he missed it. There had to be something he missed. There had to be something that he just didn't pay enough attention to that made her feel like she needed to take her own life.

Watching her, he would never understand how someone so beautiful could be so damaged. As long as he had known her, she had always had her demons. Even as a child, she never felt like she deserved to be happy. Watching her parents had beaten her spirit to an almost-irreparable state. Being with him had almost brought her out of it, but she still had her moments. Even when they were at the peak of their happiness, he would catch a glimpse of that insecure girl he used to wrap his arms around all those years ago.

Watching her sleep, so unsettled, so uncomfortable, he felt an ache in his chest. That she felt like she couldn't come to him before was what bothered him. He thought they shared everything. He thought he knew her better. He thought she knew him. He thought. . . .

He paused in his ramblings when she sat up. She was still asleep, but he saw how flustered she was. The anxiety must have been eating away at her. Watching her, he tried to be as still as possible until he saw her head hit the pillow.

How could she have not come to him? How could she have kept that secret for so long? How? The more he thought about it, the clearer it became. He had frozen when she blurted it out. He hadn't been the man he promised to be. He had let her down. He had to admit, he was shocked when she said it, and a part of him was angry. He was angry that the woman he pledged his life to felt like she had to keep something from him, but could he really blame her? With the way he reacted, he'd be lucky if she ever told him anything again. He really blew it.

Deciding to swallow his fears, he tugged at the thick comforter and revealed his sleeping wife. He longed so badly to reach out and touch her, but he was afraid she would feel it and wake, forcing him to own up to his earlier cowardice. He loved her. He loved her more than he ever thought it was possible to love another person besides his son, but she also scared him. She held in her palm the key to his world, and she had the power to flip that very same world upside down by taking herself out of it. He needed her almost as much as the air he breathed. How she didn't know that was a mystery.

Just as he thought, as soon as his body found comfort in the cool sheets, her eyes fluttered open. He could see the red outlining her eyes and knew she had been crying. Without a thought, he ran his hand down her cheek, and she just stared back. She was silent, but her eyes were screaming at him. Her eyes held all her fears, all her doubts about him. Smoothing his hands over her flawless cheeks, he felt her stiffen. He closed his eyes. He couldn't look at her without falling apart. She was everything to him, and he knew that without her he would never be the same.

He could feel her eyes on him, and even though she didn't speak, he could feel her willing him to make the first step. Slowly peeling his eyes apart, he looked at her, really looked at her. He searched her eyes, looking for the woman he married, but she wasn't there. All he saw was the scared little girl who used to sneak off in the middle of the night and into his bed when her parents fought. He saw the unsure teenager who never felt as beautiful as she truly was. Looking into her eyes now, he didn't see his fierce, fearless wife. He saw the exposed interior she displayed only when she was afraid. She was afraid, and he hated himself for that.

Without words, they had the most powerful conversation they would ever have. He could tell she was searching his eyes, and he made sure to let her know the love was still there. He stroked her cheek and kissed her forehead like he had done so many times before and she slid closer to him. He hadn't realized the abandonment he felt without her close. Burying his hand in her long, dark tresses, he pulled her head back and lined his lips with hers. The kiss wasn't like their usual lustful, intense kisses. It was sweet and gentle, just like it had been so many years ago.

Tyree looked across the room and out the window to notice the rain beginning to fall. As the rain danced across their roof, it lulled him into a soothing memory, a memory he would never forget. Holding his fragile wife tightly in his arms with a storm brewing made him think of a night many years ago. It was the night that meant everything in his young life.

The phone rang in the dead of night, and he knew it was her. He didn't even have to hear her voice to know she was upset. It had just become the norm. Looking at his bedside table, he read the clock and realized it was five past midnight, and he reached to retrieve the phone. He heard her sniffling when he answered, and he sat up suddenly.

"What's wrong, Mia? What happened this time?"

It took her a minute to calm down enough to speak, but when she did, he could tell she needed him. "They were screaming. I heard the door slam, I walked out to see what was going on, and I saw her."

He didn't have to ask who the "her" was. He knew she was referring to her mother. Things had gone from bad to worse between her parents, and every time they fought, Mia seemed to be the one to hear it. "What was she doing?"

"Ty, it's bad. She's using drugs. I've heard him call her a coke whore, but this is the first time I've seen it with my own eyes. I didn't want to believe it was true. I just . . . I don't know what to do. I just want to leave this place."

He sighed and ran a hand over his head. He had promised they would be out of there as soon as graduation was done, but they still had three weeks before that could happen. Things were just happening too fast with her family, and he couldn't protect her from everything like he had hoped. "I'm sorry. I know I promised you it would be over soon. I wish we could go tonight, but we have to graduate, and then we can go anywhere we want before college starts."

"You promise?"

"I promise. I just wish I were there with you now. You sound so sad, and I just want to be next to you."

He could hear the silence on her end, and when he went to say something, she spoke up. "You could just come over."

He wasn't sure if it was a good idea. He had been trying to respect the boundaries in their relationship, but it was growing harder with every minute they spent alone. Their friends and siblings had served as a buffer between them, but when they were alone, he wanted to touch her, to feel what it was like to really be with her.

"I don't know, babe. It's the middle of the night, and it's raining."

"Please?"

There she went with the begging. She knew he always caved when she asked in that voice. She sounded so weak. He couldn't leave her like that, not tonight. "Okay, I'm on the way." After throwing on his basketball shorts and a tank with a hoodie, he grabbed his keys and walked out, shutting the door. He got as far as the stairs when he heard a voice behind him.

"Going out?"

He turned to see his mother standing with her arms folded over her chest.

"I need to see . . . My girl needs me. Her parents are crazy, and she needs someone. I promise I won't be out long."

Karen studied him, and it felt like he was under a microscope for those few seconds. When she let out a sly smile, he grinned back at her. "Thanks, Mom. I knew you would understand." He rushed to give her a hug, and she kissed his cheek. He turned and walked a few steps down before she called out to him again.

"Give Mia my love, and tell her it will get better."

He stood frozen for the moment and looked at her, noticing the weird grin she held.

"What? You thought I didn't know? I see the way you look at her, and if her parents don't notice it, they're damn fools. I know it's been a struggle for them, but they have to know what it's doing to their kids."

"Either they don't, or they don't care. I just want her happy."

"Then don't keep her waiting. If you need to, bring her here and get a room fixed up." She turned, and he could tell something clicked in her head. "One of the guest rooms, not yours."

He laughed and sent her a wink on his way out. Once he made it out the door and to his car, he turned, looking at his house, and he felt a wave of sadness. True, he wanted to take Mia away from her problems, but he would miss times like this, where he just talked to his mother. She always seemed to know what was going on with him, and he loved her for her concern. He needed Mia away from her mother and father, but he also needed his mom. He started his car and drove away, trying to figure out what he was going to do to make things right for everyone when an idea came to him. He wasn't sure she would go for it, but he had to try. Their futures were at stake.

Driving through her back gate, he found humor in the fact that no matter how much security they had, he always seemed to be able to sneak in undetected. So many nights he had taken the same route to get to her and was never seen. He would sneak in the back, with the gate code Mia had given him, through the servants' entrance, and up the back staircase that led straight to her room. For some reason, her parents had their rooms on the other side of the house and only Mia, Janelle, and Rick, when he was home from college, were on the west end.

Tyree parked his car and took his normal passage to her, and before he could reach the stairs, he saw her coming down. Looking at her short white silk gown made his heart leap in his chest. He had seen her in next to nothing many times before, but seeing her like this was different. She was beautiful. The gown hugged every curve, displayed every perfect crease her body had to offer, and gave him an excellent view of her delicious legs. His hormones were raging. He wanted those legs wrapped around him, squeezing him, pulling him deeper inside her. Shaking the dirty thoughts, he looked into her eyes. He had to admit his girl was gorgeous.

Standing, staring at her, he only made a move when he felt her hand grab him and pull him toward the stairs. He followed her quickly, and when they made it to her room, the door closed, and he felt himself being pushed against it. He was caught off guard by her aggressiveness and fell into her kisses until he found himself getting overly excited. Pulling away, he stepped back, touching his fingertips to his swollen lips.

"Baby, what are you doing? I thought you knew we were just going to sleep. I don't think—"

He heard the deep sigh and watched her move to the bed. "Why won't you sleep with me? I thought you loved me, and I know I love you. What's the problem?"

Tyree sat down on the bed and pulled her against him. He rubbed her back soothingly and kissed her forehead before pulling her back to look in his eyes. "You know I love you,

Mia. I wouldn't have said it if I didn't mean it. I just don't want you to give yourself to me and regret it later. So much has been going on since we started this. I know we've known each other our whole lives, and there is love there, but I don't want you to mistake loving me with being in love. We've been friends for as long as I can remember, and I just can't take that step until I know it's what you truly want."

He felt her hand sliding up his chest, and when she placed her hand around his neck, his head turned to her. "I love you. I'm in love with you. How else would you explain all this? I'm eighteen, and the only boy I've kissed is you. The only boy besides my brother who has held me when I cry is you. You're the first person I call when I'm happy and the first I call when things are bad. I really feel like you would drop the world for me, and I couldn't think of anyone else I would want to give myself to for the first time or any time after that. I need you to love me that much."

He gripped the sides of her head and gave her a gentle kiss. Pulling back, he stroked her cheek with his thumb. "I already love you so much more than that. Baby girl, you're it for me. I've never wanted anyone as much as I want you. I just want to be sure you're ready."

"I'm ready. I'm so ready I could burst. I know they say young love doesn't last, but I don't think we will have that problem. I'm going to love you forever."

"Forever?"

"Forever. I hope that's what you want."

"It's exactly what I need. You're sure about this? I mean, I wanted it to be special for you."

"It's special because I'm with you. Knowing that no one else has been this close to you and that I am the only one makes it more special than you know."

Tyree laid her back on the bed, kissing her all the way down. He wanted to wait. He wanted more for their first time. He wanted candles, flowers, and music. He wanted her to feel how much he needed her. Sitting up on the bed, he saw the look that crossed her face and felt bad. He never meant to make her feel like he didn't want this, but he couldn't help feeling like he was cheating her.

He stood, pacing the floor, and she sat up, crossing her arms over her chest. The rain was beating against the window, and the thunder crackled, being followed by a bolt of lightning. It was then that he saw the tear streaking her cheek. Moving slowly from the bed, she stood and crossed the room to the door. He reached for her, but she brushed his arm away.

"Stop, Ty. You don't want me. I see that now. I know they say sex is not as fun if you're with a virgin, but I thought you would understand. I guess you'd rather be with someone who knows what they're doing."

He grabbed her wrist and pushed the door shut. Pressing himself against her, he felt her breathing hitch. He knew she felt his bulge, and he placed his hands on her hips. Pulling her back enough to turn her around, he attacked her neck, pressing her against the door.

"I want you, baby. I want you."

"Ty." She hissed his name between kisses and wrapped her arms around his neck. He picked her up by the hips and carried her back to bed while she wrapped her legs around his waist. Walking to the front of the bed and kicking it to be sure of the location, he slid her down and stepped back to admire the scene. When she sat up, he ran his hand down her lips and kissed her neck, trailing his tongue to her ear.

"I swear I want you, and I don't know what I'm doing either. If you won't hold it against me, I want to try something, but you have to trust me."

She nodded, and he abandoned her body, walking to the dresser, shuffling around until he found what he was looking for. Placing a CD in her player, he turned to find a smile on her face.

"Leaving your music here now? How sneaky."

Walking over and pulling her up, he ran his hand over her smooth skin. Everything about her was perfect, from her flawless skin to her round, supple ass. He couldn't wait to dig his fingers into it and grip it, pulling her against him. He felt his erection growing, and he knew he needed to take care of himself before he ended everything prematurely. He hadn't actually had sex before, but he had done things, with other girls of course, but he wanted this time with her to be everything she dreamed of.

Sliding his fingers up her body, he pushed the straps of her gown over, and she pushed him back, lowering her feet to the floor. When she stood, the gown floated away from her body, revealing her in nothing but black lace panties. He swore he had never seen anything more perfect than this until she hooked her fingers in the sides of her panties, sliding them down.

Watching her sent him into a daze. He wasn't sure this was real. He wasn't sure this was all happening, that the girl he had loved his entire life was standing in front of him, ready and willing. It was a dream. He convinced himself none of this was happening until he felt her lips *on his neck. For a virgin, she had a handle on this teasing thing. She sat on his lap and pulled at his hoodie bringing the tank along with it. His chest was bared to her, but she wasn't stopping. Standing from the bed and pulling him with her, he lost his breath when he felt her small hand pull the strings of his shorts and drop them to the hardwood floor. His boxers were next, and in removing them, her fingertips grazed his hardened shaft. The moan that escaped him seemed to have startled her, but she kept going until they were both completely naked.*

Now, with nothing separating them, he could feel her hesitancy. He couldn't tell at first because her touches were demanding, but being chest to chest, he could feel her uneven breathing. Pushing the hair behind her ear, he reached behind her, hooking his hands under her ass and lifting her into his arms. Being this close gave him the chance to feel her heated core pressing against him. He felt his pulse race and knew he needed to take action before he was useless in the situation.

He pulled her sheets back, and they tumbled to the bed. The kisses were getting too heated. He felt himself twitching against her and knew he needed something to slow himself down.

Leaving her mouth, he slid down her body, kissing a trail to her center. When he got to her waistline, her head flew from the pillow, and she looked at him breathlessly.

"You don't have to, Ty. I mean, we can just . . . I don't need that."

He pushed her back down and stayed in place. "I want to do this. Just trust me." He knew what this was about. "You don't have to do it back." His head disappeared underneath the sheet, and he ran his tongue over her. This was new territory for him, and he hoped he was doing it right. Stroking his tongue over her already-wet folds, he tasted the sweetest thing ever. She moved under him, squeezing her thighs around his face and he knew he was on the right track. He never thought he would like this. Even though the girls he had dated before her did it to him, he never returned the favor. This, with Mia, was special.

He continued to do what he thought she liked, flicking his tongue over every crease until he felt her body convulsing beneath him. All the while he had been stroking himself, trying to get rid of his first climax. He had heard enough from Terence to know that the first time could go fast if he hadn't prepared himself, and he didn't want that as a memory. Everything had to be perfect when Mia was involved. She was everything to him.

Her hushed moans were music to his ears, and once she stopped moving, he began slow kisses up her body. When he reached her mouth, he stopped short, feeling like she wouldn't want to kiss him after what he had just done, but she pulled his mouth down and claimed it for her own. Pushing her tongue past his lips, she intensified the kiss. Pulling back, reaching for his shorts, he fished out his wallet and pulled out a condom. Before opening it, he stopped to survey her eyes to make sure she was still game.

"You ready, baby?"

"I'm ready."

"You know, we can stop whenever—"

"Ty, come on. I'm not going to stop."

He resumed his position between her thighs and kissed her hard. He knew what happened next would be painful for her, so he tried to distract her with his kisses. He traced her entrance with his tip and felt her wetness through the condom. He knew it was going to feel amazing to be inside her, but the pain was going to rip through her, possibly making her want to tap out. He prayed she didn't, because if he didn't have her at this point, he might go insane, but he was prepared to do whatever she needed.

With one hand holding her head to his and one on his erection, he pushed his tip into her. He felt her flinch and dig her nails into his shoulder, and he paused, but she urged him on with her eyes. Her nails were still digging into him as he inched farther and farther until he was completely submerged. He stilled his movements, allowing her to adjust to him, and he watched as the pain flickered across her face. At that moment, he hated himself. He never wanted to hurt her, but he knew it was inevitable. All he could do now was try to make her as comfortable as possible. He remained still until she let up on his shoulder.

Holding her to him, he whispered into her mouth, "Just relax. I know it hurts, but that will end soon."

Making slow movements, he felt her kisses growing stronger. It gave him the confidence he needed to do more. Soon, she started moving with him, and he smiled against her lips. Taking his time, kissing every part of her he could reach, he reveled in the feeling. He was finally having sex, and it was with the girl of his dreams. Actually, he was making love to the girl of his dreams, listening to her moan his name softly, uttering incoherent ramblings, and he was the cause. He was the reason for the pleasure he saw dancing in her deep brown eyes. It made him confident. Confident enough to move his mouth to her nipple.

Pushing himself in and out of her, holding her hips in his hands, digging his fingernails into her because she felt so good was all he could think of. She had his brain so clouded, he couldn't even remember his name. All he knew was he loved her, and he was willing to spend the rest of his days making sure she knew that. Feeling himself reach his peak, it all felt bittersweet. He wanted this with her, but he never wanted it to end. She had her hands on his shoulders, pulling him against her, and he lost himself in the sensation.

He allowed himself a few more strokes before he felt her walls clamping down on him. She was so tight, so wet, and when she got to her peak, he felt himself being pushed out. Gripping her hips, pushing harder, he buried himself as far as he could and rode out wave after wave of pleasure. The throbbing between them caused him to spill out everything his body could handle into the condom. He was glad at that moment he had taken the time to protect them.

Letting the waves subside, he rolled off her. For the first of what he hoped would be many times, he felt what it was like to miss the feeling of her. He never wanted to leave her body, but he knew she needed time. She needed to recover before they tried that again. Looking down, he saw the red liquid between them and went to move. With her hand on his chest, she held him down. Rubbing circles on her back, he kissed her head, which was now resting on his chest.

"We will shower in a minute. Right now, just hold me. I just need to be held."

He lay quietly until his nerves took over. "Baby, how do you feel?" He was shaken when she remained silent. He hoped he hadn't made a mistake, that she didn't regret it. His heart was racing until he felt her palm resting above it.

"Do I do that?"

"What?"

"Make it race like that. Your heart, I mean. Do I make you feel that way?"

"Every time I see you, my heart races, but after this, baby, it will never be the same. I love you so much, and I always want to feel this way."

"I love you too. I'm sorry I didn't answer your question, but I feel great. I'm sore, but I've never felt more loved than I do now. You were so gentle with me, and I can't imagine it being any better."

"Oh, it can get better, but you were perfect baby. You're always perfect."

"How can you love me the way you do? I swear I don't deserve you."

Tyree never understood why she was so down on herself. She was his angel, perfect in his eyes. She was untouched by any man other than him, and now he had a claim he wasn't willing to give up. He could now say he was the only one to have her, and he wanted it that way, always. *"Mia, baby, you love me enough to be with me, right?"*

She laughed at his question and sat up a little. *"Baby, I'm with you right now. I was really with you just a few minutes ago. What is this all about?"*

"Am I who you can see yourself with?"

"You're the only one I see myself with. What are you thinking?"

"Marry me."

"Whoa, what? Ty, we're still in high school. We're only eighteen. We . . . we've only ever been with each other. Are you sure you can be satisfied with just me?"

"You're the only woman for me. I know we're young, but we can make it. We will graduate and go to college just as we planned, but I want you to be mine. I want to be able to call you my

wife." Tyree was on pins and needles waiting for her answer. The longer it stayed silent, the more worried he became. Letting her head rest on his chest, he heard a soft sigh fill the room. "Maybe I was a bit premature. I know I can live with you just being my girl for a while, but at some point—"

His ramblings were stopped by her lips crashing against his. He grabbed her hair, kissing her harder, and he felt when she pulled back. Even without looking at her, he could feel her smile. Running her fingers down his chest, she looked him in the eyes. "Yes."

"What? What are you saying, baby?"

"I'll marry you. I want to be your wife."

Tyree had never felt the joy he did at that moment. Pulling her closer, he buried his face in her hair. "God, I love you. We're going to be happy, and I'll always be here for you. I promise you will never hurt the way you have been living here."

With his statement, something clicked in her, and he saw it. Her happy grin went grim in just a few seconds. "Oh, God. Ty, my dad will never let us get married. He doesn't even want me dating. What are we going to do?"

"Just leave that to me. I will talk to your parents and mine. Everything will be fine."

They both went and got in the shower, while Tyree contemplated what he was going to say to Richmond and his dad. He knew John wanted him to run the company, but he thought maybe he could postpone it for a while and get settled with Mia. He had no doubt John would understand, because they had been talking about how the right woman could change everything. Tyree just never thought the right woman would find him so quickly. Hell, the right woman found him when he was just a kid.

After getting out of the shower, Tyree settled into the bed for the night and ran his hands through her hair. He stayed, watching her until she fell asleep, and he kissed her forehead. He watched her and listened to the rain, swearing that for as long as he lived, the sound of the rain would always take him back to this night, the happiest night of his life. The night she agreed to be his forever. He just hoped forever lasted as long as they thought it would.

"I love you," Tyree whispered into Mia's hair. "It's been fifteen years, and I still love you as much as I did that night. You're still it for me, baby girl."

Her voice was muffled, and he could still hear a trace of sadness. "I love you too. I'm . . . I'm sorry."

"You don't remember, do you?"

"Remember what?"

"Our first time, that night, the rain." He grinned. "Every time I hear the rain, I think of the night we first made love."

"You mean the night you asked me to marry you."

They were quiet for a few moments with him running his hands down her sides. "It took a lot to get us here. Some of it was bad, but we're still here. I'm sorry, kitten. I never should have left you the way I did. I wasn't the man I promised to be all those years ago."

He felt a shift in the bed and saw her looking down at him. "You're who you always promised to be. You protect me, you protect our son, and we would be nothing without you."

"Don't ever do that again. If I lost you, I would fall apart, and our son . . ." He paused, feeling tears well up in his eyes. "He could make it without me, but you're his hero. I couldn't be what you are to him. You are the one who makes him who he is. I can't do that alone."

She touched his face. "Baby, when this happened, you were gone, our son was gone, and I was going through some things. I thought I was never going to see either of you again, and I just blamed myself for everything. I sent you away, and if you never came back, it would have been my fault. At first I blamed myself, and then I eventually got around to blaming you. It was a rough patch in my life, and you know I would rather be dead than like my aunt Evelyn."

Mia's aunt Evelyn, Milan's mother, had struggled for a long time with depression and bipolar disorder and had suffered a mental breakdown. He supposed it may have been passed to her mother, and it could explain the drug usage and possibly Janelle, but he knew Mia had always been terrified to be that way. He knew this, but it still didn't ease his guilt.

"I should have been there."

She laid her head on his chest, and his arm came around her. "It wasn't your fault. You're perfect, sometimes too perfect for me."

"I'm not perfect, but I want to be for you."

"Just never let me go. No matter what happens, no matter how bad things get, no matter what I might say to you, never let me go. I need you to fight for me with everything you have. Promise me you always will."

Tyree wasn't sure where this was coming from, but he had a feeling there was more he didn't know. He wanted to say he wouldn't react badly, but he couldn't lie to himself. Now, he was feeling terrified of what was to come. He looked out the window into the raging storm and realized it wasn't the only one brewing. He knew there was something coming their way, but he also knew he loved her enough to do what he could to save them.

"I promise, kitten. Get some sleep." He closed his eyes and let her settle on his chest. In a few short moments, he felt her drift off, and he kissed her head. Letting her breathing lull him into a peaceful state, he fell into a dreamless sleep, leaving the problems in his head for another day.

Chapter Fourteen

He was nervous. After all this, he was nervous walking into his mother's house. After all they had been to one another, he still hadn't had a one-on-one conversation with her after everything came to a head in the restaurant. He knew she would always support him, but he also saw the disappointment in her eyes when it was all said and done. He needed to see where her head was. Only she could make sense of the thoughts clouding his brain.

Walking in, kicking his shoes off at the door, he searched the front for his mother. She usually greeted him there when she knew he was coming. He had phoned to let her know he was heading over just after he rolled out of bed. He hated leaving Mia so early before they had to be at the office, but he needed to do this. Whatever was going to happen, and he was sure there was something, he knew he needed to be on the best of terms with Karen.

Walking into the living room, taking a seat, he was soon greeted by Kiyoko, and he offered her a warm smile. "Gran." He stood, kissing her cheek. He helped her to a seat. "How are you feeling this morning?"

Kiyoko poured herself a glass of coffee and settled on the couch. "I'm wonderful." She looked around the room and sighed. "You know, I really love it here. Being in Tokyo was nice, but this"—she waved her hands around—"feels like a home. There is so much love among you."

"We love you too, Gran." Looking at her, he felt horrible. He and his siblings used to go to Tokyo when they were younger, but the older they got, the more sporadic the trips became. After his grandfather died, they were very infrequent until they stopped altogether. Karen still went, but he, Asha, and Miguel had gotten so busy with their jobs, spouses, and children that they hadn't taken the time to visit. "I'm sorry we didn't make sure you knew that."

The older woman smiled at him, and he saw so much of his mother in her. She was exactly what he thought Karen would be like when she was that age. "Nonsense, son. I know you have your families and your careers and, not to mention, all the barricades your father placed in your way. He made your lives difficult for no reason, and I'm just glad you were able to break free of his hold."

"It's no excuse. We should have looked after you better."

"Sweetheart, I talked to your mother every day, and she always kept me updated on what was going on in your lives and sent pictures of the children, who are beautiful, by the way. That son of yours is really impressive. He's smart and so polite. He thinks the world of you."

"You can thank Mia for that. No matter what we have going on, she always does whatever it takes to make sure things are stable for him. She is amazing."

Kiyoko grinned. "She is a beautiful woman, and I agree, she is wonderful with him, but he is also who he is because of you. He sees you, how you take care of your family, how you take care of the business, and you treat his mother like a queen. He said you always put a smile on her face, and if that child wants nothing else in this world, he wants his mother to be happy. He says you make that possible."

"I'm not always the best at it, but I try. I just—" He ran a hand over his face and stood. "I'm sorry. I know this isn't what you wanted to hear this early in the morning. Mom usually gives me these marathon talks, and that's what I came here for today."

Kiyoko grabbed his hand and pulled him back to the couch. "I would love to listen to whatever you have to say. You can talk to me. I may not be as good as your mother in the advice department, but I would love to try."

"Thanks, Gran." He relaxed and fixed himself a cup of coffee. "You know we divorced five years ago, and it was the hardest time of my life, but we got back together. I swear I love that girl more now than I ever have before, and we're happy, but there's just something in the back of my mind telling me not to get comfortable. Something always comes along and pushes us apart."

He saw the understanding wash over her, and she nodded. "You know what it's like to not have her. Can you say you will be okay if that happens again?"

"I wouldn't make it. Mia and Kyan are my life, and even if she told me she didn't want me anymore, I wouldn't let it stand. If I had to, I would stand on her doorstep every night until she took me back."

"She's a lucky girl. If your love for her is that strong, then there shouldn't be anything to keep you from being with her. You've made it through so many obstacles, and you still have that fire burning in your eyes when you speak about her."

She grabbed his hand. "You see, this passion that I see in you about your family, I never saw in your father."

Tyree's mood changed at the mention of John. He hadn't discussed him with anyone in over two years, and he knew he needed to release some things. "I hate him, you know. I know it's wrong, and you and Grandpa always taught us to love, but I hate him. I don't want to end up being like him." He had never admitted he was afraid that one day he would wake up and decide his family was no longer important. He already felt himself becoming an angrier person with each passing day, and if this had been a few years ago, he would have never gotten into that fight with Jake. He felt his hands tremble and saw the tears streaking her cheeks.

"That bastard."

"What?"

"That bastard is still causing problems from the grave. You listen to me. You are nothing like him. You may share his blood, and you may even look like him, but you are more of a man than he would have ever been. Has your mother ever told you why Grandpa never liked him?"

Shaking his head, Tyree focused in to listen to her story.

"Your mom is our only child, our pride and joy, and she could have been anything. She could have done anything she wanted, and she was her father's best friend. They were close, and she shared everything with him until your father came along. Her first year at that school she called home every day, kept her father in the loop on everything, but after she met your father, she changed. She started with the secrets, and then he convinced her to get married. We didn't even get to see it. Our only daughter got married, and we didn't even get to be there."

He hadn't known this. Tyree had always been told that Akio wouldn't talk to her because she hadn't married the man he picked out. "What about her engagement? What about the man you guys picked for her?"

"We may have wanted her to marry him, but she agreed to the engagement on her own."

"So why did it take you so long to see her again? It wasn't until I was born that you spoke to her."

"Your father called Grandpa and asked to marry her. He was stunned because he didn't even know they were seeing each other. We came to that school right after and found they were already married. He called us to ask for something he had already done. They didn't even have the decency to give us the truth. All we ever wanted was for her to be happy and she couldn't see that. She only saw that we were trying to keep her from the man she loved, but your grandfather and I saw something in him that wasn't genuine. I never saw in him what I see in you."

"Why did you help him? What changed your mind?"

"You did. Your grandfather took one look at you and your brother, and you won him over. He loved you so much that no matter how he felt about John, he could never not make sure you had the life your mother had. He wanted you to be taken care of."

Now it all made sense. He had often wondered why the company was transferred to only him and his siblings when they were of age. He always wondered how his father got no part of it when they took over. "He made sure we would end up with the company because he still didn't trust him, didn't he?"

"He never trusted your father with you kids or your mother, but if he pushed any harder, we would have lost all of you. We couldn't take that chance."

"Grandpa was smart to do so. I think Dad loved us at one point, but he let his greed overtake him.

I never want to let that happen to me. I find myself getting so angry now, and I don't want to lose control and do something I can't take back."

"You love your wife, despite everything that has happened. You love and cherish her. When you speak of her, I see this light in your eyes, you glow when she's around, and you can't keep your hands off her," she chuckled. "So you see, you're different from him. Even though he was trying to convince us he loved your mother, I never saw half the love in him I see in you. For you, it's real, and I can't imagine you will ever let that go. You married her to protect her when you were so young, and I see you haven't let any of that love die. You fought your way back to her against all the odds. You and Mia, you're destined for each other. She's your destiny, honey."

"From the moment I saw her, I knew we would be something. Even as a kid, I never thought I would spend one day without her in my life. But I'm not able to give her what she needs. We went to an appointment with one of the top ob-gyns in Atlanta, and we're having trouble. They ran some tests, and we might not be able to conceive. They say her body might not be able to handle it. We want another child so badly, and I don't think I can give her one. At least not naturally, the way she wants. Things have been tense, but she's not saying it to me. I don't know what to say to make things right."

"It's simple: you love the woman, and you make sure she knows it. Children don't always come the traditional way. There are so many children in the world who need homes. You and Mia would be great for a kid who truly needs you. Think about it."

Her words put things in perspective for him, and he leaned over, giving her a firm hug. "You are just as good as Mom with this."

"What are you talking about?" Karen asked from the corner. "She's much better."

He could tell by her smile that she had been watching for quite a while and heard most of their conversation. He stood to hug her, and she pulled him into her warm embrace.

"Mom, I'm sorry I overreacted at the restaurant."

"You really shouldn't let that ass get to you. She's your wife. You won."

"I know I won. I'm a hero. I saved the day." He smiled teasingly.

"Smart ass."

"I love you, crazy lady." He hugged her for a second longer and turned to his grandmother. "Thanks for the talk, Gran. I love you too, pretty lady." He scanned the room and then turned back to them. "I have a while before I need to be at work. Can I take you ladies to breakfast?"

When they both agreed, he escorted them to his car and helped them inside. "Hey, where's Rock? Maybe he wants to come."

Karen looked to Kiyoko, and she shook her head no. Tyree knew there was something they weren't sharing and went to probe further when Karen spoke up. "Rock is at the office. He has been working a lot since our dinner."

"Is something wrong? Why didn't you call?"

"You had your own things going on, and I knew you and Mia needed the time. After he dropped you off, he got the call."

"Is this my fault? Did he get called in because he was protecting me?"

Karen slid her hand into his lap and gave his hand a gentle squeeze. "No, sweetheart. You know Rock has been looking for Richmond, and his unit thinks they may be onto something. Don't stress about your actions. Rock loves you."

"You know, Mom, I'm glad you married Rock." He loved the smile that lit up her face. "I know at first it was weird, and you tried to pass off this 'just friends' thing, but he has been your husband for years whether you realize it or not."

"What do you mean?"

"All that time you knew what Dad was doing, you confided in Rock, right?"

"Yeah."

"He protected you and talked you through everything, didn't he?"

"Yeah." She smiled, getting where he was going in his line of questioning.

"I know he definitely made us feel like we could come to him. I talked to him more than I ever talked to Dad. He was already a part of my family before you married him."

"I was nervous about how you guys would take it. I mean, I knew you all loved Rock, but loving him and having him married to your mother are two different things."

"Stop stressing, crazy lady. We want you happy, and he does the job, so I'm all for it. You've given up so much of your happiness to ensure ours, and whatever you need, you can have it. I would give you the world."

"I love you, baby. You kids are more than I could have ever dreamed. You make me so proud, and I would do anything to spare you an ounce of pain. I always will."

Tyree grinned at his mother and then shifted his eyes to the woman in the back seat. He knew she was responsible for making his mother the loving, caring, selfless person she was, and he couldn't wait for more time with her. He wanted to know so much more about this special woman who was responsible for his happiness. He knew that without her, his life wouldn't be what it was.

"Aunt Mia," Jude called out, poking his head around the corner of their dining room. He had come over early before going to the office, and she could tell by the tone of his voice that something was weighing on him. He had called her early, even before she had gotten out of bed, and she got up and fixed breakfast for them and Kyan, who had been dropped off by Miguel thirty minutes earlier. She was sitting at the table, listening to her son go on about his upcoming science fair, and she smiled. He was so bright, way smarter than she was at that age.

"Yeah, Mama. I swear it's going to be great! You are coming, aren't you?"

"Yeah, I wouldn't miss it. Did you ask your dad?"

"I didn't get to, and he was gone this morning." He paused for a minute and looked up at her. "Are you and Dad happy?"

Jude was watching quietly and took a seat at the table, tuning in for her answer. "Yeah, why do you ask?"

Kyan looked at Jude, and he nodded, signaling for him to go on. "I know you both want another baby. I've seen you crying about it."

Mia let out a deep breath and grabbed his hand. She wasn't aware that he had been paying so much attention to them. "Yes, Dad and I want another baby, and it does make me sad sometimes, but we are happy. I just think when it's time for us it will happen. At least we have you. You're the best kid in the world."

"You're laying it on thick, Mama," he laughed. "I don't like it when you're sad. When you get sad, you guys fight more, and I don't want us to move again. I thought . . . When I woke up and he wasn't here, I got scared."

"We are fine. We are not always going to agree on everything, but we love each other. We're not going anywhere."

"Is he coming home soon?"

"He was home earlier. He just left to see your grandmother. He will be back after work." She could tell he still wasn't all the way convinced, and she brushed her hand over his cheek. "You know what you need?" He looked into her eyes and shook his head no. "You need a day with your dad. How about I call him and tell him to clear his day tomorrow afternoon and you guys spend some guy time together?"

"He can do that?"

"Sure he can. He's the boss," she giggled.

"Actually, you're the boss. We just do whatever you say to keep the peace."

"All right, silly boy, finish your breakfast and Abel will drive you to school." She turned away from him and looked up to see Jude smiling at them. Kyan took the last few bites of his food and kissed her cheek before jumping up and racing toward the stairs. After he was gone, she turned to Jude, and he grabbed her hand.

"Wow, that was intense."

"That's my little man. God, where did the time go? It seems like I was just changing his diapers and now he's doing science fairs and worrying if his parents are happy."

"Are they? I know what you told little man, but are you happy, Aunt Mia?"

"I'm . . . Jude, why did you ask me that?"

He held up his hands and sighed. "I don't know. I thought that maybe Jake being here was causing problems. I've never seen Uncle Ty lose it like he did the other night, and then Whit told me he was out of it yesterday. I worry about you, that's all."

"I'll admit, Jake being here isn't pleasant, but we will be okay. There's just some stuff we have to work through, nothing big."

"If you need someone to talk to, call me."

"I thought that's what you came here for. Come on, tell me what's going on with you."

"Changing the subject," he laughed. "Yes, I came for your advice."

"Well, talk. I can't imagine you came over here to talk about me and Tyree, so tell me what's going on."

"Can we take this over to the couch? It's a little complicated."

Mia took her coffee and walked over to the living room, taking a seat. She saw Kyan making his way down the stairs and blew him a kiss as he left with Abel on his way to school. Jude took a seat next to her, shuffling his hands nervously. She could tell whatever he was about to drop on her was serious, and she wanted to brace herself.

"What's going on?"

"Things aren't going the way I thought they would when I first proposed. I kind of feel like maybe it wasn't the best decision."

"It's only been a month, Jude. You have to give it some time."

She saw his eyes shift, and he swallowed hard. "Aunt Mia, I don't think it's going to work out. She's different. She has been since . . . She's just not the girl I love anymore."

"I know a little something about being with someone you don't love. It never works, but the difference between me and you is you do love her, or at least you did. What changed that, and how did it change so quickly?"

"I don't know. I think maybe I brought her here hoping things would get better, and they seemed to, but ever since the engagement party, things have gone from good to terrible. The only thing I can think of is that there's someone else."

Mia was taken aback. This was the last thing she expected to hear. She always thought Jude and Whitney were so in love. She would have never guessed she would be cheating. "She can't be with someone else. You're the only boy she's ever loved, the only one she has ever been with. How could she—"

"I'm not the only one."

"She's cheated on you before? Why would you ask her to marry you if you knew she was cheating?"

"She didn't cheat. Look, I don't know if I should say anything. I promised I would keep her secret."

"Secret? Jude, that's my niece. If something is wrong, I want to know about it. Maybe I can help her."

She saw him contemplating it and realized when his decision was made. "Just before we left school, Whitney was raped. She went to this party and had too much to drink, and some bastard took advantage of her. I hate myself for not being there, and I think she has finally gotten around to hating me too. It's bad at our house. She leaves, and I don't even know where she's going most nights. When I ask questions, I get this shitty response or no response at all. I'm worried."

Mia was silent as she looked at Jude. She wasn't sure what to say or what to do. She wanted to comfort him, she wanted to make it better, but she wasn't sure how. Things were just too foggy in her mind. "Who did this?"

"I don't know. She doesn't remember."

"Did he use protection?"

"We had her checked, but because we had sex afterward, nothing could be determined. She came up clean for STDs, but she was damaged in other ways. You don't know how bad it was. I had to drag her out of all kinds of crazy scenes, and it was getting exhausting."

Mia's shaky hand went over her lips. "How did we not know any of this? Her parents, they would have gone to the ends of the earth to find out who did this. Why didn't you guys tell us?"

"I promised, and I thought I could handle it, but it's too much. I don't want to lose her, but I feel like I already have. I swear there has to be someone else. I can just feel it."

"I want to talk to her. Maybe she will open up to me." She saw Jude's eyes widen and knew there was more. "What is it?"

"You can't say anything. Whit already feels like you like me more than her. She says you always take my side."

"That's nonsense. Where would she get an idea like that? I love her."

"I know you do, but you have to understand, you are the one her dad trusts. You're the one he always confides in. She just feels left out from you guys."

"He wanted to protect her. She was so young, and we didn't want her to live the life we did. Dad almost broke us, and her parents wanted better for their child. I can understand that. If I had been as careful as they were, maybe my son wouldn't have been kidnapped."

"She doesn't see it that way. She only sees that you guys are who her dad trusts, and she feels inferior."

"We love her. I would never want her to deal with what I did, but I see by trying to shield her, we created more damage. I have to talk to her. I can't have her feeling that way about us."

Just as the words left her mouth, Mia looked up and saw Whitney walking into the living room. "What the hell is this?"

"Whit, just let me talk to you." Jude stood and walked toward her, and she swung out and slapped him across the face.

"How dare you come to her with my personal business? What in the hell is wrong with you?"

"What are you doing here? How did you know—" He tried to question her, but she cut him off.

"I followed you. I had to see for myself what was going on here, and I guess I was right."

"Right about what?" Mia questioned.

"He has been telling you everything all along. No wonder you're always looking down on me and being so supportive of him. I should have known."

"Wait," Mia interjected. "You're wrong, sweetie. We're worried about you. You can talk to me."

"I can't talk to any of you." Mia watched as Whitney paced the floor and threw her hands up in the air. "God, Jude, what were you thinking? They didn't need any more reasons to think I can't do the job. You know what I'm up against!"

"What are you up against? I'm confused," Mia interrupted.

"You! You're perfect, and everyone loves you. They never question you or second-guess the things you say. People respect you in a way they will never respect me. You have it all: a son who loves you and a husband who thinks you hung the damn moon. You even have Jake still chasing you like a lost puppy. After everything that's happened, even he still loves you. I could never compete with that."

"It's not a competition between us. We're family. We're supposed to look out for one another."

"You have everyone! You have my dad, my mom, Uncle Ty, and now you even have my fiancé eating out of the palm of your hand. Why do you have to be so damn selfish?"

"Selfish?" Mia hissed. "Me, selfish? I gave up a hell of a lot for this family. I've lost more than you could dream of. You have no clue about loss, little girl." Mia was boiling. She had tried to remain calm during Whitney's ranting, but she had heard enough.

"The only real loss you've ever had, we had them too!" said Whitney. "They were my family too. I lost them right when you did, but it was worse for me. At least you got to know them. All I got were trips home on holidays and a phone call when they died telling me I couldn't come home for the funerals. I didn't even get to say my damn goodbyes."

"They were trying to protect you! Your dad didn't want Richmond ruining your life like he did ours. Why can't you see that?"

"Like your life was so horrible! You are married to one of the best men I know and are running a multibillion-dollar company with the perfect life."

Mia laughed angrily. "Perfect? My life is far from that. My sister was my best friend, and I couldn't save her. The last year of her life we weren't close at all because she was a drunk. She was getting better, but most of the year we fought about her lifestyle, and then she was gone. I regret every day the way I was with her." Mia felt tears roll down her cheek and she began to tremble.

"My mother died that year too, and we barely spoke. The night she died was the first time I ever let her be alone with my child, and then she died. I never got the chance to say I loved her or that I was proud of her, because when I went to pick my son up, she was dead. I found her lying facedown. If that weren't bad enough, then my son was taken. I went out of my mind, and my husband was gone, so I tried to numb the pain. I took a bottleful of pills and woke up two days later in the psych ward, so don't you talk to me about loss. I was here through it all."

"At least you had the option to be here. They didn't send you away like some unwanted problem."

"I would have preferred being sent away!" Mia screamed her last statement, and Tyree rounded the corner with a confused expression on his face.

"What is going on here?" He stepped into view and saw the tears on Mia's and Whitney's faces. He scanned the room. "Is anyone going to tell me what's wrong?" He walked toward Mia, and Whitney huffed loudly.

"Even when you're the problem, they still come to you first." She rushed out of the room, and Jude chased behind her.

Tyree looked completely lost as he turned to Mia and grabbed her arm. "What happened here?"

"Honestly," she sighed, "I don't know. You should check on her. You seem to be the only one she listens to."

"I'm more worried about you right now." He pulled her closer, and they both missed Whitney and Jude making their way back in the door.

Whitney walked over to Mia and paused. Mia pushed out of Tyree's embrace.

"I'm sorry, Aunt Mia. I was wrong to snap at you. It won't happen again."

Mia wiped her teary eyes and pulled her into a firm hug. "I'm sorry too, sweetie."

Whitney laid her head on Mia's shoulder and absorbed the hug. Tyree let out a deep sigh and offered a slight grin while Jude looked on. After the hug was over, Jude made an excuse and left abruptly. All three people in the room looked on in confusion, and Tyree finally voiced his thoughts.

"What the hell was that?"

"I don't know," Mia replied while Whitney watched the door, undoubtedly waiting for him to walk back in.

Chapter Fifteen

"So she just showed up at your house and flipped out?" Asha asked as she took a seat in Mia's office. "Did she even say what she was doing there?"

Mia shrugged her shoulders and pushed the pile of papers on her desk. "Yeah, she followed Jude. Even though she apologized, I still feel awful. I had no idea my niece hated me. I thought I was doing a good job as an aunt."

Asha grabbed her hand and rubbed it gently. "You are a wonderful aunt. My kids love you so much, and your son idolizes you. You have nothing to feel bad about."

Mia stood and crossed the room to look out her window. "But I do. I feel like I've failed all over again."

"You didn't fail Janelle. She looked up to you. Mia, you can't carry other people's issues on your shoulders. It will eat you alive."

Mia was about to say something, and her door swung open. When she looked up, she saw her lunch date waltzing in. "Chloe, welcome. Are you ready for lunch?"

"Yes." She rubbed her protruding belly and sighed. "When am I not ready to eat?" Chloe was a girl she met one day at lunch and bonded with instantly. Chloe was single and pregnant without much help. She was working a dead-end job at a restaurant when she and Mia met, and Mia had been helping her ever since.

"Well, let's get you two fed." Mia walked over, grabbing her purse, and gave Asha a gentle pat on the hand. Boarding the elevator, Mia watched Chloe, wishing she could share in that kind of happiness. She was having a boy, it was going to be her first child, and Mia could tell how happy she was.

Chloe had no family to speak of, and the father of her son was someone she didn't discuss very often. While most would have folded and given up, Chloe chose to look on the bright side of things. Mia was completely in awe of her and wanted to help in any way she could. At first, Chloe wouldn't accept help, stating that she didn't want any handouts, but Mia convinced her by saying that everyone needed someone. In Mia's eyes, she saw it as her chance to make up all the wrongs she felt she made with her little sister. Chloe reminded her so much of Janelle and her carefree spirit.

"So, how is he doing today?" Mia asked as they drove over.

Chloe ran her hand over her belly and leaned back in her seat. "He is kicking so hard. I swear he is fighting his way out."

Mia smiled and glanced over at the young girl. "You must be so excited. Have you had any contact with Will?" Will was the father of Chloe's baby and was nothing but trouble. From what Chloe explained, Will used to force himself on her and beat her, and when she found out she was pregnant, she ran in fear for her baby. Chloe seemed to be relieved that Will was gone, but Mia couldn't help but worry about her taking on a baby alone. That's why she took such good care of her.

"No. He hasn't been in contact, but I did hear he's back in jail."

"For what this time?" Chloe was quiet and glanced out the window. "What is it?"

"I really don't want to say. I just hate I got mixed up with him. You must think I'm so screwed up."

"I don't think you're screwed up. I just think you were in a bad situation that you were smart enough to get out of. We all have our things we aren't proud of. I can't judge you."

As they pulled up to the restaurant, Mia gave her keys to the valet and walked over to help Chloe out of the car. They were headed into the restaurant when Mia heard a familiar voice calling out to her. Trying to rush into the restaurant, she was unsuccessful and huffed while Chloe looked on, confused.

"Dimples, wait. I just want to talk to you."

"Jake, dammit, leave me alone. You being here has caused enough trouble." Mia snatched away from him, but when she turned to look into his eyes, she saw a sadness she wasn't expecting. Trying not to be taken in by his sad demeanor, she turned back to Chloe and kept walking toward their table. "What are you doing, following me now?"

"I swear, it's not like that. I need to talk to you. Just let me talk to you, and I swear I'll leave you alone. One conversation, beautiful, and I'm gone forever."

Mia sped up her walk and helped Chloe into her seat before she turned to see the broken man behind her. She wanted to be hard, she wanted to act tough, but in truth, she couldn't stand seeing him that way. She knew in her heart that her avoidance of him was her own fault. All he had done was help keep her secrets, and here she was treating him like trash.

"Look, I'm sorry, okay? I don't want you hurt, but I need you to understand that I'm married. I love Tyree, and yes, I messed up before, but I won't leave him again. I can't."

"I know, Dimples. Look, it's not about that." He paused, on the verge of tears, and she placed a hand on his shoulder. "I really need to talk to someone, and you're the first person I thought of. Please say you'll do it."

"Jake, what you're asking—"

"I never ask you for anything. I was there when you needed me, and I never ask you for anything. Please?"

Mia looked at Chloe and then back to him before nodding slowly. "Let me talk to Ty first. I don't want to lie to him. There have been enough secrets among all of us, wouldn't you say?"

"Yes, sure. Anything you need. I don't want to mess things up for you. I just need a friend. You're my friend. One of my only friends."

Mia remembered how lonely Jake said he was when they first met. He hadn't really connected with many people because of his work as a private investigator, and when they met, they had become friends before moving into a romantic relationship. If she were honest, she would admit she missed that part of things. She told him a lot about her life, and he shared with her.

Smiling and bowing out, Jake left Mia to her lunch with Chloe. Mia had taken her seat and looked across the table to see Chloe gazing at her. "Dimples, huh? So I take it he's one of those things?"

Mia sighed and picked up the water glass the waiter had dropped off in the midst of her conversation with Jake. "He is, but he also saved me. Jake is a long story. We met at a time when I was going through a really bad issue. Not only did he help me, but he saved my life. I had messed up so much. I pushed Ty away, and I was alone. I mean, I wasn't really alone. I had my family and Ty's, but in my head, I was alone. I had convinced myself that everyone was against me, and I panicked. Jake was there. He held me when I cried. He stayed with me through the nightmares. He was just there. He was so patient with me, and it took a lot, but when I finally did sleep with him, I didn't regret it. Sleeping with him made me realize that my feelings for Ty were still so strong even though I didn't want to admit it. So even though he isn't the man I love, I do cherish him for all he was to me when I needed it the most."

Chloe dabbed her eyes and let out a silly chuckle. "I'm sorry, it's these hormones, but that was sweet. I get how you don't want to hurt Tyree, but I also see why this Jake guy is important to you. I know Tyree probably doesn't like it, but I can't imagine him ever denying you something you really need. You need to make your peace with the whole Jake thing to officially move on."

"I do. I just need to hear him out and see what's going on. I've never seen him like this, and I would feel awful not being there. I mean, the sexual part of us is gone, but does that mean being his friend has to die, too? I can understand Ty not wanting us to be friends, but it's just so complicated." Mia looked up at the simple smile that Chloe wore. She was so easy to talk to, and she didn't have to feel the guilt of people picking sides. Most of her friends were the family, and they would always choose Tyree. She just needed an unbiased opinion.

"I get what you're saying. I think people can be friends after they've dated, but I know your husband isn't too big on this friend. At the end of the day, you have to do what works best for the sake of your marriage. You can get another friend, but you can't replace your husband."

Mia knew Chloe was speaking the truth. The plan now was to make sure Tyree knew about her seeing Jake one last time, and then she had to end it. She also knew that by the end of the conversation, she had to make sure Jake knew that the past was the past and there was no use bringing it back up.

Chloe sat quietly for a minute and then looked over at Mia strangely. Mia asked, "What's wrong? Is it the baby?"

"No." She shook her head, running her hand over her stomach. "I was just thinking Jake looks so familiar. I can't place where I know him from, but it seems like we've crossed paths before."

Mia shrugged. "Well, I guess he does have a common face. Maybe you saw someone who looks like him."

"Yeah." Chloe shook it off. "You're probably right."

"Jude," Terence called out, waving his hand in Jude's face. "Earth to Jude."

Jude looked up and finally saw Terence. He had been speaking to him for the past two minutes without any response. Terence could tell how distracted he was when he first came into work, and it had only gotten worse with the hours passing. Jude was usually very sharp and attentive, so seeing him this way made Terence nervous.

"Hey, my bad. I was just thinking about some things. I'll get back to work."

Terence folded his arms over his chest and sat down in front of Jude. "What's up? You want to tell me what has you so off? Is something wrong at home?"

"Home," he huffed. "My house is a war zone, and I think I know why. It's completely messed up, and I can't even believe I'm thinking this. We're all supposed to be family, but I . . ." He stood and pushed himself out of his seat.

"You what?"

"I need to leave."

Terence saw the calmness wash into anger all over his face and was confused. "You're not making any sense, Jude. What is wrong with you?"

"I can't be a part of this anymore. I love that girl, I do, but I can't be second. I know I'm not who she wants."

"I don't know what you're talking about. Who does she want, and why are you so rattled? The only men your girl is remotely close to are her dad and Tyree. Neither one of them could be an issue in that way."

"I thought in the back of my mind I could have been wrong, but lately she's been missing late in the night. I don't know where she goes. Whenever I ask, she bites my head off or flips out. It was never like this before we came back here. I never felt this doubt before now."

It took Terence a minute to wrap his mind around what Jude was insinuating. "You think there is something between Whitney and Ty? Are you crazy?"

Jude laughed nervously and shook his head. "I don't know what to think. You weren't there today. I mean, she snapped on me and Aunt Mia, and she just kept saying how her life was perfect and she had the perfect man. All the while I was sitting there watching my girl fantasize about some other life she wishes she had."

"She idolizes Tyree, yes. They are extremely close and always have been. He loves her just as he loves his little sister, hell, like he loves Milan, but he only has that crazy, 'I would do anything for you' love for Mia. Mia is the only woman Tyree sees that way. Whitney might as well be like his own daughter."

"I know that. He doesn't see her that way, but I just don't know, man. I didn't want to believe it, but this morning I saw it with my own eyes. Whitney is not who I thought she was."

Terence could see this was tearing Jude apart and felt sorry for the young man. It was true, he had always wondered about Whitney's feelings for Tyree. He had always seen it as a schoolgirl crush that would die with time, but he too had come to see in the past few months that her infatuation had grown. He was sure Tyree was oblivious to everything, but he knew it needed to be addressed. He had to call Tyree before anyone else started to feel like Jude did, especially his wife.

Taking a deep breath and standing from his seat, Terence crossed the room with his phone in hand. He turned back to Jude and offered a smile. "The one thing you can count on is that, no matter what her feelings are for him, Tyree would never cross that line. He loves Mia, and he knows it would kill her."

"I know, but that still doesn't make it any easier. Just because it's not returned doesn't make me feel better about the way she feels."

"I'm sure it's just a phase. It will pass, and reality will kick in for her. She loves you too, Jude. I can see it even if you don't right now."

Terence walked out of the office and pulled his phone up to his ear in the hallway. He hit his speed dial, and in two rings he had Tyree on the line. "Ty, we need to talk. We have a serious problem. I'll be at your office in a few. We need to do this in person." Shutting the phone, he walked over to the elevator and hit the button. The whole way down to the lobby, he was dreading the talk he was going to have with his oldest friend. It could only bring trouble.

Chapter Sixteen

"Kitten." Tyree came into the room and set his things down. He looked over to the bed to find Mia passed out facedown on a pillow. She looked so beautiful, her hair spread out on the bed and her arms crossed in front of her. It was late, later than he usually arrived home, but after his talk with Terence, he needed to unwind and did so in the comfort of a few glasses of Crown and Coke.

He could smell the liquor exuding from his pores and knew Mia would too if she awoke. He hadn't had a drink in years, but today's news prompted him to need one. He hadn't figured out how his best friend had come to him with such a ridiculous thought. Terence voiced his suspicions and Tyree snapped, telling him he was out of line and completely wrong. There was no way Whitney had any kind of romantic feelings for him. It was ridiculous.

As the day wore on, however, he began to let Terence's statements take hold. He was always so protective of Whitney, so touchy with her, and maybe it confused her. He didn't mean anything by it. He thought he was just the cool uncle she needed, but the more he thought about it, he came to see what Terence pointed out to him. He had been sharing his problems with her, and she had been advising him on how to deal with his wife. How could he have been so stupid? All this time, he had been feeding into her little crush and making it seem like there was a possibility of them. Well, no longer would he indulge. The only woman he needed was the one lying down in front of him.

Stripping off everything and sliding between the sheets, he saw that she didn't stir. He watched her for a second, running over every curve with his eyes, his mouth watering over every delicious morsel of skin. He was mesmerized. Mia was the one. She was the only one. Bending his head down to taste her, he moved her hair to the side and placed himself over her without applying his weight. With his knees spread on both sides of her, he kissed her and delighted in the sounds that emitted from her sleeping form.

A smile formed on her full lips as his mouth took advantage of her bare neck, staking his claim. When she moved her head slightly, he grabbed her hair, jerking her head to the side, and her hands braced the sheets. She still hadn't woken up, but sliding his hands down the back of her thighs and under the nightgown to find that she wasn't wearing panties, he slipped his fingers inside. He watched her back arch to him, and he placed his body on top of hers to push her back down. At this point, he wasn't ready to relinquish any kind of control. He wanted her to feel the need he felt and to know that she was the only one who could bring this out in him. He needed her to know who owned him and that he would do anything for her.

Dancing his fingers around inside her, he felt the wetness and almost came right there. The liquor in his system made him extra sensitive and, coincidentally, harder than he had ever been in his life. Pressing himself against her back, he felt when she shivered. Moving his mouth from her neck to her ear, he whispered and felt when her eyes begin to flutter. "Wake up, baby."

She let out a deep moan and gripped the sheets as he continued to rub vigorously away at her clit. "Ty, why . . ."

He could tell she smelled the liquor in the air, and she tried to flip over to look at him. Before she could move, he pushed her arms up and pushed inside her hard and fast.

"Wait." She pushed herself up, and he slammed into her, making her fall back to the bed.

"No talking, no moving. I just want to fuck you. Just let me fuck you, baby."

"What's wrong with . . . Uuhh, God." She braced herself against the headboard as he pushed himself into a flurry of hard thrusts. Tyree grabbed her hips and held her still while he continued to push into her hard and fast. Smacking her from behind, he heard her moan again, and he felt himself growing more excited. He squeezed her soft ass and dug his fingers into her skin. She had her hands planted against the headboard, pushing back because with each new thrust he pushed her closer. He was slamming into her with reckless abandon, watching her body spasm with each thrust.

Tyree was out of control. He was doing things he had never done to her, but he could tell she was enjoying it. His touches were rough, his kisses sloppy, but all he tasted was lust spilling from his drunken pores. The alcohol in his system fueled his intense hunger for her, and he pushed harder. He knew the initial shock threw her off, but now she was cooperating, and he felt her muscles relax, allowing him a better angle. She was into it. He could tell by the way she arched her back slightly, enabling him to reach a spot that he hadn't touched in a very long time.

"Fuck, Mia, damn."

She giggled at him, and he knew it was because of the colorful language he was using. He knew it was the liquor affecting his brain, but he couldn't control the statements falling from his lips. He felt like he was a little too rough, but he couldn't help himself. The way she responded to his actions pushed him further into the intensity clouding their encounter.

Letting go of her hips, he grabbed the back of her head, twisted it to him, and latched his lips onto hers. He muffled the screams that formed when he lunged harder against her. Her eyes were fluttering, and when he hit a particular spot, he felt her walls clamp down and melt around him. He had never had such a rush from being with her, but he still hadn't come.

Pulling himself out of her and flipping her on her back, he felt her hands rubbing gentle circles around his back. When his tongue started a slow creep down her body, from her neck, between the creases of her breasts, and farther to the juncture where her stomach and hips formed, he felt a twitch. Her body was so sensitized, and when he kissed the inside of her thigh, she screamed his name, causing it to echo in his intoxicated head. He kissed his way to her center and stopped, doing a slow, lingering lick across her folds. In an instant, her nails were on his shoulders, and she pushed him harder against her.

"Fuck, uuhh, Ty, dammit."

He continued to run his tongue over her, gripping her thighs to pull them farther apart. "Cum for me, baby." The vibrations of his tongue as he spoke caused her flesh to convulse, and she gripped her hands in the sheets balled up next to her head. She came hard for the second time that night, and he wasn't sure if her body could take any more, but he still hadn't climaxed. Her gasps and moans gave him the motivation he needed to finish himself off.

Pulling himself up and wrapping her legs around his waist, he pushed back inside her and took in her shallow breathing with his mouth. He grabbed her hand and intertwined their fingers, pushing their hands above her head just as he hiked her legs up with his hips. The new position allowed for farther penetration, and he saw the shock on her face when he plunged deeper. Her breath caught in her chest, and he smiled before dipping his mouth to her ear.

Capturing her ear between his teeth, he nibbled gently and sucked lightly. "Cum again, baby." He saw her take a deep breath and bite down on her bottom lip.

"What are you doing to me? Uuhh, Ty, I'm . . ."

"Cum, baby." He pushed himself deeper and clutched her hand tighter, moaning against her neck. "Mmmh, baby." He pushed his hips against her and heard the scream she let out. Her nails dug into his hand, and he erupted inside her. Still riding the feeling of ecstasy, he continued light strokes until all of his energy was drained. Rolling to his side, he closed his eyes. He didn't even reach for her this time. Instead, he drifted into a deep slumber.

Not sure what had just happened, Mia clutched the sheet to her sweaty chest. Her husband had come home, clearly drunk, and fucked her brains out. Not that the sex was bad, because it was incredible, but he had never been as detached as he was just then. They had always had this joke about sex, and he always said he always made love to her, never just sex. Well, this was anything but making love. He had actually come home and demanded that she let him fuck her. It was strange.

Never in the fifteen years of them being together had he ever used the word "fuck" with regard to their lovemaking. Never was he that rough, and he would have never finished and rolled to the side without so much as an "I love you." This man lying beside her was not the man she had always known. Something was wrong. His touches were off. His kisses weren't the same. She couldn't figure out what had changed between the morning and now, but she felt empty. She felt used. There he was lying there asleep without even trying to cuddle. She watched him for what seemed like hours, and just as the tears started to appear in her eyes, she felt his stare on her.

"Come here."

She laid her head on his chest, and he ran his hand down her back. He must have felt the tears on his chest because he swiped his thumb across her cheek and held her tighter. "Why are you crying?"

"What just happened?"

"Baby, I think you know what just happened," he chuckled, but she wasn't amused. "Come on, don't be that way."

"What's going on with you? Why were you drinking?"

"Kitten, it's nothing I can't handle."

She sat up and looked down into his eyes. "You only drink when it's something you can't. Tell me what's wrong. We're supposed to be able to come to each other."

Tyree sighed and sat up with her. "Terence came to see me. He said something that upset me."

"So, you had a fight with Terence. You two disagree and make up all the time. I'm sure it will be fine by the morning. Just give him time, and you take time to cool off."

"It's not that simple. Do you know what he said to me?"

Mia swallowed hard and hoped he hadn't said what she thought he did. "What did he say?"

"You know what? It's nothing. It was something stupid. I shouldn't have gotten all worked up."

Mia drew in a deep breath and shook her head. "No, it's something. You're all stressed out." The look on his face caused her to sit back. "Ty?" He looked her in the eyes, and she put her hand over her mouth. "Why aren't you saying anything?"

"Mia, please drop it, okay?"

Mia ran her hand over his face and forced him to look at her. "What is it, Ty? I deserve to know." She knew she had no right to sit there acting self-righteous, but she wanted to know what could have made him come in and behave the way he just had. She cast her eyes down for a second and then she saw it: his hand was scraped and swollen. "What happened to you?"

He shrugged, and Mia shook her head in protest. "No. You don't get to come in here all drunk and beaten up and fuck me all over this bed and pretend like nothing happened."

Tyree sat up, and she saw him let out a tired sigh. "Look, I had a long day, and I wanted a drink. I went to the bar and had a few too many."

"And your hand?"

"I hit a wall, Mia. Is this an interrogation?"

"Hell yes, it is. When you come in here smelling like a brewery and screw me like some ho on the street, yes, I have questions."

"Maybe I just wanted a hard fuck, Mia, and I didn't hear you complaining. Sometimes I just want a good, hard nut. Be glad I came home to get it."

"What the hell is that supposed to mean?"

"It means I got drunk, I had a bad day, and all I needed was my wife to fuck me like a wife is supposed to and not give me all this shit about it. Most dudes wouldn't give a damn, but I do. Yes, I got drunk, but I came home to you. I'm loyal to you."

"You watch your mouth. Yes, you're right I'm supposed to screw you, and I do that very well, I might add. What you're not going to do is come in here and treat me like some cheap piece of ass."

"Oh, because I forgot, your expensive ass sure cost me a hell of a lot." Before he could open his mouth again, her hand flew up, smacking him hard.

"Fuck you! I'm supposed to be happy that you came home and treated me like a ho? I don't cost you shit. I have my own things. Material things don't mean shit to me."

"So you can have meetings with that bastard, but I can't have a drink and sex with my damn wife?"

Mia swallowed hard and took a deep breath. "I called you, and you said it was fine. I haven't even gone yet, but if it bothers you that much, then I won't. I just think it's really petty for you to act like this because of him."

She saw the realization hit him, and he reached for her. It was as if he sobered up at that moment and realized all he had said to her. She turned her back to him, and he leaned over, putting his chin on her shoulder. "I'm always messing up here lately. I don't know how to deal with this. I know you're tired of hearing it, but I'm sorry."

"Stop being sorry. Just stop doing it."

"I had a bad day. There was no excuse."

"Yeah," she sighed. "You're forgiven, again."

"Why do you keep doing that?"

"What?" She turned and saw him hanging his head.

"Why do you keep forgiving me? Why are you letting me treat you like shit and turning the other cheek? Why haven't you left me?"

"Because you're my husband. I promised you forever, and this time, I mean it. I love you so much. I wish you could see that."

"I know you do. I don't know what's wrong with me. Maybe I'm pushing because I don't want to wake up one day and not see it coming when you leave me."

In his alcoholic haze, he admitted his real feelings, and she couldn't help the guilt she felt. "I'm not leaving. You can act like as much of an ass as you want, but I can't leave. I was miserable without you. You may be pissing me off lately, but you also make me the happiest I've ever been. I know how much you've sacrificed for me and our son, and I wouldn't let a few harsh words cloud that." She kissed the side of his mouth, and he gently ran his hand through her hair, pulling her head closer. She fell into his sweet kisses until she was out of breath and pushed back.

"Too much?"

"No." Her eyes fluttered, and she had to fight down a blush. As angry as she had been just then, her center was beginning to throb with need. How she let him make her feel like a sex-crazed teenager every time he touched her, she would never know. Leaning back to catch her breath, she laid her head on the pillow before her. Feeling him slide against her and pull her into his arms, she let out a disappointed sigh.

"What is it?" he whispered in her ear as he nibbled on it gently.

"Nothing."

"You sound upset. You still mad at me?"

"It's just when you came in here, you weren't yourself. I understand you were upset, but I don't like you drinking. It makes me nervous. You're not you when you drink."

Tyree sat up as if having an epiphany. He exhaled. "Damn, did I hurt you? Was I too rough?"

"You didn't hurt me."

"Maybe not physically, but what's wrong?"

"You're snapping at me all the time and . . ." She paused, and he rubbed her shoulders. "You never turn away from me, but this time you just rolled over. It made me feel cheap and used. I've never felt that with you. You usually take the time to make me feel special, wanted."

"I'm sorry, kitten. I never meant . . ." He looked away, and she slid her cheek down into his palm. "Look, I'm not perfect, I don't pretend to be, but I need to do better. I know I've been all over the place and you don't deserve it. I told you I forgave you before, but it was a lie." She ducked her head, and he pulled her back. "Until now. I know what you had to have been going through when I was gone, and I'm never going to be okay with it, but at least I can treat you the way you deserve. As a man, as your man, if I couldn't accept that you have flaws, then I shouldn't have made this commitment. I guess what I'm trying to say is I finally forgive you, for real this time."

"Ty, you can't just say it. You have to mean it, because if it's going to keep causing problems, then I don't know where we go from here."

"We go nowhere unless it's together. I'm tired of fighting. I'm sick of running. I just want you, and if you can forgive me for being an ass, all I want to do is love you."

Mia exhaled, and the tears wetting her eyes descended her cheeks.

"We have a life, a family, and I've never wanted that with anyone but you."

"I don't want you to say this and then tomorrow feel like you don't mean it. Our son is noticing the tension between us, and I never want him to feel like his home isn't happy. I had enough of that growing up, and it's something I never want for him."

"I don't want that either, but us not being together isn't an option. I won't let you go."

She didn't answer him. Instead, she spread her arms out and wrapped them around his neck. Soon, they were both headed toward a peaceful sleep. Twenty minutes passed, and all that was heard was the humming of the air conditioner until Tyree's cell phone started buzzing. Mia was the first to hear it, and when she looked over to see that it was two in the morning, she sat up and snatched it from the desk. When she looked down and saw it was Whitney calling, something bubbled up in her chest. A sudden tightness was present when she answered. She opened her mouth to talk to her niece, but was cut off by the shrieks on the other end of the phone.

Tyree sat up suddenly when he heard the raised voices, and he leaned over Mia's shoulder. Tyree was watching her intently when she hit the END button and dropped the phone on the bed. She was shaking, she felt numb, and when he placed his hand on her face, she turned to him with tears rolling down her cheeks.

"What's wrong, Mia? What happened?"

"It's Jude. We need to get over to their house. Get . . . get dressed." She jumped from the bed, and he followed, trying to slow her movements.

"What happened?"

She wouldn't face him. She kept reaching for her clothes.

"Mia!"

"Tyree, get dressed! We have to go."

"What the hell is going on?"

"Jude's dead. Whitney just found him dead in their living room. He was beaten to death." The words left her mouth, and she felt darkness overtake her. Tyree raced to catch her, and they both slid down to the floor. She wasn't all the way out. It was more like a daze as she just sat quietly trying to take it all in. No matter how hard she tried, she couldn't push the sound of Whitney's screams out of her head. She knew they were going to haunt her for a long time to come.

Chapter Seventeen

There were people everywhere by the time Mia and Tyree arrived at the house. They got out of their car and found Whitney on the lawn with Cassandra and Rick. They were all looking at the front door that was wide open, with people coming in and out. As they approached, Mia slid her hand into Tyree's, and he held it tightly. Cassandra was the first to notice them, and she turned, throwing her arms around Mia.

"What happened?" Mia asked through the tight embrace Cassandra had her wrapped in.

"Whitney came downstairs and caught the end of the fight. The bastard ran out when she showed up. He beat him so severely he is hardly recognizable."

"Who would do this to Jude? He doesn't have any enemies. He isn't even from here." Mia sniffled. "I can't believe this."

Rick walked around to stand next to his sister and wrapped his arms around her. "They think it was an attempted home invasion."

"Did they take anything?"

"No," Whitney said in a shaky tone. "And I think we all know what happened here. When people die around us, we know who did it. The same bastard who always does it!" Whitney walked over and sat in her father's car while the rest just stood quietly. There was an awkward silence among them until Tyree finally spoke up.

"You don't think . . . I mean, it's possible, but what would he have to gain from killing Jude? If he was going to go after anyone, let's face it, it would be one of us standing here. Jude wasn't a threat."

"Whitney is," Cassandra said quietly. "This probably wasn't about Jude. I think he may have taken the beating meant for my daughter. She's a part of this world now, and she is a target for Richmond. He wants us all dead because we took everything from him. He wants his whole family eradicated."

Things were awkwardly quiet among them for the next few minutes, and Mia stood there until she felt she needed a break. "I'm sorry, you guys. I need some time to myself." She backed away, and Tyree followed her.

"You okay?"

"No, Ty, I'm not okay. That boy was good and decent. Just this morning he was at our breakfast table worried about us. He had his whole life to live, and just like that, he's gone. He was disposable to whoever did this. It was like his life didn't even matter."

"He mattered. We all loved him."

"Did we, or did we get him killed? If he weren't here, he would still be alive. I don't know if you can live with that, but we promised that boy's parents he would be okay. We promised to take him under our wing, to be there for him."

She trembled with each word. "Why do we even try? Our families are destined to be unhappy. We will never have peace."

"Kitten, you can't—"

"Can't what? Blame myself? Well, it's too late for that. I knew us getting comfortable was a bad idea. We will never be happy."

Mia walked off, and this time he didn't follow her. She knew he was giving her time to cool off, and she found herself walking down the driveway. The night was a bit chilly and the wind a little brisk, but there was a full moon out. She felt like crying, but the tears were all cried out. She felt like she had been doing so much crying lately and was tired of it.

Looking at her hand, she studied her wedding ring. She still had the one from the first time they got married, but Tyree added to it after the second ceremony. He tried to get her a whole new set, but she refused, telling him that the first one meant something to her. Glancing across the yard, she saw that Asha and Terence had arrived and were standing, talking to the others. She wanted to say something to them, but something told her she needed this time alone.

With everything going through her mind, she needed to figure some things out. Suddenly, her problems with Jake seemed so small. If her father was back to his murderous ways, she had other things to worry about, like her son. He was just a kid, but it was already shown once before that he would be collateral damage if he got in the way.

Walking farther, she found herself approaching Jude's car. It was hard for her to believe he had just driven it a few hours earlier, or that he had just sat at her table. When she thought about what headspace he was in when he saw her earlier, the tears she couldn't cry flowed freely. He was miserable the last time she saw him. He felt like his life was falling apart, and now it was over.

Mia felt like she was on the verge of a real breakdown. She hadn't felt this depressed and helpless in years. Her legs felt like they were about to give out, and when she started to feel them shake, she opened Jude's car door and climbed in. She felt a smile creep on her lips when she smelled his cologne still present in the fabric of the seats. Making herself comfortable, she laid her head back on the seat, closing her eyes.

She held her eyes closed for a few minutes and then stared up at the ceiling. She had no idea what she was going to do once she got out. She just knew she needed this. She was grateful Tyree was being understanding right now. They had been arguing so much in the past month, but as soon as he heard about Jude, he was right there. She knew it was probably killing him being away from her right now, and she figured it was time she headed back.

She opened the door, but before she could get out of the car, something caught her eye. There was something in the car with her name on it. Reaching up to the sun visor, she pulled the small envelope down and was just about to open it when she heard someone approach the car. Out of habit, she stuffed the envelope into her purse, and then she looked up to see Whitney walking over. Mia had the driver-side door still open when Whitney opened the passenger door and sat down.

"You know, I was so mad at him earlier, and you. Now, I just want him back," said Whitney.

Mia turned to stay in the car, but Whitney put her hand up, halting her. "Look, I'm sorry. I never meant to snap at you. You're not even who I'm mad at, but do you think I can have a minute here?"

Mia grabbed her hand and gave it a gentle squeeze. "Anything you need." She got out and headed toward the house. Whitney called out to her, and Mia responded, "Yeah, baby?"

"Do you think I could bunk with you guys for the night? I love my parents, you know I do, but my mom is going to smother me. I don't need that tonight. I just need some sleep."

Nodding, Mia smiled at her. "Sure. Pack a bag or a few bags and stay as long as you need."

"Thank you."

Walking back to the others, Mia turned back to see Whitney looking around in Jude's car. She wanted to go back and ask if she needed help with anything but was distracted when she looked up and saw Tyree heading her way. With outstretched arms, he approached her.

"Are you ready to get out of here? There's nothing more we can do, and I really just want to get you in bed and hold you."

"We can do that." She wrapped her arms around his neck and gave him a light kiss. "But let me check on Whit first."

"Tell her we will see her tomorrow." He kissed the side of her mouth.

"Actually, she's going to be staying with us for a while."

She watched as Tyree's expression changed drastically. "Are you sure about that? Why wouldn't she want to stay with her parents? Cassie is going to be upset."

"Cassie goes overboard sometimes, babe, and she needs us. Maybe it will give me time to show her she is just as much a part of this family as anyone else."

"Babe, I don't think it's a good idea."

Mia didn't know what to make of his attitude. It was completely out of left field. "I already told her it was okay. I didn't think you would mind."

As if flipping a switch, he was wearing a smile. "It's fine. Just check on her and let's go. I'm so tired." He kissed her again and walked away, and Mia stood with a baffled expression.

"What the hell was that?"

Chapter Eighteen

"Mia."

She cringed upon hearing her name called out and was disappointed by who stood behind her. She knew she would see him eventually, but she never thought he would be crazy enough to come to their building.

Scanning her office, he leaned against the wall, waiting for her to face him. "Your office is nice, Dimples. I'm glad you're doing well."

She really had no energy to fight. It had been a few days since Jude's service, and she was drained physically and emotionally. Whitney had been with them for a few days, and she was like a zombie. She hadn't eaten much, and from what Mia gathered, she hadn't slept either. What was strange was that Tyree hadn't said much to Whitney the whole time she was there. Mia expected him to support Whitney as much as, if not more than, she was. He and Whitney had always been so close. Now he just stayed his distance, showering all his attention on Mia.

Things had gotten better between her and Tyree, and she felt like maybe he had truly let go of the past and moved past it. He was so attentive, he was gentle, he was everything he promised to be and more, but she couldn't expect it to stay that way with Jake popping up as he wished. She had to put an end to this.

Turning slowly to face him, Mia found her courage and looked him over. He didn't look as bad as he had the last time she saw him, but he still wasn't the Jake she knew. He used to be so confident, so handsome. Now, bags rested under his bright eyes, and frown lines littered his handsome face. He looked stressed. Placing her hands on the desk in front of her, she let out a deep breath, ready to engage in this long-overdue conversation.

"Jake, sit." She motioned for him to take a seat, and he did without pause. "I'm sorry I hadn't been in touch. We had a lot going on."

"Yeah," he sighed. "I heard about your nephew. I wanted to tell you how sorry I was, but then again, you haven't been answering my phone calls."

"It wasn't a good time. We had things to deal with as a family, and truth be told, I wasn't sure how appropriate it would be for me to be talking to you."

Mia saw that the comment stung him, and he tried not to let it show on his face, but he couldn't hide it. She could always read him like a book. "I'm not going to say I'm not upset to hear that, but I understand. You have a life here, and you have your husband. I hate that son of a bitch, and I think he doesn't deserve you, but if he makes you happy . . . You deserve to be happy. Even if it's not with me."

Mia watched the pain flash over his face and felt awful. "Why did you come here? Why torture yourself by being around us?"

"You're all I have. In this whole world, all I had were you and Vincent, and now you're all I have. I had nowhere else to go, no one else to turn to. I know it sounds pathetic, but I needed a friend."

She wasn't sure what to say. He looked like he was really going through something, and a part of her wanted to be the friend he was to her. "What happened to you? Why are you so upset?"

He was fiddling with his hands and wouldn't look her in the eye. She waited patiently for his answer when she saw his head sink lower. "I was wrong to come here. I can't rely on you when you have your own life to lead. I have to figure this out on my own. I shouldn't have come here."

She knew she should have let him go, but her nerves took over and she reached for his hand.

He was shaking when she placed her hand on top of his, and she knew something was terribly wrong. "What is it? You can talk to me."

"Vincent, he met a woman a few months back. He swore she was the one, he swore he was in love, and I was happy for him. At least one of us deserved to get the woman of his dreams. Things were going well, and they seemed to be happy. I never met this woman, he kept her under wraps, but I could see the love when he spoke about her. She was everything to him."

"Where did he meet this woman?" Mia didn't know why, but her chest tightened talking about this. For some reason, she already felt like she knew where this was going.

"You know Vincent. He likes to travel, he likes to go all over the world. There is no telling where they met, but I know he would follow her anywhere."

"Okay. So, he's happy. What's wrong? Why do you look like you lost your best friend?"

He stood and turned away from her. Mia was sitting quietly, waiting for his response when she saw him drop to his knees on her floor. She really didn't know what to do, how to handle her ex breaking down before her. A part of her wanted to pick him up and hug him, because no one deserved to be in the pain she was witnessing. The other side of her knew it would be inappropriate. Tyree had seemed like he was better about the whole ordeal, but she didn't want to push it. As much as she wanted to be a friend to Jake, she wanted to be with Tyree so much more.

She watched from her position behind her desk until she couldn't bear the sight any longer. He hadn't moved from his place on the floor, and when she walked over and bent down, he reached up and grabbed her hand. Allowing him a moment to gather himself, she pulled him from the floor, helping him to the couch behind them. He was still crying when she stepped back behind her desk, attempting to create distance.

"I'm sorry." He sniffled. "I didn't mean to make you uncomfortable. I had nowhere else to go. I have nothing, Mia."

"Jake—"

"I know I lost you. Truth be told, I knew I never had you, but I was hoping one day you could love me like you love him. With you, I had it all. I had a beautiful woman, and I had Kyan. I know he's not mine, but I loved him."

"Kyan was crazy about you, but—"

"He wasn't mine."

"His dad is important to him."

"I would have never tried to replace him."

"I know."

"I tried to think of the time where I was the happiest, and all those moments include you."

"You can't do this. Don't make this harder for yourself. Just tell me what happened. Where is Vincent?"

Shaking his head, Jake wouldn't look her in the eye. She could tell he wasn't himself, and she could tell he was under some kind of influence. She couldn't stand to see him like this, so crossing the room, she headed toward the door. She wasn't sure who she was going to get, because everyone in the building besides her hated him, but she needed someone. The scene was breaking her heart.

As soon as she reached the door, she felt his hand on top of hers. "Don't go. I know I'm scaring you, but don't go. Nobody understands me like you do."

"You have to stop this. Let me get some help for you." She turned and saw his eyes were bloodshot. She took a deep breath. "Are you high? You haven't smoked since college, or at least that's what you told me."

"I need you, Mia." He pressed her up against the wall, and her breath caught in her chest. "I just need to be with you."

Putting her hands on his chest, she felt like the room was spinning. She felt dizzy, and when she looked back to the door, she saw Tyree standing with his fist balled. It was as if they were both frozen until Jake hissed, and then all hell broke loose. The punch Tyree threw was loud, and she felt a gust of air whoosh past her face as Jake slid down in front of her. The hit missed her face by only a few inches, and she saw Tyree's eyes widen when he realized how close he came to hitting her.

Stumbling, Jake lifted himself from the floor and rushed at Tyree. The rage in Tyree's eyes frightened Mia, and all she could do was scream at the top of her lungs. Shortly afterward, Miguel came barreling down the hall and pulled them apart. Mia had gotten her bearings together just as Asha walked in, scanning the room. Before Asha could reach her, she walked over, drawing back to slap Jake in the face. Mia felt her body going into overdrive as she kept swinging. She felt the frustration boiling out into her hits, and after a few swings, it was Tyree who was restraining her.

"Let me go!"

Tyree had her arms, but she was still trying to get back to Jake. "Mia, baby, calm down." He wrapped his arms around her, and she felt her body relaxing. She didn't know why she snapped, maybe it was the weight of all the secrets, maybe it was the constant threat to her marriage, but she just lost it. She felt like she was outside her body just then, and when she blinked, she finally saw the situation for what it was: a complete mess.

"Take me home," she demanded, finally having had enough. Now she was ready. She had to get everything off her chest before it made her crazy.

"Baby, are you okay?" Tyree looked worried. She'd been afraid he had seen them and thought she was encouraging it, but the look in his eyes only showed the concern he felt. Shaking her head, she let him pull her into his arms. "Come on, let's go." He kissed the side of her head while Miguel pulled Jake from the floor.

On the way out, Jake became hysterical and was yelling as loud as he could, "Just kill me. I don't have a reason to go on."

"Get him out of here," Tyree growled. "Get him out before I give him what he's asking for. I want security to know that he never makes it in this building again."

Jake wasn't fighting Miguel, but he was screaming, and Mia turned to see the tears falling. She was confused. She couldn't understand why he would be making such a scene. It wasn't like him. "Just make it stop."

"The only thing that's stopping is all this drama you got going. You're lucky I'm not into kicking a man while he's down." Miguel tightened his hold on Jake and jerked him out the door.

Mia walked over to the door, and she could still hear him yelling. "He's dead, Mia. So I might as well let him kill me because I'm dead inside anyway."

Through all the madness, his actions finally made sense. Telling Miguel to stop, Mia ran down the hall and stood in front of Jake. Turning back to Tyree and seeing him nod that it was okay, she touched her hand to Jake's cheek. "I'm sorry. I'm so sorry. I know he meant a lot to you."

Jake began to sob loudly. "He was all I had left. I'm all alone, and I just needed to see you."

She let her hand linger on his cheek and pulled back when she thought about her husband standing behind her. She turned and saw him with his hands in his pockets, trying to stay composed. Walking backward, she touched him, and he looked at her with more love than she had ever seen.

"It's okay, kitten. Do what you need to do. I'm not going anywhere."

At that moment, she felt like she didn't deserve him. She didn't deserve either of them. Things had gotten out of hand, and she knew what she needed to do. It was time to get her life back on track. Kissing Tyree on the cheek, she walked back toward Jake and grabbed his arm. Miguel looked hesitant to let go, but when she gave him an encouraging nod, he loosened his grip and walked to Tyree. Standing shoulder to shoulder with his brother, Miguel leaned close enough to have a quiet conversation, which Mia overheard.

"You okay with this?"

Tyree cleared his throat before responding, "Not really, but even I won't shit on dude when he is obviously going through something. He had to be to come in here like that."

"You're going to let her be alone with him again?"

"No." He took a step forward. "I'm going too. I guess I'm giving her a minute."

"You're better than me. I'd still be beating that ass."

"Maybe I should be, but I don't know, she surprised me. I thought I would be the one who had to be restrained, but Mia went crazy. I'm a little worried about her."

"She's stressed."

"There's more. I know that woman, and I've never seen her act like that."

Tyree and Mia took Jake to his hotel after that, and though she could feel his eyes on her, she tried not to look at him. She felt like if she did, she might break. She needed to hold it together at least until they made it home. She needed to keep her head straight at least until she figured out what to do next. She felt her world slowly unraveling, and if she wasn't careful, she could lose it all and end up just like Jake. He was so broken. She didn't want that for herself. She didn't want that for Tyree.

Chapter Nineteen

She was looking at him, but she wasn't seeing him. Her eyes were vacant, and he needed the emotion to return. She looked empty, and Tyree had to admit he would do anything to get it back. He knew today was hard for her and he was partially to blame for that. He had given her so much stress about Jake, and when he actually needed someone, she felt like she couldn't be there for him.

He wasn't thrilled about Mia being the only one who could comfort Jake, but he knew what it was like to feel alone. No matter what his feelings were, he wouldn't make her be heartless and turn her back on him. He was a friend to her during a time she needed it, and he understood, even though he hated it. Jake was the one who helped her through the whole suicide attempt, and in a way, maybe he owed him for taking care of her. It would never sit well, but it was their reality. To truly be happy with her, he had to accept the good and the bad.

She had been quiet ever since returning from the hotel. She had a bottle of wine resting next to her feet as she sat on the couch. He was all for giving her space, but he was worried about her. Instead of letting their son stay home and feel the discomfort, he sent him to be with Karen and Rock. Kyan was more than happy to go, but Tyree could sense he wanted to stay with his mother. Ever since Jude passed, he had been glued to her and had even spent a few nights in their room. It didn't bother Tyree, but he was glad to have their bed back. They hadn't made love in a while, and he was missing her.

He thought things had improved since their talk, and they had, but he felt like they were walking on eggshells around each other. They were both afraid to say or do something that upset the other, and he wanted to change that. He didn't want to fight, but he wanted her to know it was okay if they did. He knew that in any relationship there were fights, and he needed it to be okay. He needed back the confidence they once had.

Standing across the room, he watched as she downed a glass of wine. He saw how uncomfortable she was. He had to admit the discomfort wasn't all her fault. He had been on edge with Whitney in their house. Nothing had happened, but he felt uneasy around her. The things Terence said to him had been taking over his thoughts when he was around her, and it was hard to act like it wasn't affecting him. She had been like a shell of herself since Jude died, but he found himself staying his distance. If she did feel different about him, he didn't want to give her the wrong idea. That wouldn't be good.

Tyree watched Mia as she poured another glass of wine, and he knew he had to do something. She was on her third glass, and he knew, as much as she would deny it, she was a lightweight. Walking over and placing his hand on the glass, he was surprised when she let him take it. Looking into her deep brown eyes, he pushed her hair back and swiped his thumb over her cheek.

"Talk to me, sweetheart." He felt his emotions bubbling in his throat. "I need you to know whatever it is will be okay."

Blinking, she shook her head, pushing his hand away. "It's all my fault. I made so many decisions that are messing up our lives. I'm sorry."

She sniffled, and he ran his hand through her hair, pulling her head to his chest. "I don't know what you think you did, but you can tell me. I'm scared we won't make it if you don't talk to me.

I haven't made it easy for you to tell me things, but it's okay. I promise."

"Stop. Don't promise it's okay. You don't know what I did. You won't forgive me. I don't forgive me."

She was breaking. He looked into her eyes and saw the pain and grew terrified. He needed her to tell him to rip the Band-Aid off, and then hopefully they could rebuild. Parting ways wasn't an option. "Baby, talk to me." He held her close to his heart for fear that if he let her go, she would be gone forever. Kissing the top of her head, he ran his hand up and down her back. He could feel the tears soaking his shirt, and he pulled her back, placing a kiss on her lips. When she pushed back, he was confused. "Why—"

"Ty, I'm the reason we don't have a baby. I messed up, and I can't fix it."

"Maybe it's not meant for us. But it's okay. We can adopt—"

"Stop, dammit!" She jumped from the couch, and he fell back. "Stop telling me it's okay. Stop being so fucking understanding. Can't you see I want to feel bad? I want to feel like shit."

"Mia, whatever you did, we can get through it." He saw her pacing, and when she finally faced him, he felt like he had been hit with a brick when he heard what she uttered quietly. "Wha . . . what did you say?"

"I had an abortion, and that's why I can't get pregnant again. We will never have another child because of what I did."

His breathing stopped momentarily. He felt sick. He felt like he was going to vomit. He did. Luckily there was a plant beside him, and he got to it just in time. He was standing over the plant, heaving as he listened to the sound of her sobbing. He tried to regain his senses, but before he could stop himself, he heard his own voice yelling. "You killed my baby? You hated me that much that you would kill my child? What the hell is wrong with you?"

"No. No, I wouldn't. You have to believe me. I would never kill something we created. I love you."

"You don't. You couldn't. To do this, you would have to hate me. You hate me that much?" His voice had gone up an octave, and he could hear it cracking. He was trying to understand, but nothing made this okay. Nothing helped the ache he felt in his chest.

"It wasn't your baby."

Hearing her admission, he stopped short. He searched her eyes for the joke he knew she had to be playing, but he saw nothing. Instead of speaking, she just stood there weeping with her arms outstretched.

"Well, who . . ." He closed his eyes, and then they flew open as he realized he already knew the answer. "I'll kill that bastard. You were having his baby, and you never thought that I should know?" He was back to yelling, and he saw her shake with each word. "Talk!"

"No! I couldn't tell you because I knew you would only blame yourself, and it hurt. It hurt so bad. I just wanted to forget it. I took those pills to forget, but it wouldn't go away."

He was hysterical. He felt his hands trembling. As upset as she was, he wanted to comfort her, but his nerves were shot. Swinging out, he connected with the wall, and she started crying even harder. "I knew there was something, but I never thought it was this. I never thought you could make me feel this way again, but I was wrong. I loved you, and I thought that if I just loved you harder, it would be okay." He was rambling when she walked up, touching his shoulder.

"It wasn't his baby." His head shot up, and he stared her down. "After you left, I was in bad shape. I needed a minute to breathe, I needed to unwind, so I went for a walk. It was dark." Her hands started to tremble, and he saw the pain wash over her. Looking at her, it all hit him, and he began to shake his head vehemently.

"No, stop. I can't hear this. I won't hear this."

"I need to, Ty. Let me talk." She was going through the story so fast, he could hardly believe it. "I never wanted it to happen, I didn't. He pulled me into an alley and held a knife to my throat and told me to be a good little fuck and I could live. He was rough, it hurt, and all I could think of was how much I wanted to be anywhere but there. He hit me in the head, hard, and I was disoriented. I don't even remember getting home. I just woke up the next morning feeling so dirty. He made me feel so cheap, Ty."

"Don't tell me this. I don't want to think about . . ." He looked at her with tears in his eyes. "Oh, baby, who did this to you?"

"I don't know. It was dark, and I should have paid more attention, but I was scared. My head was throbbing and nothing made sense to me. I know I messed up by getting rid of the baby. It could have helped them catch him, but I couldn't have a part of him growing inside me. I never wanted any of this. I wanted you. I needed you."

Suddenly it all made sense, why she reacted the way she did the last time they had sex. He had made her feel like she had that night. He hated himself. He felt like an ass. "Dammit!" He pushed a vase from the table and dropped to his knees. He hadn't cried like this in years, and he couldn't stop the tears. It was all hitting him so hard.

He felt her stroking his head. When he looked up, he saw the redness and puffiness of her eyes, and he pushed her head into his chest. "I'm sorry, I'm sorry, I'm sorry, baby. Oh, God, I'm sorry."

"I never wanted you to worry. I'd rather swallow it than let you feel like it was your fault."

"I should have been there, Mia. You needed me. Dammit, I should have been there."

"I couldn't have his baby. I just couldn't. I just wanted to end the pain. When it was over, I was scared, I was angry, and after a while, I blamed you. I know how wrong I was, but I blamed you for not being there."

There was nothing he could say. Nothing made sense. The thought of her hurting that way made him come unglued. He could hardly speak, so he just held her, rocking her back and forth, promising to never let go, and she kept her head laid over his heart. When she finally stopped crying, she reached up and made him look at her. Gazing into her eyes, he swore he would never let anyone hurt her again, and she shook her head. He only hoped she believed him, because he meant it with every fiber of his being.

That night, he watched her sleep. He felt like he had been doing that a lot lately. She stirred so many times, and he watched her toss and turn, but mostly he just stayed awake looking at his angel. She had been through so much, and she was still able to love him and their son unconditionally. Before he picked her up and carried her to bed, they talked. Well, he mostly listened.

For once, he just sat and let her talk. He let her tell him everything she was feeling. Though he hated it, he realized why she and Jake were so connected and why she felt the need to salvage their friendship. He had seen her through the pain of being violated, and he held her hand after the abortion. He had really stepped up. She told him about how when they first met there was only a friendship, and he believed her. When they moved to Paris, he was just a friend, and it developed into more a year later.

Finally, he had gotten to the bottom of the whole relationship between her and Jake, and as much as he hated to admit it, he had grown to respect him as a person. He would never like him, but the respect would always be there for how well he had taken care of Mia. At the end of the conversation, he told her that if she wanted to be friends with Jake, he wouldn't stand in her way. She was hesitant, but he assured her he meant it wholeheartedly.

They talked for hours, and after it all, she fell asleep in his arms. He had never felt more content in their relationship. Now that they had all the problems out of the way and all the cards were on the table, they could get back to being everything to each other. It was finally the way it should have always been, and now he loved her more than he could ever put into words.

Chapter Twenty

"Whitney, sweetheart, can you come here for a minute? I need to talk to you." Mia had been trying, she really had, but nothing she did seemed to break Whitney out of the funk she was in. She had been going to work and staying out until late in the night, and Mia had no clue where she was going. Where she seemed to worry, Tyree kept her at arm's length. It was confusing, but she just went with it.

Watching Whitney come over and join her at the table, she felt her heart breaking for the young girl. True, she had been separated from her son and Tyree before, but no matter how bad things got, she knew in the back of her mind they would be together again. She never realized it until a few days ago that she had never truly given up hope. She'd just tried to dull the pain. Now that things were back on track with them, she needed to do what she could to fix her niece, although there was nothing she could do to make up for the loss.

"What can I help you with?"

"Honey, I need you to help me figure out what I can do to make this better. I know we have a lot to make up for and I know I haven't always been there, but I'm here now, and I want to fix it."

With hesitation, Whitney looked into her eyes. "Can we? Can we fix something that's been broken for so long?"

Mia was confused. Up until that moment, she thought she was reaching out about Jude. She thought he was the main reason for the pain in her niece's eyes. "Broken?"

"For years, this is all I wanted. The chance to sit down with you and have you see me. Not as your twenty-five-year-old, kid niece, but as a person, as a woman. I needed that. I needed you all to take me seriously, to love me."

"We love you, we do. You just have to understand that your mom and dad were so afraid for you. They saw what happened to Mom and Janelle and wanted so much more for you."

"And all I wanted was to be home with my family."

Although it felt like they had done the right thing by shipping her off, Mia saw what it had done to Whitney's trust in them. "You know, your mom was the reason I initially went to Paris." Whitney wore a look of confusion, and Mia nodded. "After everything that happened, she saw that I needed a break from here. She suggested that I take a trip and then return home with a clear head. Once I got there, I took the coward's way out and ran from my problems even though everyone begged me to come home."

"Do you regret it?

"Yes and no," Mia answered honestly. "It helped in the beginning. It gave me a new outlook, and toward the end, it showed me that everything I ever needed was right at home. Even if I was too stubborn to admit it, your uncle was and still is my soul mate."

"But you were with Jake for all that time. Did he mean nothing to you?"

"He meant a lot to me. He still does." Whitney's eyes widened, and Mia shook her head. "Not in a romantic way. He was a friend when I needed one. He was a comfort when I needed to be held. I can't say that I regret him, because I don't. I needed to have that someone else to make me realize that Ty was the one I could never be without. Jake made me feel alive when I felt so dead inside, but Ty is the one who put my world back into focus."

Before speaking the words just then, Mia had never realized that was what had happened. She always knew that Jake wasn't the one, even when she was trying to convince herself he was. With him, there was always something that held her back, always a sense of trepidation. She didn't know it at the time because she was so clouded with hurt and anger, but it was her love for Tyree. She had loved him since she was a child, even when they were just friends. She couldn't find it in her heart to be with someone else. Tyree had dated other girls and had even messed around a little, but the real experiences he saved for her. They were each other's firsts, and nothing compared to that.

They had overcome a lot to be together, and now things between them were stronger than ever. All the doubts he had about her and her loyalty were gone, and he had even given her his blessing to continue a friendship with Jake. Although he still wasn't too fond of him, Tyree took a step back, allowing her to make a huge gesture on Jake's behalf. Because Jake had explained to her that he wasn't ready to go home and face the loneliness that would greet him, he resolved to stay in Atlanta. She offered up their old house in place of a hotel. Jake, of course, protested, but she was persuasive and won out in the end. Jake ended up moving into the house after striking up the compromise that he would at least pay rent for the time he was there.

With things falling back into place as far as her marriage, she needed to get through to Whitney, or she would never have peace. "How could you leave though? Do you know how bad he took it? Uncle Ty was a mess, and he did some stupid stuff to get over you. You do know he almost killed himself, wrapping his car around a tree, right?"

Mia saw the resentment in her eyes and took a deep breath. "Not a day goes by that I don't think about what it did to him, but what I can't do is keep holding on to it. We have worked through it and agreed to live in the now, not what we used to be."

"How do you do that? How do you shut off the pain and replace it with love? Is it even possible?"

Shaking her head, Mia took Whitney's hand and gave it a squeeze. "No. You try really hard to suppress it until it eats you alive, and then you release it. It's not easy. It took us five years to come to terms with the things we did. Even with all the love we still had, it took us screaming at each other to finally get to a good place. Before now, we were just going through the motions trying not to shake things up because we were afraid to let go."

"And now? Did all of that help?"

"I love that man with everything I have, and I can honestly say I've never been more confident in what we have."

"But how could he just get over your betrayal? I swear, as long as I live, I will never understand it. He was so good to you."

Mia felt the sting of her words and was taken by surprise. She hadn't expected this conversation to be extremely pleasant, but she hadn't expected this. It was like Whitney was blaming her for everything that went wrong instead of seeing the big picture.

"How can he act like you did nothing wrong?" Whitney asked.

"He knows what I did just as well as I do. He loves me, and we have forgiven each other for all the hurtful things." Mia felt her temper and her voice rising, and witnessing the look in Whitney's eyes, she had to pull back. "What happened between your uncle and me is not what we're supposed to be discussing. I understand you have questions, but frankly, it's really no one's business but ours. What I wanted to do was check on you. You haven't mentioned Jude once since he died, and I don't want you keeping it bottled up. You have to talk about it, or you'll go crazy."

"I don't want to. I don't want to say his damn name because I'm so angry. How could he leave me? How could he just abandon what we had?" Tears were sliding down her cheeks, and Mia saw her body trembling. "We were getting married. We were supposed to be happy."

"He loved you. He was so worried he might lose you. He was out of his mind wondering if you were about to walk away."

"I wasn't. I messed up, and I just wanted to know if his last thoughts of me were bad. That morning I was so angry. I was jealous . . . of you."

"Me? Why?"

"He never said anything to me. Instead of talking to me, he confided in you. When I needed to know what was going on with him, he came to you."

"He was afraid. He thought I could give him some advice. He was just lost."

"Well, I should have been the one he came to."

Mia slid over and pulled Whitney against her chest. "Sweetheart, I'm sorry. I truly understand, and I get why you're angry. I just want you to know that I'm going to do whatever it takes to fix what's wrong between us. If I had done better, maybe it would have been easier for you two to talk to each other."

"Why do you care so much?"

"Because I love you. You're my niece, but you're more like my sister. Growing up, your mother was everything to me, and I owe her so much. I know how she's been feeling not knowing if you're okay, and I want to be able to assure her that I'm taking care of you."

"You don't have to do that. I don't deserve it. I have been so horrible to you. I'm sorry."

Mia just held her closer with her eyes closed. She knew what they went through was different, but she and her niece had another bond. She needed to let her know everything would be okay. "Whit, Jude told me what happened to you." Mia felt her stiffen. "It's okay. I promise one day you will wake up and it won't seem so bad."

Whitney sat up, and Mia could tell she was searching her eyes for answers. "How do you know? How could you possibly understand?"

Since talking to Tyree about it, Mia felt a weight lifted from her shoulders. It seemed like the revelation helped her understand it wasn't her fault and that she hadn't asked for it. She just wanted the same for Whitney. She wanted to be her sounding board. What better way to reach her than sharing her equally painful past? "It happened to me too. When it happened, I was ashamed, and I blamed myself. I thought maybe I deserved it for how I treated Ty, but I know now that no one deserves to be violated. No one deserves to be treated that way."

The tears began flowing freely, and Whitney held Mia's hand tighter. "I'm sorry that happened to you. I never knew. I just thought you were mad at Uncle Ty."

"I was so broken, and yeah, I blamed him after I got over blaming myself. I was destructive. I tried to do so many things to numb the pain. I only made matters worse."

Her eyes widened, and Whitney shook her head slowly. "What did you do?"

Mia hadn't ever wanted to discuss her suicide attempt again, but she needed Whitney to understand that what she did wasn't the answer. "I took a bottle of pills. When I felt myself getting tired and I thought it was ending, I went and lay down in my bed. I thought I had died, but two days later, I woke up in the hospital with Jake sitting by my side. I had met him a few times before that. He had offered to help me with Kyan. For me to wake up and see this familiar stranger sitting next to my bed was crazy. I was alone, or at least felt like it, but it was my fault. I had done this. I pushed everyone away, but Jake was there. He never left."

"But you left him."

"We were never meant to be that. We were meant to be what we are now. I will never regret meeting and getting to know him, but Ty is my love. Jake and I were meant to save each other and make room for the right people to enter our lives. Mine I already had, and he will find his soon."

"Save him? What were you saving him from?"

"His wife died, and he wasn't dealing with it. He was keeping his feelings hidden. When he met me and after what I tried, his feelings of guilt transferred over to me. He didn't know anything about me other than my son was missing and my husband was gone, but he developed this protective feeling about me and never left my side. I know I was wrong, and I never should have let it get as far as it did, but I let my gratitude trick me into feelings that were never there. I let him get in so deep that he wanted to marry me, and I couldn't say yes. At the time, I thought it was because I couldn't commit again, but I think in the back of my mind I knew it was because my love for Tyree never died. I couldn't marry someone else when my heart was still here."

"But he was going to. How did that make you feel? I mean, you turned Jake down, but Tyree asked that girl to marry him."

"It hurt, but could I really blame him? After everything that happened, I was lucky he even gave me another chance."

"He loves you so much. I wish I were capable of that kind of love."

"You loved Jude. He loved you back."

"Yeah, but it wasn't the same. Jude and I, we worked, but I messed up so much where he was concerned."

Mia studied her face and realized what she had been seeing and mistaking for sadness was actually guilt. She thought she had an idea of what was going on, but she needed to hear it for herself. "Did you ever cheat on Jude? I mean, I won't judge you if you say yes. God knows I've made my share of mistakes and I—"

"I did," she said, interrupting Mia. She dropped her head. "It wasn't anything serious, and he wasn't anyone special, but I messed everything up."

"Who? Where?"

"I know what you must think of me, but I swear I never meant to hurt him. I felt horrible after it happened, so I lied. Every time he tried to make me feel better about it, I felt like such a fraud. I never meant for it to get this far or for it to be his last thought of me."

"Are you still seeing this man?"

"Not intentionally. We met years ago and had a thing, and we met up again just before we moved here. Jude and I held off on sex for the majority of our relationship because of it. This guy, he was rough. He wasn't gentle with me in the beginning, and it made me afraid of sex. I thought if I pushed it out of my mind, I could go back to when I was a virgin and give myself to the right person, to Jude. That night, I skipped the party because I saw him. He found out where I was."

"You weren't raped?"

"No. I was scared, so I lied. This guy, he knows things about me. He knows my weaknesses. He knew exactly what to say to get into my head, and I was stupid. All those years of being with Jude were washed down the drain because I couldn't say no to him."

Mia felt the air leave her lungs. She never knew her niece was so vulnerable, that her sense of self-worth was so low. "Whit, what you did, I understand. I know what it's like to doubt yourself and not feel worthy of anything real. You have to make yourself believe you're better than that, better than he makes you feel."

"I've made so many wrong choices. I think it may be hard if not impossible to find my way back."

Mia's hand touched her face gently. "You can, sweetheart. I'll help you, and I want you to know you're not alone. You will always have me, and you have our family. If you let them in, they can be pretty great."

"After everything I just admitted to you, you're still able to be around me and not feel like I'm a horrible person?"

"Like I said, we've all made mistakes and done things we aren't proud of. We never expected you to be perfect. We just want you to be happy."

"It's going to take a while for that."

Mia stood and kissed her on the cheek before heading for the stairs. "Good thing we have time." Mia retreated to the stairs, and then she pushed herself against the wall and sighed. She wasn't expecting the revelations she had just heard, but she was glad they were making progress.

Making her way into her room, she reached for her purse and pulled out the letter. Now it seemed even more tempting to read, but still, she just held it between her fingers, looking at it before stuffing it back in. She still couldn't bring herself to open it. Now she wasn't even sure if she should. It would probably only contain the harsh truths Whitney had just relayed, and she sure didn't want to think about it again.

Deciding to put the letter out of her mind, she tossed her purse on the bed as her cell phone lit up with a call. Looking at the caller ID, she noticed it was Tyree and picked up. "Hey, you. When are you coming home?"

"I'm going to pop in on Kyan and make sure he's good at Mom's, and then I will be there to you. You want me to get dinner?"

He had been incredibly sweet since the talk they had, and he was doing everything he could to make sure she never had to lift a finger. She was grateful, but she was beginning to feel like they should go back to normal, including bringing their son home. She was glad Kyan loved spending time with Karen, Rock, and Kiyoko, but she wanted him home. Honestly, she missed the conversations they had. Things were great between her and Tyree, but she needed him to not try so hard. It could get exhausting.

"No, babe. I'm cooking, so just bring that sexy self home."

"I can pick something up if you want to rest. I just want you comfortable."

"I am, and I'll be more comfortable cooking for my guys tonight."

"Guys? I thought you wanted Ky with Mom and Rock for a while."

"I did, and now that Whitney and I have had a talk, it's okay. Plus, I miss him."

"Okay," he laughed. "I'll get the boy, and I'll be home."

"Okay, babe."

"Love you, kitten."

"I love you too."

Chapter Twenty-one

"So I think the flowers should be in silver vases in these corners and black here," Asha pointed out. "But it is your choice."

Tyree looked at the pictures she had and nodded. "I agree. Whatever you think is fine. I'm just glad you had time to help me put this together." He had enlisted his sister in putting together an anniversary party for him and Mia. They had been through so much, and he wanted to reaffirm the love they felt in front of all their family and friends. He was planning to do it in less than a month, so they had to get a move on, and it was proving to be a difficult task keeping it from Mia. She was always so involved in everything he did.

"No problem, big brother. I'm just glad things are good for you. I was worried for a while."

"I was worried too, but now things are great. I want to show the world how much I love my baby. It's been hard as hell, but she deserves this party and so much more. I'm so happy, sis."

Asha smiled and winked at him. "Well, I think it is going to be fabulous, and the fact that you're having it at Rick's is very helpful because she doesn't know a thing. She is going to be so surprised."

"She'd better be. Her nosy butt has been all up in everything around the house. Hell, I had to squirrel the boy away at Mom's to keep him quiet, and now she wants him home. I have to talk to him and make sure he knows it's a surprise because she will definitely grill him if she suspects anything."

"You know your wife, but Kyan will be okay. He won't let her crack him." She laughed and grabbed her bag, heading toward the door. "All right, I'll see you tomorrow. I'm going home."

"All right. You be safe."

"You too. Go home."

"On my way out." He watched her leave and made a few phone calls before packing up his things to leave the office. He was well out the door when his cell began to ring. He looked down and saw his home number and smiled. He knew Mia would be calling soon since he hadn't made it home. He knew she would be antsy after over two hours had passed. He picked up the phone and smiled at the silence he heard at first on the other end.

"Hey, kitten, you ready for this sexy ass to get home?"

"Hmm. So is that what you're calling yourself nowadays? I don't know if I like my daughter with someone so vain."

Tyree gripped the phone so tight he swore something broke off. "What the hell are you doing at my house, Richmond? Where is Mia?"

He heard a loud sigh and found himself speeding up to get to the elevator. "You can rush here if you want, but she isn't home, and I'm a bit disappointed. I really missed my dove."

"What are you doing at my house? Do you think this is a game, old man?"

"It's not a game, son, I can assure you. I need to see my daughter and I will soon. Don't try to make it here. You will never catch me. Let her know I will be seeing her soon. You need to do a better job at this whole protection thing. Anyone could just walk in this house as they please, just like I did."

Tyree heard the phone click, and even though he had already pressed the button to hit the ground floor, he pressed it again, several times. Staring at his phone like it was going to explode in his hand, he thought about Mia. He thought about where she could possibly be, and he hit the speed dial to call her cell. He hoped she would answer, that Richmond hadn't taken her and just called to gloat.

After three rings, he began to get frantic. Finally reaching his car, he almost burst into tears when she answered. He heard his voice cracking and could hear the confusion in her voice. "Where are you, baby?"

"I had to run to the store. I finished all the food and was waiting for you, but you were running late, and I realized we didn't have wine. You know how I feel about steaks with no wine," she laughed, but he still couldn't joke around with her.

"I need you to meet me somewhere. Can you come to the hotel across the street from here?"

"Come to a hotel?" she huffed. "I have dinner cooked. And where does our son fit into that equation?"

"Baby, please. I just . . . Please?"

He heard a pause, and after a deep breath, he heard her voice speak. "Fine, Ty, but I need to go to the house and get—"

"Just come. You don't need anything. I don't want you going back there tonight."

"Is someone anxious to see me?"

"Yes. I need you right now, and I want you to hurry, baby."

"Just so you know, you're not off the hook about dinner."

"I'll buy you the whole damn cow if you just get here now."

"Okay, pushy. I'm coming. Order a bottle of wine because I feel like I'm going to need it tonight to loosen you up."

"Whatever you want, baby. Just be safe, okay?"

"I will, Ty. I don't like this mood you're in. Whatever it is will be okay."

Tyree had spaced out, but when he heard her statement, he focused back in. "Huh? What did you say?"

"It's going to be okay. Whatever happened, it won't matter once we're together."

As much as he tried to fight it off, a smile appeared on his face. "I'll see you soon, but do me a favor. Don't hang up until you're at my door. I'll be in our normal room, 315. I want to make sure you get here okay. Hold on. It's going to get quiet for a little while because I need to make another call, but don't hang up."

"It's not that far, Ty. I'm like fifteen minutes away. I'm sure nothing will happen between now and then."

"Humor me."

Switching over to his other line, Tyree called Rock. He answered after two rings, and Tyree quickly went over what had happened and asked that he call Rick and Cassandra. Throughout the conversation, Rock was surprisingly quiet, and Tyree got the sense there was more he didn't know. At the end of the call, Rock assured him things would be fine and pushed him to spend time with his wife, not worrying about the impromptu visit from Richmond. Rock let him say good night to Kyan and urged him to enjoy the rest of his day. After a few protests, he caved, remembering he had Mia waiting on the other line. When he clicked over, he could hear her in the car, and he smiled. She had followed his request.

He walked into the hotel and got them their room before covering his phone to keep her from hearing what he was setting up. He was worried about her, but he didn't want to ruin her entire night. He knew any mention of contact from Richmond would make her want to react. She probably wouldn't even leave home like he asked. She had told him she wasn't afraid of Richmond any longer. First, he wanted to do something special before he told her about Richmond. He was tired of having to soften her up for the blow. He often wondered if they would ever have a normal day; if they would ever just be able to enjoy each other.

After getting everything set up and going up to the room, he could hear her in the car singing along to one of her favorite songs. He always loved her voice, and nothing had changed. She was beautiful in every way, and even with all her flaws, she was his perfect woman.

Dropping to the bed, he was surprised to hear a knock at the door. He swung it open expecting to find his wife but saw room service. He hadn't expected them so soon, but they had arrived with the bottle of wine and the rest of the surprises he had ordered. Pouring two glasses, he sat on the bed, waiting for Mia to arrive. He could still hear her shuffling around on the phone, and when he heard another knock at his door, he jumped up and swung it open.

His breath caught in his chest when he saw her smiling face. He hadn't realized how tense he was until he saw her. When she reached out to touch him, he pulled her inside. Watching Mia push her coat aside, he felt himself growing crazed with each movement. He pulled her down to the bed and clutched her hand.

"So, now do you want to tell me why you wanted me out of the house?"

He should have known she always knew when something was bothering him. Remembering his promise to her about always sharing, he sighed and wrapped his arm around her small waist. "I got a call from the house just before I called you."

"So, I guess Whit went back. I thought she was staying with her parents tonight. No biggie. I know you wanted us to have some alone time, so I get that."

"It wasn't her. Babe, don't freak out, but Richmond was in our house. I called Rock, and he's going to handle it, and Ky is fine. He's having fun with Mom and Grandma. Rock also called Rick and Cassie. Everyone will be fine." He saw the fear flicker through her and touched her chin. "Hey, don't look like that. We're fine. Everyone is fine."

"He's not that stupid, Ty. He will never let them catch him, and him being in our house means he is up to something big, something dangerous."

"He can't hurt you. I will never let him get close enough for that. Earlier you told me we would be okay as long as we were together, and from here on out, I'm not letting you out of my sight. If I have to move my office to your floor, that's what I will do." He attempted it as a joke, but she didn't crack a smile.

"What about our son? You said he's safe?"

Tyree nodded. "Somehow, I think this is all about you. He doesn't seem concerned with Kyan, so him being with Rock and Mom is the best thing for now. They won't let anything happen to him."

"I hear what you're saying, but—"

He grabbed her chin and forced her lips against his. His tongue traced the outline of her lips before surging inside her mouth. He held her to him, gripping the side of her face until all her resistance was gone. Sliding his hands down her sides, he grabbed her hips and pulled her closer.

"No worrying. Let's eat, unless you want to find other ways to entertain ourselves."

"The food will get cold." She pulled back, catching her breath. "But truthfully"—she winked at him and placed her hand on his chest, pushing him back on the bed—"I'm not hungry anymore."

He sat up, twirling her over on her back, and hovered over her. "I am." He started his slow creep down her body and let her moans urge him on. He knew she was afraid, but he also knew he wasn't going to let Richmond do anything to harm her. Now, his focus was on making her forget their problems. Her nails digging into his shoulders let him know he was getting closer. Now he just had to finish the job.

"What were you thinking?" Lenae yelled, throwing a pile of clothes off the bed. "Why would you go to their house?"

"I don't explain myself to you. I did what I needed to do. I'm tired of living like an outsider to something I built! I built that business. I built that family! How dare they toss me out?"

Lenae walked up and got right in his face. "You did this to yourself! All your lies, all your bullshit did this. You are the reason we have to hide, the reason my child has to bounce around like a nomad."

"No, dear, that would be you. You had to open your mouth. You ruined everything I had going."

"I won't apologize for what I did. I still feel like it was the right thing to do."

Richmond saw the tears in her eyes and felt himself calming down. "I'm sorry. You're right. It set us back a bit, but you are right, dear." He stroked her hair, and she laid her head on his shoulder.

"Is it always going to be this way? Will we always have to look over our shoulders?"

"No. Soon enough, you will have everything and so will that beautiful girl in there."

"You promise?"

"I promise. Just give me some time."

"Time is something we don't have much of."

"I know, sweetheart." He kissed the top of her head. "I know."

Chapter Twenty-two

"You want any help?" Chloe asked, looking at Tyree struggling with the ribbons for their invitations.

Glancing up and chuckling at the frustration he was displaying, he reached over and handed her a stack of envelopes and a bundle of ribbons. "Thanks. I told Asha I had it, but now I see that was a mistake."

"It's cool. I don't mind helping." She picked up an envelope and stuffed a finished invitation inside. "You know, this is awesome what you're doing for her. She's going to love it."

Tyree looked up with a silly grin. "Yeah, she will, and she will be pleased to know how much you helped out. I really appreciate it. Usually, my sister is the one who puts up with my crazy events, her and Whitney." Saying Whitney's name, Tyree felt a little guilty. He had been keeping his distance, and now he felt like it was all for nothing. She hadn't made any moves that suggested she thought of him as anything other than her uncle. She actually had become really close with Mia. He was glad for them, but he kind of missed the bond they once shared.

In the past few weeks, he had been spending a great deal of time with Chloe, and he now saw why Mia liked her so much. In spite of her situation, Chloe was very bright, and she was genuinely concerned about others. A few weeks earlier, she had come to the office in search of Mia and had run into him trying to hide the evidence of his party planning. She helped him smuggle everything into his office. Afterward, she stayed and helped him get some other things under control. Today, she had been planning a lunch with Mia, which got canceled when Rick insisted that he needed her. It was all a ruse arranged by Tyree before he knew she had plans, so Chloe offered to help him.

Ever since receiving the call from Richmond, Mia had been at his side unless they were in their offices. He was fine with her being gone as long as she was with Rick, Miguel, or Rock. He hated it, but she had also been spending time with Jake. He knew no matter how he felt about him, Jake still cared for her and would look out for trouble. They hadn't really gone anywhere. They just had food brought down to the house and hung out watching TV. This had been going on for the past two weeks or so, and he had come to terms with the fact that they were going to be friends.

"So, did you get everything squared away with the caterers? I know the last time we talked there was an issue."

"Yeah, they got it after the tenth time of being told. It had to be perfect. It's how it was the first time." He had ordered the same cake they had at their first wedding reception, which she'd loved. It was a white chocolate cake with strawberries. The cake part was flavored to taste like chocolate, and she was crazy about it. She always raved about it and said she wished they could have had it the second time, but he was unable to give it to her. This time, he made sure they knew exactly what to do.

"Great. It sounds delicious."

"I hope so. I swear I didn't know how much went into this kind of thing. It's no joke." He saw a distant look on Chloe's face and stopped what he was doing. "Hey, you okay?"

Snapping out of her trance, she looked up with a forced smile. "Yeah, I'm fine."

"You know you can talk to me, right? I know I'm not Mia, but I have been known to be a good listener."

She looked at him for a second and then dropped the invitation she was holding. "I look at your lives, at you, and wonder why you guys are giving me the time of day. I mean, your families are two of the wealthiest in Atlanta, and you have all kind of options I could never dream of. I just hope I'm not your charity case."

"Mia sees the good in people. When she looks at you, she doesn't see someone who doesn't have anything. She sees a sweet and wonderful person who happens to remind her of someone she lost. She sees so much of her sister in you, and despite the similarities, she also sees the differences and appreciates them."

"How do I resemble her? She was rich and beautiful."

"Your kind nature, your ability to smile despite all life has thrown at you. Janelle was a fighter, and she was so much fun. She brought out a side of Mia that I see when she talks about you."

"I guess I just wonder what I did to deserve you guys caring about me so much."

"Look at what you're doing right now. You're eight months pregnant, but you're here helping me put together her party. I'm sure you're tired, and little man is probably wearing you out, but you still came because you knew I needed help."

"Tristen."

"Huh?"

"His name is Tristen. Tristen Tyree Davis."

"Really?"

"Yeah. You and Mia have made me feel more welcome than anyone I've met since I moved here. Without you guys, I don't know where we would be. Probably in a cardboard box," she joked. "It's a small gesture, but I hope you like it."

"I love it. I'm stunned. I don't know what to say."

"You could say thank you," said another voice.

He looked up to see Whitney standing in the doorway.

"And if I were you," she continued, "I would hide all this stuff because your wife is about to walk through the door."

"Damn. Go stall, Whit. Chloe, you help me get rid of the evidence."

Tyree and Chloe pushed everything back into the boxes they came out of, and Whitney rushed over to keep Mia away from the dining room. She was only able to hold her off for two minutes before she came barreling through the door. When she arrived in the dining room, Mia looked around, trying to find any clue about what they were doing, and only saw Chloe and Tyree sitting at the table, laughing. She walked over and took a seat on his lap and gave Chloe a simple smile.

"You're early, kitten, I thought you had at least a few more hours." He said this, meaning he had instructed Rick to keep her for a few more hours. He knew he had probably tried and she put up a fight to get home. He knew her too well to think otherwise.

"He didn't want anything really. I think he's just trying to watch me, like someone else I know." She narrowed her eyes at him and smirked. "I have told you both that I'm fine. If he comes anywhere near me, I have my stun gun."

Laughing, Whitney took a seat next to her. "You have to get close to use it. What if he has a real gun?"

"Oh, you hush up, Benedict. I know they sent you to watch me too."

"Actually, they sent me for us to watch each other. They still think he wants to kill me too."

Tyree placed his hands on Mia's thighs and gave them a squeeze the other girls didn't miss. "Look, I'm not about to argue with either one of you. If we say stay together, we mean stay together. I don't know why it's so hard to get you women to follow directions." His tone was comical, and he pulled Mia in for a brief kiss.

"Besides, you were the ones complaining about not getting to go anywhere without me."

"Uncle Ty, you are so not my favorite person right now," Whitney teased and stood, smacking him on the head. Tyree was surprised by her playful gesture, but he had to admit it was a pleasant change. It was as if she had been able to sense his discomfort and stayed away. Now, things seemed to be falling back into place.

"It's okay. You think everyone likes the president? Obama has haters coming out of the woodwork, but do you ever see Michelle disrespecting him in public?"

"So you're the president now?"

"In this house, yes." He grinned and held his breath, waiting for it. He looked at Chloe and saw her laughing as they both waited to see which one of the ladies would strike back. When Mia sat up, he knew she had something, and he closed his eyes waiting for it.

"Bullshit."

"What was that, foul-mouth wife of mine?"

"I said bullshit, clearly delusional husband of mine."

"You see, this right here is why we got divorced the first time."

"What, you're an ass?"

"No." He smirked. "You have no respect for a real man. I put in the work around here to keep us all safe. Now give me my props, woman."

Mia tilted her head to the side with her finger on her chin. She sat there pretending to be thinking before letting out a boisterous laugh. "All right, you win. Who could ever argue with a face like that?"

"No one." He turned his face up, causing the other two girls to break into laughter.

"Well, okay, I think it's time for me to head on home," Chloe said, standing from her seat. "I'm feeling a little tired now."

"Well, come on, I'll drive you. You don't need to be taking a cab."

"Tyree, really, I'll be fine," she protested.

"No, please, Chloe, let him take you. It's no trouble, really."

Whitney watched for a second before she threw her hands up, stopping the three-way argument. "Look, I'm heading back to see my mom, so how about I take her? That way the president and first lady can have their alone time."

"Smart ass," Mia hissed.

Whitney stood waiting for her answer and placed her hands on her hips. "Well?"

"If it's not too much trouble," Chloe said quietly.

"It's not. Let's go."

Whitney grabbed her hand, pulling her toward the door, and they disappeared into the living room. When they heard the door shut, Mia turned to Tyree, wrapping her arms around his neck. "So, Mr. President, what's on the agenda for today?"

"Sex in the Oval Office," he laughed, picking her up and throwing her over his shoulder.

"What if I say no?"

"You can't. My house, my rules." His hands crept up her thighs, and he felt a warm sensation shooting through him.

"Damn, I think I like these rules."

"You better." Once he reached the bedroom, he dropped her on the bed and kicked the door shut. "Lights on or off?"

"I want to be able to see the flag to salute it, Mr. President." Her voice was low and seductive as he stood unbuttoning his shirt.

"On it is."

"I think it will be fun, but you can spank me if I'm wrong. Uumh, I really hope I am."

"Damn, Mrs. First Lady, how can I argue with that?"

"You can't." He dove over her body, smothering it with kisses while she purred in his ear. Completely blocking everything else out, Tyree drowned himself in her and got lost in the sensations expelled from her mouth. Burying himself inside her, he knew he was home. No matter what happened, she would always be home to him.

The car ride between the girls was awkwardly quiet. Chloe kept flipping through her cell phone while Whitney drove and glanced over every so often, waiting for her to say something, anything at all. After over ten minutes of silence, Whitney cleared her throat and Chloe looked up. Gripping the steering wheel tighter, Whitney looked over in her direction.

"So, how do you like Atlanta?"

"It's cool. Most of the people I've met seem nice."

Whitney offered a small grin. "You know, I never caught where you moved here from."

Up until then, Chloe had been half in the conversation. When she heard that statement, Whitney saw her head jerk to the side, and her phone was discarded in her lap. Not saying a word, Whitney just watched her, staring her down.

"You couldn't catch something I didn't throw your way."

Whitney wasn't prepared for her response. Actually, it took her by surprise. "What's with all the hostility? I only asked you a question."

"I know where your questions are leading, and I'd rather we skipped this part."

"If you think so little of me, why accept my offer to give you a ride?"

"I didn't want to inconvenience Mia or Ty. I could tell they wanted some time alone, and I'd rather not fight with them about it."

"Ty, huh? If you don't mind me asking, what are your intentions with my aunt and uncle? They are good people, and I don't want someone taking advantage of their kindness."

"I know what this is." Chloe let out a sarcastic chuckle. "You're a little jealous someone else can be of help to Tyree. You're used to him coming to you. I could see the way you turned up your nose at me the other day at the office."

Chloe and Whitney had run into each other while she was helping Tyree with the party plans. They had met several times before in passing, but that day was the first time they ever stopped and had a conversation. To say it was a pleasant one would be a lie. The circumstances they met under were questionable, to say the least.

Whitney felt like she was only looking out for her aunt and uncle. She had seen them through too many rough times to let some random girl come in and blindside them. She wanted to know all there was to know about this girl, and she was going to start by knowing exactly where she came from and what brought her to Atlanta. She wanted to know just what it was that brought her into their lives.

"I wasn't looking at you like anything. It was an honest mistake, and I apologized. Can we move past it?"

"Move past it to what? A friendship? You accused me of trying to steal from your family the first time we met. You don't like me, and I don't trust you. I know you want to put on this protective rant, but I don't have time for your games."

"I'm not playing any games, I swear. I want to know that you are around them for the right reasons. I apologize for making the wrong assumption about you. Can't you understand that I'm looking out for them? They are great, and they don't deserve the things people have done to them, the lies they've been told." Whitney got a look on her face and glanced down for a second.

She saw Chloe's expression grow softer, and she felt like they were making progress. "Look, I get it. Mia and Tyree are great, and you want to be protective, but I'm not out to hurt them. When I say they really helped me and all I want is their friendship, I really mean it. I've never known kindness like theirs except once before in my life. I'm grateful, nothing more."

"And naming your kid after him? You've only known them a few months. Why give your child his name?"

"He is strong. In the time I've known them, so many things have happened that could have broken what they had, but he didn't end up walking away. I've never seen him treat Mia with anything but love. I know they've had their problems, but that kind of devotion can only come from great strength. I want my baby to have at least an ounce of that."

"You really mean that, don't you?"

"Yes. I don't admire them for the things they have. I couldn't care less about all that. I admire them for the people they are inside. The caring people who opened their hearts and home to me and my baby without knowing a thing about us: that's who I care about. I don't know how to repay them."

"Naming your baby after Uncle Ty made his day. You know when Kyan was born, he said he didn't care what his name was as long as he got his son, but I think he secretly wanted a kid named after him." She smiled at Chloe, and she finally smiled back. "Now he has one."

"He does." She ran her hand over her protruding belly. "You know, maybe I was wrong about you. I get defensive because it's all I know how to be. I wasn't always this tough, but life changed me. I've made some bad choices, and they cost me."

Whitney completely understood where she was coming from. The resentment she had for her family had led her to do some ridiculous things that changed the state of her future. "I was wrong about you too. I'm sorry. I know I said it before, but I mean it this time. I had no reason to jump all over you, and I shouldn't have judged you."

"My life wasn't always like this. I had someone, family. My sister, Delilah, she was the best. We were never rich or anything, but she never let me feel like we didn't have things. She worked hard to take care of us."

"What happened to her?" Whitney saw the look wash over her face and drew in a deep breath. She wasn't sure she was ready for the answer.

"Delilah always took care of us, but she wasn't always legal in her methods. She took on these crazy jobs and met crazy people. I don't know much about her life, but she got mixed up in some stuff that got her killed. She always wanted better for me, but she never saw that she needed better too. Our mom was always no account and our dad, well, no one knows what happened to him, so we were it for each other."

Whitney saw the tears slipping down her cheeks, and she grabbed her hand. "I'm sure she loved you, and that's the only reason she was in that life."

"I wish I could believe that. The truth is, she just didn't know how to be normal. She couldn't accept living average. She was always looking for the next big thing. Her appetite was greedy." Chloe paused for a second before going on. "Look, I'm not downing her. She took care of me. I just wish she could have appreciated the person she was instead of letting that world she was in change her."

"If you don't mind me asking, how did she die?"

"I was off at school when she disappeared. She sent me money, and I got calls, but one day they stopped. When I got back to where we were from, three years ago, I found out she was dead. My mom had her buried and didn't even call me. I had to find out from one of her old associates."

"Wow."

"Yeah. After that, he promised to help me, to look after me. I should have known he was up to something, but before I could get my head straight, I was already in too deep. By the time I knew what he was, who he was, I was already pregnant, and he had control over my life. I had never been a person to be controlled that way, but I couldn't fight him. He was just too strong."

"How did you break away?" Whitney was actually anticipating the answer. After having had her own experiences with men like that, she was anxious to hear how she got out.

"I met someone." A smile graced Whitney's lips, and Chloe quickly threw her hands up in protest. "No, not like that. Not a man, just a really good friend. She pulled me out of it all and gave me a fresh start, here."

Now Whitney was confused. She thought her family was the only people Chloe knew in town. "How?"

"She bought me a plane ticket to here and set me up with an apartment. The job I have, she told me to apply for it. She said the owner was nice."

Whitney realized whoever this person she was might be someone she knew. She had a job at Gina's, and Gina's had been a place all of her family frequented for as long as she could remember. Gina's was small and most of the people in their business circle probably never heard of it, but her dad discovered it when she was a child. She remembered it fondly, one of the few memories she had of being home. "Chloe, this woman who helped you, who is she?"

"I really shouldn't . . . Well, it's just that she seemed to be outrunning her own demons when she reached out to me. I'm not sure if I should be talking about her business."

Finding it a bit odd, Whitney just decided to drop it. She had gotten more out of the girl than she ever thought she would, and she now understood why her aunt cared. The honesty she gave about her life before meeting them was refreshing.

As they pulled up to her complex, Chloe rolled herself out of the passenger side and looked down, offering Whitney a gentle smile. "Thanks for the ride"—she looked toward her building and turned back—"and the talk. It made me feel better to be able to share that with someone."

Whitney smiled, and when her phone rang, both girls looked down to see the screen. When Whitney looked up, the smile on Chloe's face had disappeared, and she was backing away from the car. Whitney opened the door and called out to Chloe, and she froze her steps without turning around.

"Hey, what just happened there?"

"I just remembered I have to go. Thanks again."
She still didn't turn around, and Whitney was
puzzled.

"Hey, Chloe, what's your child's father's name?"

Chloe had started walking again, and when
she heard the question, she stopped suddenly.
"Why?"

"Just curious. I don't know, it kind of seemed
like we were bonding and I just wanted to know.
It's not a big deal, and if you don't want to tell
me, I understand."

"Will. His name is Will, but I have to go.
Thanks for the ride. I'll see you soon." Chloe hur-
ried through the archway that led to her steps,
and Whitney sat back in her car with questions
swimming around in her head. She felt like she
knew more about this girl than she first thought.
It was almost as if they were the same person,
minus the baby, of course. Something about
her story drew her in and she wasn't sure how.
Putting her car in drive, she looked back over to
the phone she had previously ignored, and she
sighed. Why her life had to be so complicated,
she would never understand. She picked up the
phone and dialed the number back. Something
clicked in her head, and she gasped, not thinking
it could be a coincidence.

"We need to talk," she said into the phone.

"That we do. Get over here now," the voice responded before the phone clicked off.

Driving her car in the direction of her parents' house, she felt sweat beads arise on her face. She knew this wasn't going to be pleasant. She knew because she had so many questions that needed answers. She had so many theories running through her mind, and none of them made sense.

"Seriously, you gotta be kidding me. Nothing?"

"Nothing." Terence shook his head as Miguel poured himself another drink.

"I swear I expected something. At least a charge for disturbing the peace for as annoying as his ass is. So you're telling me there is nothing on Jake's record? Not even a parking ticket?"

"Not even a parking ticket."

"Damn, so dude really is on the up-and-up? I wanted to hate him and to be able to convince Tyree to keep Mia away from him. Guess I need to just let it go, huh?"

"Seems to be that way. Look I don't like him being around any more than you do, but maybe we just need to learn to deal with it. I mean, they all seem to be getting along fine, and he hasn't tried anything crazy since that day at the office, and I think that was only because he was out of it about his brother."

Miguel was silent before nodding. "Yeah, I guess I'm just trying to make up for last time. I had no idea things were getting as bad as they were until I found her passed out in the bed. It still freaks me out that I let her lie there so long before I did anything. They said any longer and she wouldn't have made it."

"I don't think any of us knew. Asha blamed herself for the longest time because she said she should have seen it coming. After the abortion and the . . . the rape, Mia just went into this isolation. Asha tried, but she wouldn't let her in. I guess with Jake's loss, they just bonded."

"I still feel like it should have been us she confided in. We're family."

"You know, she didn't tell Tyree what happened until recently, and I guess after he knew, it was okay for the rest of us. Asha only found out because she found her in the shower the night it happened. She wouldn't talk to her about it, she only opened up to her when she made the appointment for the abortion. Asha thought she was getting rid of Tyree's baby and confronted her, and she had no choice but to come clean. To this day, Asha never told a soul what she knew, not even me."

"That's a hell of a secret for little sis to keep."

"You know her. She's loyal to a fault. It's what we all love about her. She's always been that to all of us."

"Yeah." Miguel smiled. "I guess I understand. They weren't her secrets to tell. At least Mia finally told Ty. I swear, keeping the little I did know from him felt dishonest. Me and my bro don't have secrets like that, and I was starting to feel bad."

"Me too. I mean, I didn't know much, but I could see him struggling with everything, and I had to keep my mouth shut."

"Well, at least that's over, and I guess I have to get over this Jake stuff."

"Yeah. So, what's up with you? Anything new?"

Miguel laughed and shook his head. "No, after Mia came over and ran the last chick off, I've been lying low. It's too much work learning new names every night."

"What'd you say to that girl? I got half the story, but Mia wasn't sure what all you said."

"Man," Miguel huffed, "don't make me go through this again. It wasn't my finest moment. I went off, and I'm sure she didn't really deserve it, or maybe she did. Hell, I really don't know."

"Well, she pissed Mia off, so whatever you said to her was probably warranted."

Miguel stood with his signature smirk and sighed. "Fine. I heard when she told Mia I didn't want to see her, and I hit the roof. I mean, who the hell was she to be speaking to my family like that?"

"So you said what?" Terence was smiling like a mindless idiot, and Miguel rolled his eyes.

"Look, I threw three hundred dollars at her and told her to get her shit and leave because her services were no longer needed. She started crying, and I told her to stop acting like she was anything more than an average piece of ass."

"Damn, now that's cold. Bro, do you seriously practice being an asshole or does it come naturally?"

"It's all natural over here," he chuckled. "But seriously, after I got over my hangover, I did feel bad. I wanted to apologize, but I didn't even know her name." He shrugged. "Oh, well."

"Dude, how do you sleep with a girl and not know her name?"

"Easy," he chuckled. "You know we never had problems in the 'getting ass' department. You and Ty got all settled on me and left me to handle all these women by myself."

"Well, you can't play forever. Have to grow up sometime."

"Yeah." He looked off sadly. "You know I see her sometimes."

"Who?"

"Janelle. Sometimes, when I'm doing something I know is stupid, I see her face. When I do, I feel like maybe she would be ashamed of who I've become. I just feel like every day I keep going like this, I'm letting her down."

Terence poured himself a drink and took a seat next to Miguel. "She knew who you were and she still loved you. We could apologize for every little thing we do, but then where would that get us? We have to own up to our shit, but we also have to take them as learning experiences."

"I don't know, maybe if I were"—he paused with a serious look on his face—"nicer, maybe I would have a wife and kids." They both stared at each other before breaking into a fit of laughter.

"Bro, the woman who comes along and tames you is going to have to be a hell of a woman."

"Yeah, she has big shoes to fill. My baby had skills."

"That she did." He nodded, knowing no woman handled Miguel like Janelle did.

Chapter Twenty-three

"Thanks again for coming with me." Chloe smiled back at Mia as she stared at the monitor. They were at one of Chloe's appointments, and Mia was just as excited as Chloe was. They had been there for twenty minutes waiting for her doctor to arrive in the room. Today would be the first time Mia got to see Chloe's son up close.

"It's no problem. I'm ready to see him."

Mia felt a wave of sadness wash over her, and then she looked to see Chloe grab her hand. "I know this has to be hard, you having trouble getting pregnant, I mean. Well, at least you will have your godchild to keep you busy."

Mia's head snapped up, and she saw the incredible grin spreading across Chloe's face. "What? Really?"

"Yeah. I want you and Ty to be his godparents. I hope that's okay."

"Of course it is, sweetie." Mia touched her face. "Ty is going to be thrilled, and I'm so honored. Why us?"

"You're the only people looking out for us, and I thank you so much."

Mia felt tears slipping down her cheeks and went to brush them away. "This is amazing." Just as she went to hug Chloe, her doctor walked in, giving them both a huge grin.

"Well, hello. I don't think we've met." She extended her hand to Mia.

"Hi, I'm Mia. I was just coming to check up on these two."

"Well, I think that's great. Chloe was telling me she didn't have family in town."

"She does now." Mia watched as the tears swelled in Chloe's eyes. She grabbed the young girl's hand. She couldn't imagine going through this alone. Even though she was young when she got pregnant with Kyan, at least she had Tyree. She had Tyree, and she had her family. Everyone was great during that time, everyone except Richmond.

Richmond loved Tyree before he knew they were dating. He seemed to like him more than his own children, but when he found out they were together, his whole attitude changed. After discovering Tyree and Mia's relationship, Richmond tried everything in his power to end it, including trying to blackmail Tyree. Mia had only recently heard everything her father had said to Tyree, and it made her hate him even more than she already did. She knew they were young, but she also knew, even back then, that he was the one. For her father to stand in the way of that was unforgivable. She never got past it. She never would.

Looking down at Chloe, she saw the anticipation in her eyes and grinned. When the doctor spread the cool gel on her stomach, Chloe gripped Mia's hand tighter. "I never like this part," she chuckled nervously.

"It's okay. Squeeze as hard as you need to," Mia reassured her. They both watched quietly as the doctor slid the probe over Chloe's stomach and sighed. Mia didn't like the sounds she made as she looked at the monitor. "Is something wrong?"

"Hmmh, he seems to be a stubborn one today. I can't get him to turn around." She pressed a little harder and looked up at Chloe. "That doesn't hurt, does it?"

"No. Is the baby okay?" Chloe asked nervously.

She moved the probe over and lit up with a huge smile. "Well, I don't believe this."

"What?" both Chloe and Mia asked quickly.

"We commented on your weight gain, and I was concerned until now."

"Why? You said I gained too much weight."

"You did, for just one baby. Good thing you're having twins."

"Twins?"

"Yes, a girl and a boy, see?" She pointed at the screen. "We couldn't see her because she was always hiding behind him, but now she's where we can see her." She turned it around for Mia to get a good look.

"Twins?" Chloe asked frantically. "How could we not have seen her? Is she going to be okay? I mean, how did we go eight months without knowing I was having two?"

"We heard two heartbeats, and I always assumed it was yours and your son's. It's not common, but it's happened before. Based on your labs and from what I can see here, I think she will be just fine. There is no need to worry."

Tears streaked Chloe's cheeks. "I can't do this. I can't take care of two kids. It was going to be hard enough with just him, but now . . . I can't."

Placing a hand to her cheek, Mia wiped the tears away and bent down to give the fragile girl a kiss on the forehead. "You can do this."

"I can't." She shook her head, and Mia's smile deepened.

"You can. You can do this, and you will be great. Do you know why?"

"Why?"

"Because I got you. We got you. Do you think me and Ty did it alone?" Chloe shrugged. "Hell no. We had our families. I was scared of Kyan when he was first born. He was so little, and I was just a kid myself. I was only twenty-one when I had him, and I didn't know a thing about babies. Karen taught me how to hold him and helped me so much. So you see, none of us are perfect, but as long as you have help, you can do it. You have help. Never think you don't."

"I can't ask you to do that."

"Then don't, but I'm not going anywhere."

"You're such a good person. I don't know how I ever got so lucky. You know, you remind me of someone I met before I moved here."

Mia let her laughter fill the room while the doctor concluded the exam and gave Chloe more instructions. When Chloe was getting dressed, Mia stepped outside and fished out her phone to call Tyree to tell him the news. Before she could do so, her mind began to wander back to what Chloe said about meeting someone like her before. She was curious because Chloe rarely talked about who or what she was before they met.

She was standing outside the room, in her thoughts, when she heard the door creak open. She saw Chloe step out and smiled. "Ready to go?"

"Yeah." They walked to the car, and both were quiet until they strapped in. Before she put her car in reverse, Mia turned to Chloe and asked a question that was floating around in her head. "When you said I reminded you of someone, who was she? I was just sitting here, and I realized I don't know much about your life. I know it's selfish that I never asked, but I just assumed it wasn't a pleasant subject for you." She looked up to see the horror on Chloe's face and put her hands up in protest. "I know I'm rambling, but I'm here if you ever want to talk about it."

"I know you are, and I appreciate you respecting my privacy, but I didn't say much because I didn't want you guys to think less of me because of where I came from. My life isn't as glamorous as yours."

"Sweetheart, you are not where you come from. I should know. My mother was a drug addict, and my father is a murdering bastard. If people judged me on that, I wouldn't be much either."

"That's what I admire so much about you. You look past appearances. She said I would meet nice people here and that I just needed to be open to accepting help."

"This 'she' sounds wise. Who was she?" Chloe hesitated for a second, and Mia patted her hand gently.

"My friend. My friend Lenae. I just have to ask that you don't mention her name to anyone. She risked a lot to help me, and I think she had problems of her own."

"This Lenae . . ." She paused. "When and where did you meet her?"

"Six months ago in Tuscany. Why, do you know her?" She held out her phone, showing Mia a picture, and her eyes widened. She felt a sense of familiarity wash over her, and she wasn't sure why. The girl had her face covered and was wedged underneath a beautiful little girl, the same little girl Mia saw years earlier in a picture she found at Janelle's grave. Something was off, and she couldn't quite put her finger on it. Had Chloe been in contact with her father and this woman? So many thoughts were racing through her head when she heard Chloe's voice break her out of her trance.

"I wasn't supposed to take this. She was sleeping here, but it was too funny not to catch." She pointed to the little girl next to the woman, and Mia's breath caught in her chest. "You see, her daughter, Jenna, fell asleep on her chest, and it was too cute. She's like five, but she still sleeps with her mother. How funny is that?" Mia was too busy jumping to conclusions in her head to pay attention to anything Chloe was saying until she felt her hand squeeze tightly. "Hey, do you know her?"

"I don't know. I might," Mia choked out and threw her car in reverse, swearing the drive home would be the longest she ever had.

Chapter Twenty-four

Mia knew she should be home, but something drew her there. The last call she received from him was a little disturbing, and she needed to be sure everything was fine. She knew Tyree wouldn't mind, but she felt bad for not going straight home with her suspicions. Knocking lightly, she didn't get an answer. After about three tries, she pulled out her spare key and twisted it in the lock.

Scanning the living room, she realized he had left their house exactly the way it was before he moved in. The only thing she saw out of place was a bracelet that obviously belonged to a woman. She was surprised but glad to see him moving on with his life. Calling his name quietly, she heard her voice echo off the bare walls. When they moved, she took down the art, and only the large furniture remained. She called for him once more, making her way through the quiet house, and was startled when she felt his hand on her shoulder.

"God, Jake, you scared me."

"I'm sorry. I didn't hear you knock. I was in the kitchen making a little snack. You want something?"

Shaking her head slowly, she turned and walked back toward the living room. "No, I'm all right. Just checking on you. How are you doing?"

"I'm good, why? Is something up with you?"

She could tell he was studying her face and saw the confusion. "I'm fine. I just thought, well, when I called you sounded off. You sure you're okay?"

"You know every day is a struggle, but I'm making it. How could I not be with all this concern from everyone?"

"Everyone?"

"You, Rick, and even Cassie have been checking in. I thought that was really cool of them considering our history."

"They can be really cool." She smiled. "So, have you met anyone here? Any women?"

A shy smile crept over his face, and she relaxed. "I met someone, but it's nothing serious. Honestly, I don't know what I was thinking. I'm too old for this."

"For dating?" she laughed.

"Not dating, smart ass. Dating someone in their twenties. I feel like an old man trying to keep up."

"If it makes you feel so old, then why not find someone your own age?" She was laughing hysterically and put her hand to her mouth.

"I mean, I tried that and struck out, so I thought, hey, let's try something new. Plus, she's so damn good at making me feel good."

Mia stopped in the middle of her laughter, and her eyes widened. She stood from the couch. "Hey, I just remembered, I need to get over to Karen's. She's expecting me."

With a baffled expression, Jake stood, touching Mia's ice-cold skin. "Hey, you okay? You don't look so good."

"No." She threw her hand up in protest and backed away. "I'm okay. I just need to hurry, I don't want to hold up her day. I'll call you." With that, she was out the door, and Jake stood scratching his head.

Outside the door, Mia rushed to her car and shut the door quickly. Starting her car up and pulling out of the yard, she stomped on the gas and sped down the driveway. She was almost past the main house and out the gate when she saw Rick stepping out. She slammed on the brake.

Wiping the sweat from his forehead as a result of their almost collision, Rick let out a sigh and walked over to her driver-side window. "Sis, what's going on? You almost ran me down." He could see her shaking and opened the door to embrace her. "Come in the house, calm down, and I'll drive you home."

"No, I'm okay." She tried to argue, but he wasn't hearing any part of it.

"Get your ass out of the car. Talk to me." As he led her through the house, she noticed it was decorated for some type of event.

"Cassie having a party?"

Looking around the house, he nodded. "Oh, yeah, I forgot to mention it. Everything was so last minute. You and Tyree are invited, so don't make plans for tomorrow night. It's just some little thing for one of the charities."

"Yeah, okay," she responded distractedly.

"What's going on with you? I thought things were great at home."

"No, they are. We're wonderful."

"So why do you look like you just saw a ghost?"

She turned, finally focusing in on the conversation with him. "Rick, have you ever felt like you were completely wrong about something and didn't know what to do?"

"A time or two. I never thought Mom and Janelle would die so young and that Dad would be the reason. I always knew he was shady, but I thought it just applied to the business. I never thought it would be just you and me left."

"What if . . . what if we were wrong?"

"About Dad?"

"About everything. What if we had a whole other family out there we didn't know about?"

"Mia, what are you talking about?"

"I didn't want to say anything to you because I thought you might get upset, but I think Dad has another child out there." She pulled the picture out of her purse and showed it to Rick.

"What is this?"

"I found it after Dad was arrested, in the grave-yard."

He flipped it over and ran his finger slowly over the name.

"She looks like us, like me." She pulled out a small picture of her as a child, and he nodded.

"Why are you thinking about this now? That was years ago."

"Chloe met someone who told her to come here. They set her up with a place to live and really helped her out. She pulled out her phone with a picture, and it was this same little girl, a few years older, but it was this girl. I want to know what the connection is. You know I love Chloe, but I'm scared, Rick. What if she's just a part of his big plan to screw with us?"

"Is that what had you so out of it? Little sis, I've only been around her a short period of time, but she is sweet. She wouldn't endanger her kid getting mixed up with him. She loves this kid, and she loves you."

"I know, I'm crazy. She would never hurt me or this family, but she's a good kid, Rick. I'm afraid for her. People around us are disappearing. He is taking everything. I don't want this sweet girl sucked into our messy lives." She tried to still the tears. "I'm a mess today."

"God, sis, go get yourself together. You look awful," he chuckled, pulling her into his arms. "I don't want you worrying. You got me, we have each other, and nothing is stronger than that. I never worry because I know as long as we stick together we can do anything." He was too calm, and she wasn't sure why. Even though she was wary of his attitude, it calmed her down.

"You're right. I love you, Ricky-D. Thank you."

"You're welcome, sweetheart. Remember, your life is good, and you have a husband and son who both adore you. Never let the bad outweigh the good."

"How are you okay? I mean, it's still freaking me out that he was in my house."

"I'm okay because I know that man of yours would die before he ever let anything happen to you."

"That's what I'm afraid of. I don't want him hurt protecting me. This monster is ours to deal with."

"When are you going to realize we are all family? When you say 'ours,' your husband, my wife, and all the in-laws are included. We have been dealing with things together for so long now, there is no longer just you and me. It's all of us now. Be thankful for that."

"I am. God, I love them all so much. I just know what he is and I don't want them hurt."

"Baby girl, don't worry. Go home, spend time with your family, and come back here tomorrow night and enjoy what we built. There is nothing wrong with fear. Just don't let it consume you."

Hugging Rick one last time, she took a deep breath and headed back to her car in a much better mood, but it still didn't stop the worrying. As hard as she tried, it was in the back of mind. It wasn't going away.

Chapter Twenty-five

Tyree looked at his watch before stripping his clothes off to get into a hot shower. He wasn't sure his body had ever ached so much or been so exhausted. After work and her appointment, Chloe got Mia to drop her off at home and called to have Tyree pick her up to finish some last-minute details for the party. They had been working hard, but Tyree was sure it would be an incredible night for her.

He had just returned from dropping Chloe off when Rick called to tell him Mia knew there would be a party. He was nervous at first, thinking she had figured them out, but Rick explained she thought it was a charity event, and he was calm again. The only thing left was to have the rest of the decorations sent over and for everything to be set up. It was a hard task that he would never volunteer for again, but his wife was worth it. She deserved nothing but the best.

Stepping into the bathroom and turning on the water, he saw the steam clouding the room and smiled, feeling his muscles already relaxing. Stepping into the stream, he placed his hands on the wall, letting himself get drenched from head to toe. The heat felt good, and he felt rejuvenated, reaching for a sponge to lather. Running the soapy object over his body, he paused when he felt a gust of wind on his back. Feeling her reach for the sponge, he relinquished it, letting her run it aimlessly over his back.

Falling into the slow strokes over his back, he leaned against the cool marble, letting Mia work her magic all over him. As much as he wanted this to be just a shower, he felt himself growing excited. Having her so close, running her hands all over him, made his mind run into all kinds of lustful thoughts. He let her get one last stroke before he turned, pinning her against the wall, latching his mouth to hers.

Grabbing the sponge from her hand, he took his body wash and soaked the sponge, running it over her body. She turned her nose up at him, and he knew she was wondering why he used his shower gel instead of hers. "It makes you smell like me," he said, answering her question before she could even ask it. "I love it when you smell like me." He ran his hand up and lifted her into the stream.

"Babe," she squealed when the water hit her hair, returning it to its natural curls. "Come on, watch it." By this time, her hair was already drenched.

"What, you don't want to get wet?" He ran his hand down and touched her heated core. "Well, you're already wet, and I can't wait to get inside you to enjoy it. Damn, you're so wet, baby." He slid his hand over her folds and pulled her legs tighter around his waist. Shutting the water off and taking her with him, he found a towel, running it over her hair. Kissing her, sliding his tongue into her mouth, he sat her on the sink, running the towel over her wet body. "I'm sorry about your hair."

She ran a hand through her curly tresses. "I'll straighten it later." She grabbed his head, crashing their lips together. Walking to rest between her legs, he deepened the kiss. When he felt her move the towel that was between them, he pressed himself against her, giving her a chance to feel how hard he was. "Uuhh," she moaned, breaking the kiss when his fingers found their way inside her. "Oh, God, don't stop."

He kissed her neck, running his lips up to her ear as he pumped his fingers in and out of her. "I love it when you beg for me, and I love it when you're loud, but today I need you to be quiet. I didn't get to call you, but I have a surprise for you. The boy is here."

Mia's eyes fluttered as a result of his continued finger movements, but she managed to display a smile at the mention of her son. He knew she had been wanting to spend some one-on-one time with him and decided to bring him home for the night. If she had known how much time they had been spending together, she would undoubtedly be jealous. With all the planning for the party, Kyan had been helping after school, and they had spent a lot of father-son time together. It was nice.

Letting his mind wander back to the beautiful woman in front of him, he took a deep breath and closed his eyes, listening to the soft moans filling the room. Tyree felt like his entire body was slowly catching fire when she placed her hands on his ass. Her touch sent electric currents through every orifice of him, and he didn't know how much longer he could take it. Her lips lingered near his ear, and he locked his eyes on hers. He was hoping she wouldn't notice how shallow and labored his breathing had become from the moment he stepped between her soft yet firm thighs.

Losing the battle between his head and the throbbing between his legs, he gazed deeply into her warm brown eyes, getting lost in the intensity of their color. Damn, he wanted her. He thought before that, maybe over the years, the want he had for her would fade, but with each day it only grew stronger.

Tyree kept staring in her eyes. The way they glittered was hypnotic, holding his attention like some kind of trance. He lowered his gaze to her lips, taking his free hand to reach up and touch them with his thumb. He felt the heat radiating from them and the pulsations at his touch as he leaned and kissed her.

"Tyree," Mia murmured, trembling from his touch despite the smothering heat blanketing the bathroom. Tyree cupped her chin in his hands and shook his head.

"Shhh," he whispered, descending on her lips, feeling a moan escape from them as his mouth covered hers. It was sweet but aggressive. The fire her touch had ignited before was now a raging inferno, and he was desperate for more. His mouth searched hers hungrily, ravenously, as his fingers threaded through her soaked hair.

"Mia," Tyree moaned, his hands clutching at her back, holding her tightly against him. "Baby, I need you to get off this sink before I slide you all across it," he mumbled as his lips continued to meet hers. Mia responded to his request by pushing his lips insistently with her tongue, begging him to give her access. He groaned and parted his lips, unable and unwilling to deny her more. Allowing her access, he loved how her tongue pulsed against his, dueling and challenging him to deepen the kiss. Tyree sucked her tongue hard, eliciting a small gasp from her as he maneuvered their tongues into his own mouth, daring her to meet him stroke for stroke.

"Tyree . . . Oh, God," Mia whimpered as Tyree broke the embrace. "You don't really want to stop, do you?" she asked hopefully, her chest heaving from her ragged breathing. His head was screaming at him to stop because he was too amped up to be quiet enough not to alert their son, but the rest of his body had other ideas. He shot her a wicked smile, and his eyes gleamed with desire. He reached behind her and pulled her closer, burying his fingers deeper inside her.

Mia closed her eyes and bit her lower lip hard. Tyree could tell the sensations were already starting to overwhelm her. "Do you like that?" he hissed into her ear, tracing the crevice of her earlobe with his tongue.

Mia shivered, and another moan escaped from deep in her throat. "Yesssss." She clenched her eyes shut as Tyree's teeth nipped at her ear. He grinned and sank his fingers farther. His other hand wandered to the nape of her neck, and he cradled her to him for another passionate kiss. Mia crushed her body against his, her hands running along the planes of his stomach and up over his defined pecs. "You feel good."

"And you're beautiful. I don't tell you that nearly as much as I should," he breathed, his eyes roaming up and down the length of her body. Mia's eyes sparkled at the compliment.

"Make love to me, Tyree," she begged. The mere tone of her voice, as she asked the question, increased his arousal. He nodded and cupped her breast his palm, massaging it lightly and eliciting a low moan from her. She threw her head back, reveling in the pleasure that washed over her in waves as he touched her. Tyree smiled and circled his thumb over her nipple, peaking it against his finger.

Mia clawed at his back, her nails digging into his shoulders as his lips took possession of one of her nipples. She moaned in ecstasy as his teeth grazed over it and his tongue rushed to soothe it. A devilish spark crackled in his eyes as he released her from his mouth. Mia desperately tried to regulate her breathing, but no sooner had she gulped in a much-needed breath than Tyree took it away again. She writhed against him as she felt him shift to her other breast, rubbing his tongue over her aching nipple. "Tyree," she moaned, the heady sensations dizzying her.

Feeling his body beginning to spiral out of control again, he clung to her, her breasts flat against his own bare chest, the dampness of their skin increasing the friction between them. He knew she could feel his erection pressed insistently against her stomach. He was ready. He needed her now. He moved to lift her from the counter, wrapping her legs around his waist. When she shook her head, he stopped.

"I need you now, right here." Her slick fingers closed around his arousal, and he groaned with pleasure as they began to stroke him. "Please, Tyree, make love to me." He slowly entered her, smiling at the gasp of pleasure Mia emitted as he did. She cried out his name and bucked her hips up to meet his, driving him farther inside her. A guttural groan escaped from Tyree's throat as she began to thrash against him with his steadily increasing thrusts.

He made her promise to be quiet, but he had a hard time keeping himself in check. She felt so good, and her body was so warm. She was so soft. He had to stop before he caved and came entirely too early. Running his hand down her face, he saw that her eyes were closed. "Mia, open your eyes." He smiled as her eyes met his.

Rolling her body against his, she held on to him, keeping his head against her neck. "Oh, baby, uuhh!" Her words were caught in her throat, and he reached down to dig his fingers deep into her supple ass. With her mouth calling his name and her insides screaming for more, he brushed his lips over hers, muffling the shouting he knew was sure to come with his next movement. Grabbing her legs, pulling them apart, he pushed into her slowly, smashing against her thighs with his hips. Just as he thought, she went to scream, but he thrust his tongue into her mouth, quieting her impulses.

"Dammit, Mia," he grunted, closing his eyes to block out the blurriness affecting his vision. Running her fingers over his lips, her eyes closed when his tongue swirled around them. He could feel her body contracting and shaking lightly, and he desperately wanted to hold on. He knew she was cumming no matter what he did, and he also knew that as long as he hadn't, she would keep going. With her legs spread around him, her mouth slacked open, and he leaned in, claiming her moans, feeling them vibrate against his tongue.

Despite the orgasm ripping through her, Mia continued to meet him thrust for thrust. Everything started out slow and sweet, but as she came closer to ecstasy, the pace quickened, leaving them out of breath. Mia reached down and pulled Tyree up into a deep kiss, continuing her rocking motion. She wrapped her arms around his neck and began to nibble on his earlobe. Tyree was biting her shoulder ever so lightly, driving her more insane, causing her to lose all sense of control.

He could feel her warm breath on his neck as he nibbled lightly at her shoulder. Pulling away from her shoulder, he looked into her eyes once more. He saw all the pleasure, desire, and passion in her eyes, and he felt something in himself he knew was only meant for her.

He was amazed that he had put so many raw emotions in her soul in one night. Their eyes connected and he brought his mouth back to hers. With each thrust, the kiss intensified rapidly as if they would never be able to share a kiss again. Mia dragged her nails over Tyree's back as she began to climax for the second time.

As she climaxed, she said his name, repeating it with so much lust in her voice that he sped up, sending her back into the mirror behind them. Everything going on added to the pleasure for Tyree. Her nails digging into him, her swallow breathing against his neck, the breathless whispers for him to keep going made him twitch. He was coming, he felt it. His body went into over-drive, hitting every sensitive inch of her warm, wet core, and she folded in his arms just in time for him to bite down on her shoulder, muffling his screams. His climax exploded inside her, and all he could hear were her soft moans.

Pulling her into him without disconnecting, he walked past the entrance of the bathroom and into their room. Kissing her swollen lips, he lowered them to the bed slowly, finally pulling out of her. Placing a gentle kiss on her forehead, he swept his hand over her smiling face.

"Do you know how long I've wanted you, baby?" He saw her open her mouth and placed his finger on her lips. "Not this time. I meant, do you know how long I've dreamed of being the man for you?"

Mia's eyes drifted down and then back up. "Since senior year, you told me."

He shook his head and gripped her chin, giv-ing her a slow, lingering kiss. "Try sophomore year."

Her eyes bucked and she sat up slowly. "But you were with Sharon then. She was gorgeous, and she never made it a secret that she was willing to do whatever it took to keep you."

"Yes, I was with her, but I always wanted you. I didn't realize it until the day I saw Roland trying to kiss you." He remembered that day well, and he could tell by the smile on her face that she did too.

Roland Sharp was the son of one of her father's friends and one of the only guys he let come around besides Tyree and Miguel. They had all been hanging out around the pool while her father was away on business and her mother was shut away in the house, probably high. She and Janelle had invited some friends over, and they were enjoying the heat of a sunny Atlanta afternoon. Roland had been all over her the entire day.

Tyree was there along with Miguel and Terence, and he had that girl with him, Sharon. Mia was disgusted watching how she sucked on his neck and ran her hands all over him. They were dating, and he had been interested in her, but he was tired of her fawning all over him like he was some prize to be won. It was gross and ridiculous, and he was over it.

While watching Mia watch him, Tyree saw how she continuously had been fighting Roland off. She looked so annoyed until he decided he had seen enough. She had a mean scowl on her face until she felt his hand on her shoulder.

He wasn't sure how, but any time he touched her, he felt it everywhere. Turning slowly, she offered him a cute grin, and he stared at her for a second. He had liked her for a while but never thought she looked at him that way. They were locked in the trance together until Sharon came over, throwing her arms around him. Roland draped a heavy arm over Mia's shoulder, and she looked uncomfortable. Tyree saw the look, grabbed Roland's arm, and pushed it to the side. Roland stiffened in protest. The guys were toe-to-toe when Tyree shoved Roland in the chest.

"She doesn't want you touching her, so keep your hands to yourself."

"In case you missed it, your girl is behind you." Roland pointed to Sharon, and Tyree huffed without looking back. "Look, what me and Mia do is our business. If she doesn't want me touching her, let her tell me that."

"Mia," Tyree said sternly without turning away from Roland, "do you want him touching you?"

Mia opened her mouth, saw the glare she was receiving from Sharon, and closed it suddenly. When she didn't say anything, Tyree turned, his look growing softer. He said in a lighter tone, "Mia, you can speak up. Don't be afraid. Stand up for yourself. Don't let this asshole intimidate you."

Looking more confident, she let a grin show, and he smiled back. "Keep your filthy hands off me, Roland. I don't care that your dad is my dad's golf buddy. If you put those grubby paws on me again, you'll be eating through a straw."

Roland stomped off, mumbling, "To hell with you," while Sharon tugged at Tyree, pulling him away. He walked off but not before sharing one last glance with Mia. While they made it to their position on the other side of the pool, he looked back over at Mia, swearing he had never seen her as beautiful as she was just then.

"I never knew you felt that way then. I just thought you were a nice guy. I thought you were all about Sharon. I mean, who wasn't? At the age of fifteen, she had hips, ass, and breasts for days. Perfect bitch," she chuckled.

"She was stacked. Probably one of the fattest asses I ever held in my hands." He grinned, and she threw a pillow at him. "But she didn't matter. I liked you. Even then I thought there was something so incredibly cute about you. You were this sweet girl who could hang with the guys and still be sexy as hell when you stepped out. You listened to every story I ever told, and you became my best friend. I found myself thinking about you every minute of every day."

"You never said anything until senior year. Why?"

"I didn't know how to approach you until then. Here was this perfect girl, so sweet, so innocent, and she got me like no one else did. It freaked me out how much I thought about you."

"I was never perfect. At that time, there was so much going on in my family."

"They had their issues. You were perfect. My perfect woman, and you still are. I wanted you to know that. I don't know where the feeling came from," he laughed. "I guess I have these moments when I think back on all the things I should have said before, and I don't want to make that mistake again."

"You're getting so good with this feelings thing, babe. I remember when it used to be like pulling teeth to get you to open up."

"I guess I surprise you every day then, don't I?"

"That you do." She leaned in, brushing her lips against his, and then stood from the bed, reaching her hand out for him. "Let's get dressed. I need to get dinner started for my two guys."

He stood, smacking her on the ass and then caressing it, letting his hands linger. "I take my comment back. I think you just might have Sharon beat in the ass department. The years have done you good, kitten." He gave her a gentle squeeze before turning her around, placing a rough kiss on her lips, and gripping her as he did. Pulling away from the kiss with her ass still in his hands, he put his forehead to hers. "Yep, I'm sure you won. Damn, my baby got back."

Letting out a silly chuckle, she pushed away from him, rummaging through the dresser for clothes. "Come on, silly man. Get dressed. I'm hungry."

"Okay." He smiled. "Whatever my baby wants, she gets." He watched her slip a shirt over her head, and he moved over to pick up the clothes she laid out for him. She was always taking care of them, and he would never take that for granted. He would always cherish the little things. He knew looking at her that he made the right choice all those years ago. He would never regret loving her.

Chapter Twenty-six

"You never explained to me why it was so important to you that we got here at eight. I mean, come on, Ty, it's not even our thing. They wouldn't have noticed us being a little late. The idea I had was so much better than being in a roomful of strangers," Mia complained as they walked into Rick's house. Tyree grinned at the confused expression she held when she noticed the lights off. "Okay, so I'm not an elite party planner or anything, but since when do you have a party in the dark? I saw cars outside, so where are the people?"

Tyree just laughed and pulled her hand to his lips. "For someone so beautiful, you sure have a lot of questions, kitten. Let's walk inside to see what all the fuss is about before we make judgments." He pulled her toward the huge banquet room, and her eyes lit up when the music started and the guests jumped out.

Turning to him, she let out a beautiful laugh. "This is crazy! Thank you, baby."

"You're welcome, sweetheart."

She leaned to him and kissed his lips, holding them together for a few more minutes before they made their way around the room, mingling with all the friendly faces. He had invited almost everyone she knew, and he could tell she was touched. He had even extended an invitation to Jake, and he was standing over with Cassandra and Rick, laughing at something one of them was saying.

She and Tyree stopped and danced to a few songs and were observed by most of the room. They swayed to the music and stole a few kisses. Mia placed her head on his shoulder, telling him how grateful she was for a night like this. He watched as she looked around. He noted all the happiness in her eyes and knew he had done well. Everyone was there, all their family, all their friends, and it felt right, like something would finally go their way.

In her resumed scan of the room, Mia's eyes landed on Chloe. She had noticed pretty much everyone else when they first arrived but hadn't spotted her until just now. She was standing off to the side alone, and something looked off about her. Mia watched as she tried to plaster on a fake smile that didn't quite meet her eyes. Making her way over after glancing back to see Tyree with Miguel and Terence, she stopped before the girl and raked her hand over her arm.

"Hey, what's with the look? You okay? Is it the babies?"

"No." She shook her head, finally registering that it was Mia speaking to her. "I need to tell you something." Running her hand through her hair, she sighed and closed her eyes. "What am I doing? I'm ruining your party. I just didn't want to go on with this on my chest. I feel like you've been too good to me to not know the truth."

Mia's heart sank witnessing the distress on the girl's face. She wasn't sure what to expect. She didn't know how it would make her feel. All she knew was that whatever it was seemed bad, and she wasn't prepared to hear it in a houseful of people celebrating her marriage. She needed some air, some space. She excused herself from Chloe and went over to let Tyree know she was stepping out. He told her to stay close before turning back to the guys.

Placing her hand on Chloe's shoulder, Mia nodded toward the door, and the girl followed her. The wind from the night air blew up against them as they walked the grounds. They were well past the house when Mia looked over to see tears drifting down the young girl's cheeks. When Mia looked back up, she saw they were in front of the old house. She pulled out her key to unlock the door. She knew Jake was up at the main house and wouldn't mind them talking there.

Stepping inside and sitting down on the couch, she motioned for Chloe to join her. When Chloe shook her head in protest, she reached out for her.

"Whatever it is you want to say, I need you to sit down. You're stressing, and it can't be good for the babies."

"How can you worry about me? You don't know me. I'm sure you won't want to when you find out who I really am."

Mia was lost, and then something clicked. Shaking her head, she stood from the couch in disbelief. "No, no, no. You can't be. Did he send you here?"

"I was scared. I needed to get away from him, and I knew if I didn't, me and my baby would end up like my sister. I didn't know what he had done until it was too late. I didn't know he was a killer."

"Chloe, how did he find you? How did Richmond get his hooks into you?"

"Richmond? Mia, I think . . . Hold on." She went digging through her purse and pulled out a picture, holding it to her chest. "I don't know Richmond. I was running from Will because he killed my sister. They were into some crazy things together. I was afraid to tell you because of what she did to you and Tyree." She flipped the picture around.

Mia's breathing stopped for a moment, and her heart fluttered. "Renae? Renae is your sister?" The woman who had infiltrated Tyree's life and slept with both him and his father was this sweet girl's sister. Renae had made their lives a living hell. She had helped Tyree's father, John, kidnap their son.

"I swear I didn't know. I never knew your history with her until I saw a picture up at the house. I asked Rick who she was to you guys, and he told me everything she had done before she died. I'm so sorry. She wasn't always so vile. Delilah, that's her real name, she used to be the nicest person in the world until she met up with Will and his friend Anderson. I didn't know what kind of person he was until I heard them one night talking about how they killed Delilah for fucking them over. They said she was cooperating with the police. They thought she would turn them in."

Mia was overwhelmed with everything being laid in her lap. All this time, she thought it was Richmond who ordered the attack on John and Renae. Now she didn't know what to think. Looking up to see Chloe's broken face, she reached for the girl, pulling her into a strong embrace.

"It's okay." Mia rubbed Chloe's hair as she sobbed. "You didn't know. It's not your fault."

"I'm sorry. I never would have bonded with you and let you bond with me if I had known. I didn't know she was the one who caused so much pain in your life."

"She didn't," Mia answered quickly. "She may have been a pain in the ass," she chuckled, "but she didn't break us up. There were so many other factors, so many other participants. I don't blame you for anything, and you have nothing to feel guilty about. Sweetie, I'm glad you came to me. Now I can tell you not to worry."

"Mia, what are the odds of us meeting like this? I never questioned Lenae and her motives, but now do you think maybe she was involved in all this? Was it some sick joke to push us together?"

The same thought had been running through Mia's mind, and she was afraid to say it out loud. "You know what? It doesn't matter. We met and got to know each other, and I have a fondness for you and these babies." She touched Chloe's stomach. "I'm not ready to give that up yet. You're stuck with me. You all are."

"I don't know what I did to deserve you, but I'll take it. I can't really refuse help at this point, now can I?"

"No, you can't." She looked around the room and drew in a deep breath. "You feel like partying tonight?"

"Honestly, no. I really hate to bail on you, but I'm so tired. I think after this, I'm going home. These babies are wearing me out."

"Well, how about you go lie in the bed and rest here until the party is over? Jake doesn't use the master. He's weird like that," she chuckled. "It's comfortable and clean. Get you some rest, and I'll pick you up after the party and drive you home. That way if you need anything, we're close."

"Oh, God, you're an angel. I really didn't want to wait for a cab."

Mia winked at her and motioned for the stairs. "Get settled in, and call my cell or the house if you need anything."

"You're too good to me."

Mia walked out of the house, not sure if she wanted to tell Tyree all she had learned. She knew he would probably be put off that Chloe was Renae's sister, but she knew he wouldn't take it out on Chloe. Renae had been a woman Tyree almost married. She had lied about being pregnant with his child, and now they were all sure Renae was being paid by Richmond as revenge. Everything Richmond did seemed to be about revenge.

She walked the trail back to the main house and was surprisingly excited when she heard the music. She could tell the party was still in full swing, and when she hit the door, she saw the one person who always made any day brighter.

Leaning over and placing a kiss on Tyree's cheek, she pulled back as he shot her a questioning look. "How's Chloe?"

"I have so much to tell you, but it can wait. Right now, I want a dance with the most handsome man in the room."

"Well, damn, babe, let me get Jake for you."

"Tyree," she scolded, not liking his joke. "There could be a roomful of underwear models in here and you would still be my number one choice. I love you."

"I love you, kitten," he replied, twirling her out to the dance floor. "Let's show all the wannabes how a real couple dances."

They moved together like they were one, once again being observed by the room. Tyree took his hand, slid it down her back, and leaned to her ear. "You look beautiful, kitten. I can't wait to get you home and under me." She let out a small giggle, and he claimed her lips. They were lost in the moment, only seeing each other. They entranced the room, so much so that no one saw the couple sneaking out the side door.

Chloe woke slowly, swearing she heard voices. Looking around the comfortable bed, she lowered her feet to the floor, feeling the cool wood. She scanned the room, swearing that she had never slept so good. She was a little angry that she had been awoken. Making her way to the door, she pulled it open quietly, trying to make out the voices, and she instantly recognized Whitney's.

Letting out a small yawn, she stepped out into the hallway, making her way to the stairs. She was halfway down the staircase when she heard Whitney's voice yelling. Running back to the top, she leaned against the wall, listening to the heated discussion.

"You promised it would end there. I can't keep doing this!"

She heard the man's voice, and her eyes widened, realizing she knew who it was on the other end of the argument. She had suspected as much when she saw his name on her caller ID the other day, but she had pushed it out of her mind.

She thought she had just imagined it. "We had a deal, and you can't back out just because you're feeling sentimental. Do I need to remind you that they shipped you off? They haven't given a damn about you until now, and that's only because your little boyfriend is dead."

Chloe heard a loud slap and whimpered.

"Jude was better than you could have ever been to me. He loved me."

"Stop acting like you miss him. You sat there and let me do whatever I wanted to him. Face it, you love me."

She could hear the pain in Whitney's voice as she spoke. "I don't. I made a mistake with you, and now I'm done. I'm out."

She looked down in time to see him grab her and force her against the wall. "You're not out until I say you're out. You are going to finish what we started. I want them to suffer."

"I can't! How could you do that to her? How could you rape my aunt?"

"She asked for everything she got, and you will get worse if you try to quit on me now."

The tears were streaking Whitney's cheeks, and Chloe pulled out her phone to text Mia. Without trying to, she pushed a button, and the phone made a loud noise. His head snapped over to where she stood. With fury in his eyes, he marched over and grabbed Chloe, dragging her down the stairs. She was only able to send off a two-letter text before he snatched her phone.

"Looks like we have an audience, Whit. Now it looks like none of us are going anywhere."

"You can't keep me here. Mia and Tyree know where I am and will come looking for me."

"Oh, I'm counting on it. I want Mia to find you. She and I have unfinished business. I wanted to wait, but it looks like I'm going to have to kick things into gear early."

"You can't hurt her. You love her. Jake, stop this." Chloe was pleading with him, but she could see that nothing she said was affecting him.

"Still with the Jake shit," he laughed. "Stop pretending like you don't remember me."

Chloe tilted her head to the side and searched his face. She always thought there was something familiar about him, but she still wasn't sure where they knew each other from. Whitney was looking at them questioningly, and when she saw Jake turn, completely facing Chloe, she tried to reason with him.

"Come on, Jake, let her go. She's just a kid, and she's pregnant. She has nothing to do with this."

"She has everything to do with this." He turned, snapping in Chloe's face, "Look at me, dammit."

"Stop this! Just let her go. She's scared, and it's not good for her babies."

"She is staying right the fuck here." He laughed sinisterly. "I suggest you start cooperating."

"No, not like this. I can't hurt her. I can't hurt Aunt Mia or Uncle Ty."

"You weren't worried about hurting her when you were bouncing on my dick. You can get all forgetful and act like you care so much about them now, but where was all that concern when you were helping me?"

"Whitney." Chloe's body was trembling as she looked at the girl she was beginning to see as a friend. "What have you done?"

She reached over, and the girl snatched her arm away. "Chloe, I thought they didn't love me. I thought they didn't care. I wanted them to see me, and when I thought they didn't, I wanted to make them pay. I blamed Aunt Mia the most because she was the one who always got all the attention. I thought that if I could be like her, people would see me the way they see her. I thought if he looked at me like he did her, it would make me feel special, too."

"You're crazy. They love you. All she does is brag on you."

"I know. I know that now. I always wanted a man to look at me the way Uncle Ty sees her. He loves her so much."

"He loves you too."

"Not the way he loves her. She always got everyone. I met him"—she pointed at Jake, and he smiled wickedly—"and he made me feel like a woman. I knew it was wrong to be with him, and when I found out about him and Aunt Mia, I should have walked away, but he's like an addiction to me. I couldn't walk away until now. No matter how he makes me feel, I can't hurt them any longer."

"Do you honestly think it's that easy?" Jake snarled. "Do you really think that your perfect aunt and uncle will accept you after she tells them everything you just said? You have been fucking me for six years behind their backs, and don't forget everything you've helped me do."

"I didn't mean . . . I never thought we would be this close."

"All you had to do was fuck Tyree and make sure Mia found out about it, but you screwed that up just like everything else. Anyway, now me and little Miss Chloe have unfinished business."

"What are you talking about?" Whitney's eyes bucked.

Instead of answering her, he turned back to face Chloe and pulled a gun from his waist. "Now I'm going to ask you again. Do you remember me?"

Looking at him again, she shook her head, slinging tears away. "I don't know. I'm sorry."

"You leave, you take the last piece of my Angie, and you act like you don't know me?" He cocked the gun back and aimed it at her face. "You better say my name. You better acknowledge me."

Chloe's mind was in overdrive, and suddenly it all clicked to her. He had changed his hair, and his eye color was different, but it was definitely him. She had only seen him in pictures, but she recognized him now and felt the fear rising in her chest. Blinking her eyes with the realization, she whispered his name. "Anderson?"

"Yes, they know me by Jake, but you know who the real Anderson is. Now get comfortable because we're not leaving until the guest of honor gets here."

"Why are you doing this?"

"They took everything from me. Now I'm taking it back, starting with my niece and nephew. How in the fuck did you think it was okay to make that dude their godfather?"

"They've been there for me. I owe them."

"They're nothing, and as soon as you give birth, we won't need you."

"What did I ever do to you?"

"You ran off with the last piece of her."

"I don't know Angie. I swear I don't."

"Angie was Will's sister. She was my wife. She killed herself and my kid, and now all I have to hold on to from her are those two kids. I won't lose them too. You see, I came here for you. You let that bitch filling your head convince you to come here not knowing I know this place like the back of my hand. I have eyes here." He winked at Whitney, and she cringed. "I will always find you."

"You can't tell him where I am. He will kill us," Chloe cried.

"He can't do anything. He's dead. It's funny, you ran from him, and all he wanted to do was protect you from me. He died trying to protect you."

"He was your friend."

"He was a liability. I claimed him as my brother, but he was soft. He caved for you, and I couldn't have that. Now my only concern is those babies."

"You can't have them. I'll die before I let you have my babies."

He shrugged and cocked the gun. "Well, I guess that means you die then."

Chloe closed her eyes and heard Whitney's high-pitched wail. "No, don't!"

After that, everything got quiet. Chloe took a deep breath, waiting for everything to be over. She exhaled deeply while the tears continued to pour down her face, and then she heard the gun go off and felt herself falling to the floor. Her hands were soaked with what she assumed was blood, and she lay there, waiting, waiting for the darkness to overtake her.

Mia and Tyree parted after a series of dances, and Mia swore her legs felt like they were about to give out. "Can we sit now?" she chuckled. "I am exhausted, baby."

"Anything you want." He tugged at her hands, pulling her into a nearby seat. "You want something to drink?"

"No, I'm okay." She leaned in, catching her lips on his. "Just sit with me a minute." He pulled her head to his shoulder. Leaning against him, taking in his scent, she closed her eyes until she felt her phone vibrating. She pulled it out of her bag and looked down at the screen, laughing quietly.

"What is it?"

"Chloe. She sent me a text with nothing but a couple of letters. She must be enjoying that bed."

"I can think of some other people who have enjoyed that bed." He squeezed her thigh, and she squealed. "You texting her back?"

"No. I think I'll pop down there and make sure everything is okay. I just get nervous about her being alone."

"Here, come on." He stood and offered his arm to her. "I'll walk you down there, and then we can get ready to start wrapping this thing up. I mean, they can keep partying if they want, but I'm ready to make a quick exit with you." He smirked.

"That sounds like a plan." They began to walk toward the foyer when they saw Rick and Rock walking briskly to the library. They could tell by the expressions they wore that something was up, and when Asha appeared, they knew there was more to it.

"What's going on, sis? Why are Rock and Rick looking so serious?"

"I don't know," Asha sighed. "They asked me to clear the house and took off."

Tyree looked at the door to the library and then back at his sister. "Then do as they said." He turned to Mia, and she nodded. "Go check on Chloe. You'll be safe there until I come and get you."

"Be careful." Mia kissed him.

"Go ahead, get out of here, babe. I'll be down there soon."

Tyree watched Mia walk out the door and ushered Asha to clear the party before heading toward the library. Once he reached the door, he felt his hands shake. He had no idea what was on the other side, but it made him anxious and afraid all at the same time. Pushing the door open and turning to close it, he felt his heart racing, and when he turned to see Rick and Rock, he knew something was off.

"What's going on?"

Rock held his hand up. "Son, I need you to remain calm. No matter what happens next, remain calm."

"Tell me what's going on," Tyree snapped, feeling his anger taking over. When the side door to the library creaked open, Tyree flew off the handle. "Motherfucker! How could you bring your ass in here?" He rushed toward the older man, and Rock grabbed him.

"Tyree, you don't understand."

"Make me understand why you have this murdering bastard in here. Rick, how could you? He killed your mother and your sister!"

Tyree was fighting through Rock's restraint when he heard a familiar voice. He dropped to his knees when she came into view, and she ran her hand down his face.

"Tyree, it's good to see you."

He was shaking his head in disbelief. "No, you can't be here. How can you be here?"

"I'm here, brother. I'm here." She wrapped her arms around him.

He buried his head in her shoulder, whispering, "Janelle." There she was in the flesh, Janelle Lenae Livingston, and Tyree was thrown.

"I know this is crazy, but you have to believe me when I tell you that Dad had nothing to do with anything. He was set up. All of this was a setup."

"I don't understand, J, what happened? How are you alive? We searched for you."

"Dad found me after the accident and kept me safe. He has been keeping me safe for all this time. He figured out it was one of the companies he overtook that was plotting against us, but he didn't know which one. If we had told you, we could have risked tipping them off. We needed you in the dark. Dad tried to talk to you, and you wouldn't hear him out. None of you trusted him. I tried to tell him to talk to you guys the right way, but he's stubborn. He's still angry at you guys for kicking him out of the company, but he wanted you safe. That's why he called Rock."

"Who did this? Who would try to kill you, sis?" She swallowed hard, and her eyes glistened with tears. He saw her hesitancy to tell him, and he stroked her face softly. "J?"

"Jake."

"Jake?"

"Jake." She nodded.

"Mia!" he yelled, remembering where she went.

"Chloe," Mia called into the quiet house. "Chloe, you up?" She walked around the corner, and her eyes fell to the bright red stain on the floor. She bent down, looking at it closely, and ran her fingers over it just in time to hear the lock click behind her. She turned and saw Jake with bloody hands.

"Mia," he breathed out frantically. "I tried. I tried to stop her, but I . . . She just came at her. There was so much blood." He was trembling, and she put her hand on his face.

"Who did what? Where is Chloe?"

"She's in the living room. Mia, it's bad." She ran around the corner and felt her stomach grow weak as she looked at the blood-soaked floor and the two saturated bodies. She went to reach down, and he grabbed her hand, snatching her back, laughing harshly.

"You can't help them. You see, Mia, none of us are walking out of here."

"What did you do?" she screamed, swinging at him. "Whitney. Chloe! Get up!"

"They can't hear you." He grabbed her by the hair and threw her on the couch. "You're going to sit here, and you're going to listen to every little detail. You're going to hear the shit I've been holding in before I use these last two bullets. One for me and one for you."

She could smell the liquor on his breath and let the fear swell in her chest. "Why are you doing this?" Asking this, she saw Chloe move and let a joyful tear roll down her face. "You're not like this. You can still save her. It's not too late."

"She's going to die. Whitney's already dead. Stupid bitch jumped in front of the first bullet." He tapped the gun across Mia's face, and she felt the chill of the cool metal. "Like I didn't have more. Nobody is leaving this place alive, including you and me."

"I know you must hate me for leaving the way I did. I was wrong. I didn't think of your feelings, and it wasn't fair. I'm sorry," she pleaded.

"Shut up. Just shut up! You know as well as I do that's not what this is about. You figured it out yesterday. It's why you ran out of here."

"I don't know what you mean."

"Bullshit, bitch! You're lying, and you know it! You remembered what happened. Stop lying and tell the truth for once in your life."

Mia thought she remembered something, but she wasn't sure. The night was filled with hazy memories, and nothing jumped out at her until yesterday. When he touched her and laughed about the young girl he was sleeping with, the line he said stuck with her. Looking down at Whitney, things began to become clearer to her. "Say it again."

"What?"

"What you said yesterday. Say it again."

His lips curved into a devious smile, and he gripped a handful of her hair, pulling her face to his lips, looking down at Whitney. "She was so good at making me feel good, just like her aunt. Just like you."

Mia's lips trembled, and her throat got dry. "You . . . you were the one that night in the alley? You raped me? Why? Why did you do this? I thought you loved me."

"I love you. You better believe I do. If I didn't love you, you would be dead right now, like your mother, like Jude, like Vincent."

"You killed them?" Mia shook her head as it filled with the realizations. She thought she knew this man. She had slept with him, told him things. He had sat by her bedside and held her hand and helped her through the destruction he caused. She felt herself getting dizzy and her eyes drooping. Just when she thought she would pass out, she felt him jerk her by the head.

"Wake up! You don't get to faint. You're going to sit here and listen to me. Lord knows I've heard enough of your whining over the years."

"How are you so evil? What made you this way?"

"Your family. Your father and that bastard father-in-law of yours took everything from me. My dignity, my pride, and my wife. My beautiful Angie killed herself because they took it all. They took her company, and she killed herself because of it."

It was all starting to make sense to Mia, but the one question that floated in her mind was how Whitney and Chloe fit into all this. "Why hurt the girls? Why not just come after me, after Rick and Tyree? Why them?"

"Don't do that. Don't act like you care about anyone other than your ass of a husband. I don't even think you spend as much time caring about your son as you do bending over for him. Before I pulled you into that alley and showed you what a real man was like, I watched you. I watched your whole family, and I figured out what I could do to ruin it. All I had to do was ruin you."

"Why me? What made me so important?"

"You see, killing your mother didn't work. She was already too strung out, and she had been away so long you didn't miss her long. Buddying up to your gullible niece didn't have the effect I thought it would, so I knew I needed to go harder. It felt good, fucking her, it felt damn good, but I needed more, so I got her to tell me everything she knew about all of you. Janelle, she hit home for you for a while, and then you and Rick were back at the job like nothing happened. You know, Whitney was the one who led me to Janelle that day, and she was the one who brought me back here to find Chloe. She hated you, you know."

"That's a lie. All of it is a lie. I loved Whitney. I loved Mom and Janelle. I miss them every day."

"You might, but they didn't cause the ache in your heart that losing your precious Tyree did. When I took your son and gave him to Renae, you lost it, but nothing compared to when he left. You were roaming the streets like a lost puppy. I was going to kill you and take you away from Rick, but when I saw how you hit rock bottom, I actually felt something. I let you and your little 'pity me' attitude suck me in. I fell in love with you. I sat next to you, holding your hand, while you killed my baby!" He smacked her in the face with his palm, and she whimpered. "And you still left me like the selfish bitch you are."

"You're crazy."

"Maybe I am, but you have to admit it was brilliant. Killing your mother, running your sister off the road, and pinning it all on your father was genius. You gotta admit, Mia, sending in Renae, I mean, Delilah, to fuck up your marriage was smart until she fucked us over. We had the perfect plan until that bitch grew a conscience. She let your husband and father-in-law weaken her. I had to shoot her. Killing John was just for fun. He was as dumb as they come and never suspected she was working for us. She wasn't my idea, though. Vincent always had a soft spot for that ho, just like he did for her little sister. It made him weak. He saw what my feelings for you did to me, and he still got this bitch pregnant."

"Vincent? The father of her baby is named Will."

"William Vincent Tussant. My brother-in-law and those kids were the last link to my Angie. I gave her the chance to save them, and like you, she chose to be a shitty mother. She chose her own stupid whims over those kids. They're better off dead than with her."

"Why tell me all this? Why admit to all the things you did?"

"I thought there should be nothing but honesty between us before we died, and I wanted to see the look on your face when you heard that your sister is still alive."

"Don't do this to me. Don't tell me lies now."

"I have no reason to lie to you. I only just figured it out, but yes, she's alive. I saw them tonight, at this party. I thought when they didn't find her body it just washed away, but I should have known. The only thing that makes me happy about the whole situation is knowing you will never see her or your niece."

"Wait, the girl in the picture, she's my niece? Little Jenna is my niece?" Mia thought about the picture she had found years ago at her sister's grave. She once thought it was a child her dad fathered and was enraged.

"Yes," he answered in a singsong voice. "And you're never going to meet her."

Mia was bawling, and all she could hear was his laughter. She had been through so much in her life that she had no fight left. She closed her eyes when she heard the gun cock and shivered when she felt the metal on her face. If this was going to be the end, she had to say one last thing.

"I never loved anyone the way I love my son and his father. This may be the end for me, but I was lucky. I had a great life with a great family, and I experienced that once-in-a-lifetime love. I feel sorry for you because you're going to die here today never knowing what that feels like."

"Shut up. That's what you think, but I've seen you with him. I've watched how he fucks you. It's that slow, gentle shit and it's not what you like. The one time he came home and fucked you like a real man, you loved it. I saw your face. You enjoyed every second of it, just like you did in that alley."

"How do you know any of that? Were you in my house?"

"Whitney gave me an all-access pass to your house. Cameras everywhere. Every moan, every scream, every orgasm I heard, but nothing compared to that night he came home drunk and smacked you around. Face it, you like it rough, *kitten*."

She hated the way he used Tyree's name for her. It almost made her never want to hear it again, but then she thought about how good it sounded rolling off Tyree's tongue while he was inside her. She thought of the passion in his eyes as he ran his hand over her face and whispered it in her ear. It gave her the strength to strike back. "I didn't enjoy anything you did. You hurt me. You almost ruined my life."

"Kid yourself all you want, Dimples. You loved it. It took you so long to give yourself to me again, and when you did, I memorized all the moans. The pants of my name were proof of that."

"Oh, so that's what you stake your beliefs on?"

"I know your body."

"Well, did you know I hadn't had an orgasm in over two years before I saw Tyree again? All you did was make me miss him. I tried to pretend like it was the same, but no one compares to him. You may think you know my body, but he owns it. The spots you think you touched, he discovered. The pants and moans were there to make you feel like you were doing something. I may have moaned for you, but I scream for him. He has taken my body places I never thought it could go, and just when I think he's done, he makes it explode with nothing but sheer ecstasy. You never accomplished that and you never will. Now, die with that on your mind."

He aimed the gun at her head. His hand was shaky, and he tried steadying it but failed. She could see the hesitation, and the gun slowly lowered, but when the front door opened and Tyree's voice called out to her, she felt the gun back at her head. His hand was no longer shaking at this point, and with teary eyes, she looked up just in time to see Tyree. When she didn't respond, he ran around the corner and froze, witnessing the scene.

Mia saw the sick look on Jake's face and found her voice just in time for Jake to aim at Tyree. "Shoot me! Leave him out of this. Just shoot me." With a sadistic laugh, Jake fired off a shot, and Tyree crumpled to the floor. Mia saw his eyes shut and she let out a gut-wrenching scream. "No, Tyree!"

Her eyes were swimming in tears, and it took her a second to notice the arm around Tyree's leg. He had been pulled to the floor. She kept looking at him to see any sign of blood and didn't. That was when she and Jake both realized that Richmond had pulled him out of harm's way. Realizing he was about to be carted out, Jake raised the gun to his own head. Before he could pull the trigger, Richmond fired off a shot that went straight through the shoulder. Within a few seconds, he was on top of Jake, pummeling him with his fists. With all this going on, Mia jumped to the floor, touching Chloe's bleeding body.

When Chloe moved, Mia cried out happily and grabbed her hand, stroking it soothingly. "You're going to be okay. We're going to get help." They called the ambulance, and within minutes they were there, loading Chloe inside. Just as Jake had stated, it was too late for Whitney.

When the coroner showed up, Cassandra and Rick broke down in the driveway.

To everyone's dismay, Jake was still alive, bleeding heavily, but alive. Once they pulled Richmond off him, he was loaded into an ambulance, shackled to the bed. They were assured that after leaving the hospital he would be detained, but for Mia, it wasn't enough. She wanted him dead.

Through all the confusion, Mia had scanned the yard. She had to know. She had to see her for it to all be real, and when Janelle stepped in front of her, she broke from Tyree's embrace and threw her arms around her sister. Both girls shared tears and clung to each other while Janelle rubbed her hair.

"I'm here, Mia. I'm never leaving again. I'm finally home."

"I don't know what to think. I can't believe this is real."

Stepping back and gripping her hands around Mia's face, Janelle displayed a shaky smile. "It's real, big sis, so real."

"You promise?"

"I promise."

Chapter Twenty-seven

"I need to know," Tyree sighed. "How did this happen? What the hell is going on around here?" They all rushed to the hospital from the house, and Mia was in with Cassandra, Rick, and Janelle, so he had the opportunity to talk to Richmond and Rock. They had all been there for over two hours, and he still couldn't wrap his mind around the night's events.

Rock took a seat next to him, and Richmond just stood against the wall. "When I was first assigned to the case, something felt strange about Richmond's involvement. I knew he was a part of the shady business deals, but the murders seemed off. They weren't his style. He's the kind of man who doesn't like to get his hands dirty, and when the evidence started turning up, I knew I was on the right track. I couldn't tell any of you. I needed you to all suspect him if I was going to flush out who was really behind everything. I always suspected it was someone close to home. After John was killed, we knew it needed to look like Richmond was behind it, and it had to look like we knew, so we staged his arrest and escape. Everything needed to look real."

"How long?" Tyree said quietly.

"What?"

"How long did you know and not tell us? Mia has been terrified of him. She was afraid every day that he was going to hurt her."

"I know, and I'm sorry. I had to let you think he was at fault. If you had known, it would have tipped Anderson off."

"So he was really the one behind it all?" Tyree laughed sarcastically. "I knew he was full of shit and I shouldn't have trusted him around my wife. She thought she owed him so much, that he was so good."

"He fooled all of us. It took a minute to discover what he had done. He was very meticulous and efficient in his actions and never slipped up until Jude."

"Jude?"

"Jude figured him out. He had been following Whitney and saw them together. That's why he died. He came to Jude and Whitney's house that night, and in the midst of the fight, Jude got plenty of Anderson's DNA on his body. It was good because we were able to identify him that way, but we had no way of knowing Jake was this Anderson person until we started following him around. Something about him always rubbed me the wrong way. Maybe it was just me being protective of you."

"I never liked him, but Mia wanted to be a friend in his time of need. Things were going so well for us, and I didn't want to upset her. I can't believe he was the one who did this to Jude. Hell, who did all of this."

"Jude put up a good fight, but Anderson wasn't fighting fair. The last blow to the head came from something blunt and did the trick." Rock swallowed hard and looked back at Richmond. "Whitney was there. She may have even helped."

Tyree shook his head in disbelief. "No, she wouldn't. Not the little girl I watched grow up. She wasn't like that." Rock reached into his jacket and pulled out an envelope, placing it in Tyree's hands. He opened it slowly, pulling out the contents, and let out a loud sigh. "What the hell is this?" He held up a picture and Rock shrugged.

"I received that the day Jude died. He had it sent over with a few other things."

The picture was taken the day Whitney and Tyree had gone to lunch. It was snapped right when Whitney was sharing her food with him. "Nothing happened," he supplied quickly. "Mia and I had a fight that day, and we went to lunch. I could tell something strange was going on with her, and I tried to get her to talk to me. Terence said that she had feelings for me, but I blew it off. I never thought she could do anything like this." He looked further and saw more pictures. There were several pictures of Whitney with Jake, and he threw them from his lap. "I let her in my house, around my son. Dammit!"

"You could have never known what she was involved in. None of this is what I expected when the case first began."

Tyree was overwhelmed, and through all his grief, he still had questions only one person could answer: the man standing quietly across the room. "I know he says you didn't kill them, that you were innocent in that sense, but what did you do to make him hate you so much? What made him come after my wife?"

Richmond had remained silent through the whole conversation, but when Tyree asked the question, he took a seat. "Look, I made mistakes, so many mistakes, but I never once meant to put my kids in danger. I tried to keep them away from this life."

"You tried to keep Mia from me. You made it damn near impossible for us to be together."

"It wasn't about you. It was about who you would become. I knew John wanted you to take the crown and run Johnston, and I needed Mia far away from that. I went about it the wrong way, but I just wanted you to take her and leave here."

"You have to be kidding me," Tyree laughed. "You may not have done all this, but it is your fault. You threatened me, told me you would ruin everything if I didn't walk away from her. How the hell is that encouraging me to take her away?"

"I knew you. I practically raised you with them, and I knew if I pushed, it would only make you fight harder for her. I saw you, the way you looked at her, the way you always stepped in whenever she needed you. You thought you were keeping a secret, but I saw it. Even before you did, I saw how you felt about her, and I knew you would be there for her. I knew you would be there for her better than I ever could. It's why I set you up with that trust fund."

"You did what?"

"John cut you off. You had nothing. I needed my daughter to be okay, and I knew you wouldn't take the money straight up. I set it up with my lawyer for all three of you to get trust funds so it wouldn't look suspicious to John. He always thought it was a gift from his dead father."

Tyree couldn't believe what he was hearing. Everything he thought he knew had been lies. He wasn't sure how to feel about Richmond, but he did know one thing for sure. "You are the reason she needed to be protected. She was afraid of you. She saw what you did to Helen, and she was scared. You may not have killed Helen, but make no mistake about it, you were the villain in her story."

Richmond let out a few tears and Tyree was surprised. He had never seen this much emotion in this cold man and had to take a step back. Gathering his anger, he tried to understand what Richmond was saying to him. "You're right, I messed up her life. I drove her to drugs, and I damaged that wonderful woman. That's all on me, and never think for a second that I didn't love her. She was everything to me, and I hate I didn't see it before it was too late."

"You were in the house that night she died, why?"

"I had been getting these warning messages that if I didn't pay what was owed, someone I loved would pay the price. My first thought was of her, and so I went to warn her. She brushed me off, telling me I was crazy, so I left. A few hours later, she was gone. After that, I knew the kids were in danger, and I watched them. When

Janelle's accident happened, I had been following her, and I found her unconscious on the road. I took her and kept her safe until I could figure out who was behind this. I just hate I was too late to help Helen and that I couldn't protect Mia. I need my daughter to know how sorry I am, all my kids. Janelle knows how much I love her, but it may be too late for Mia and Rick."

"Even with all the things she thought you did, she never once said she didn't love you. She was afraid, but she still loved you. She just wanted her dad."

"I've missed so much of their lives, and it's my own fault, but you have to know that Jake, Anderson, or whoever the hell he is was way off base. His hatred for our family is unwarranted. Once he hears what really happened with his wife, he is going to feel like an ass. He did all this, and things are not as they seem."

"What happened?"

"You know, I could have killed him back at the house. I hit his shoulder on purpose because this is a conversation we all need to have together. I want to look him in the eye and give him the truth about his wife. She wasn't who he thought she was."

"Well, let's go down there." Tyree stood. "I want to stare that bastard down." Tyree was the first to charge out of the room, and the two guys followed closely behind him. They took the elevator up to Jake's room, and once they reached the door, Tyree paused, and Rock touched his shoulder.

"What is it, son?"

"I can't go in there."

"Why not?"

"I can't touch him. The officers will never let me get close enough, and I want to kill him. He touched my wife, he forced himself on her, and I want him dead."

"He is going to get what's coming to him," Richmond hissed. "You just go in there and control your anger for now."

"I can't promise that."

"You have to. Mia needs you." Rock walked into the room, leaving Richmond and Tyree in the hall.

Tyree turned to Richmond and sighed. "How are you handling this? He killed your wife, raped your daughter, and corrupted your granddaughter. You should be more pissed than anyone."

Richmond walked up and whispered in Tyree's ear, "I'm just thinking about how much I want to be with my family, and that is enough to silence the voice in my head screaming to kill him."

"I guess I need to think those thoughts," Tyree said, "because the voice I'm hearing is telling me to break his neck."

"I wouldn't expect anything less, but come on. We have something to settle here."

Tyree walked in, and Richmond hung back for a second before walking in. Once he saw the armed guards walking out, he went in, saw Tyree's livid expression, and put a hand on his shoulder. "It's going to be okay."

Richmond was eerily calm, and Tyree got a bad feeling but brushed it off once he heard Jake's laughter. When Rock walked over and closed the door, he knew something was up. Watching the two men conversing back and forth, Tyree scratched his head and turned back to Jake. "All right, bitch, let's talk. Tell me why you put your hands on my wife."

"Have a seat, boys," Jake hissed. "Let's kick this show off."

"You have to wake up, kid," Janelle whispered against Chloe's forehead. "If you don't wake up, I'll never forgive myself. I can't believe I got you in this mess."

Mia had been sitting back, watching in disbelief. She still was amazed that her sister was

sitting in front of her. They had all been talking
for hours, but it still didn't seem real. After leaving the morgue with Rick and Cassandra, Mia
and Janelle had come up to check on Chloe, who
still hadn't woken after her emergency Cesarean.

The babies were both underweight, but
healthy. The doctors were hopeful with a few
tube feedings they would be fine, but they were
going to keep them until they got up to at least
five pounds. Little Tristen was already at four,
but the girl was only three. Both Mia and Janelle
had been to see them and even given the doctors
the name for Tristen. They weren't sure what to
call the girl. Chloe hadn't decided on a name for
her yet. Mia said she would leave that honor
for when she woke up. She was sure Chloe
would wake up.

"You know it's not your fault, right? She would
have never been in that house if I hadn't told her
to stay there. I was so sure he was a good guy,
and I let him around her."

"If I've learned anything these past six years,
it's that you can't read everyone. I used to think
Dad was this monster, but never once in the
past six years has he let me or Jenna fall in
harm's way. I think we may have been wrong
about him."

Mia nodded slowly. "If he saved you, I know I was. I thought I would never see you again. I never thought you would be standing in front of me, and with a baby, no less." She laughed with tears rolling down her cheeks.

"Jen is hardly a baby. She's five going on thirty-five. She's so smart and such a sweetheart. I can't wait for you to meet her. She's going to love her aunt Mia."

"Where is she?"

"With Karen. I thought, well, I thought they should meet, and I didn't want her here."

"Why?"

"I didn't tell her Jenna was Miguel's, but I'm sure she figured it out. She looks like a mixture of you and him. I swear, how do all the kids in our family come out looking like either you or him? If I didn't know any better, I would swear Kyan was his." She was trying to lighten the mood with jokes, but Mia was shocked by her admission.

"Miguel is her dad? Does he know?"

"No, and before you judge me, I haven't seen him. We haven't talked, and I'm not sure if I want to. He never wanted kids, and I didn't want to blindside him. I wanted to think this out before the time came that I had to face him, but things got crazy, and we had to come. Once Dad figured out Jake was the one behind everything, he had to warn you and Rick. He came to your house one night to talk to you, but you weren't there."

"Tyree freaked out. He kept me out of the house the rest of the night, but you're wrong about Miguel. He has changed so much since he thought you died. He went through a bad patch, but he is a better guy now. I think meeting his daughter will mean the world to him."

"I don't know, Mia. I don't want to bring him into her life and have him freak out. She's my world, and I can't have him disappointing her."

"Let him surprise you. You should see him with the kids. He is the best uncle, and I just know he would be a good father. I can't believe you're a mother. My baby has grown up."

"You're not that much older than me," Janelle laughed. "You always did try to act all old." Janelle wrapped her arms around Mia, and she sank into the hug, enjoying the moment.

Mia let Janelle go and looked back at Chloe, brushing a hand over her cheek. "How did you meet?

"By mistake. I left the house one day, Dad was livid by the way, but I ran into her, and she was crying. I sat and talked to her and figured out that she was afraid of this Will guy. I never put it together that she was Renae's sister or that the Will guy was Jake's brother, but I'm not sure how we missed the Renae thing. They look so much alike. Anyways, she would come over to the house and visit me, and Jenna and Dad saw her one day and flipped. He said we couldn't have visitors or interact with people we didn't know, but I couldn't turn my back on her. She was just an innocent kid, and I needed to make sure she would be okay, so I gave her money and told her what to do once she got here. I knew if you met her, you would click. I just know you so well, and that one day you would see her at Gina's and speak."

"You had that much faith in me?"

"I was right, wasn't I?"

"Yeah. I saw her one day trying to juggle one too many plates and grabbed one. We have been cool since then. She said she met some-one who reminded her of me, and she even showed me a picture of you and your daughter. I thought . . ." Mia started laughing and Janelle's eyebrows raised.

"You thought what?"

"I thought your daughter was our sister and that you were some woman Dad was dealing with. I couldn't see your face in the picture, and I had no reason to think you were still alive. I was pissed because she had Mom's middle name.

She was calling you Lenae, and it never clicked with me because you hate that name. I never thought in a million years you would be calling yourself that."

"First of all, I wasn't my idea to use that horrid name. Dad just thought it up because he didn't want to have to explain to Jenna why my name suddenly changed. He knew it would be easier to explain a middle name rather than a whole new one. Second of all, gross. Who would have another kid with Dad?" She laughed. "People think he's a murderer."

"Really? You know some women find that sexy," Mia chuckled. "But really, though, how did you know about Renae, or even Jake, for that matter? Although I think we should be calling him something else. Isn't his real name Anderson or some shit? Hell, how did I not know who he really was? I lived with that man for two years."

"Just because you couldn't see us doesn't mean we weren't there. We would pop in on you guys from time to time, and I would sneak off to see you guys sometimes in the middle of the night. And as for him, he is a con artist to the fullest. Dad says he has been living this lie for over six years."

Mia took on a look like she remembered something. "A few years back, my first night back here, was that you in Kyan's room? He screamed that someone touched him. Tyree and Miguel saw this figure on camera, and they never figured out who it was. I never even knew where the cameras were, but Anderson said Whitney helped him set them up."

"That little dipshit. She was always jealous of us. Her parents treated her like a princess and kept her away from this bullshit we had to endure, and she's jealous because we got to live this dangerous life? I swear I would have traded with her any day."

"You never liked her, and you didn't get to know her like I did. I think toward the end, she regretted everything. Look, you're getting me off subject, was it you or not?"

"Yeah, it was me. I missed you guys, and I couldn't risk you seeing me, so I waited until you were asleep. I don't know if you took Dad seriously, but really, your house was easy to get into."

"Okay, okay, I get it. I need to do something about security."

"Well, duh, you act like you don't have the funds. Stop being cheap and invest in a high-dollar system."

"I kind of feel like I shouldn't need it now that Anderson is caught and I know Dad isn't trying to kill me." Mia saw a sadness wash over Janelle. "What's wrong?"

"I hate that you thought that, because he really loves us. He made mistakes when we were growing up, but you should see him with Jenna. He's her hero. She worships him. I just wish Kyan could have had that and that Jenna and Kyan could have grown up together."

"I'm open to getting to know him, but I'm not so sure about Rick. They have shared a lot of bad blood over the years, and I just don't know if they can bounce back."

"I hope they can because I can tell Dad misses you both."

"Yeah, me too." Mia looked back at Chloe and sighed. "What if she doesn't wake up? How are those babies going to know about their amazing mother?"

"Don't think that way. She will. We just have to have faith. I can't make myself believe that she came this far just to let it end like this." Just as Janelle finished her last statement, she heard a faint call behind her. She turned to see Chloe's eyes opening slowly, and she formed a gorgeous smile. "Hey, kid."

"Lenae? What are you doing here?"

"This is my family." She reached for Mia's hand. "This is my big sister."

"Wow, small world." Chloe managed a laugh.

"Yeah, it is." Mia brushed the hair from her forehead. "Now on to business. There is a little girl in there who needs a name. What's it going to be?"

Chloe pulled herself up in the bed, and Mia gave her the water glass between them. "Thanks." She took a drink of the water, and Mia smiled. "I think her name should be a mixture of the two women who mean the world to me. Now the problem is figuring out which name goes first."

"I have first dibs," Janelle snapped, and Mia rolled her eyes. "What? I've never had a kid named after me, and I just thought it would be nice." They all started laughing, and Mia stopped to look at her cell phone. While looking down, her attention was quickly snapped back when she heard Janelle's screams and the beeping of the monitors.

Chloe was coughing and shaking, gasping for air. Janelle was trying her hardest to calm her down, but nothing she did worked. In the middle of everything, Mia walked over and grabbed Chloe's hand. As if things slowed down for a minute, Mia heard the words falling from the girl's lips clearly and allowed tears to roll down her cheeks. "Take care of the kids. Don't tell them about me. Just love them like your own."

Shortly afterward, the nurses and doctors raced in trying to bring her back, but it was too late. Mia and Janelle watched as Chloe's gown was ripped open and the defibrillator pads were pressed to her chest. The doctor screamed, "Clear," and the whole room went silent for a few seconds. Mia could hear her heart beating in her ears. Janelle was gripping her hand tightly. Her palms were sweaty.

"Clear!" The doctor's voice sounded through the room once again as the first attempt to revive her didn't work. Chloe was lying there, helpless, with the life draining out of her, and all Mia and Janelle could do was watch.

The monitor began to flatline, and after several attempts with the defibrillator, they called it. Mia and Janelle were both drenched in tears, and the only thing Mia could think of was the kids. She would do as Chloe asked and take care of them, but she couldn't agree to the other part. She would always make sure they knew everything Chloe did to bring them into the world, and she also knew exactly what name to give her new baby girl: Chloe Janelle Johnston.

Standing outside the room, Mia felt herself hyperventilating. "I have to get out of here."

"You want me to come with you?" asked Janelle.

"No." Mia squeezed her hand gently. "I need a minute. Go call Miguel. Don't miss one more second with the man you love and your daughter."

"How did you know I love him?"

"I know you."

Janelle nodded and walked down the hall, turning back to Mia once as she reached the elevator. As soon as she disappeared, Mia dug her hand into her purse and pulled out Jude's letter. Finally convincing herself to read it, she tore the envelope open and sat down in a vacant chair. Reading the neatly scribbled words, she found her emotions taking over.

> *Aunt Mia,*
> *Well, I'm not really sure if I can still call you that after this. I wanted to write you because I needed you to know how much you changed my life. You and Uncle Ty were the first to show me any kindness in this family, and I know it was mostly because of you. Know that I love Whitney. The rest of this is going to be difficult to say, but I need it out in the open.*
> *I came across these pictures, some with Uncle Ty and some with Jake. I'm not sure*

what it was all about, and I never wanted to be the one to tell you my suspicions about her, but I think she's up to something. I didn't want to believe it. I wanted to think she loved me and only me, but I fear I'm wrong. God, I wish I could have found what you guys have. You give me hope. If I hadn't witnessed it for myself, I would have never known that kind of love exists.

I may be leaving here soon, but know that it in no way changes anything about us. I still want to be able to visit and call you with my asinine problems. I want you to still see me as family even though things with Whitney have failed miserably. Tell Uncle Ty I'm sorry I couldn't keep my promise to always take care of her, but I can't do this with her any longer. There will always be a part of me that loves her, but I can't get married to a woman I can't trust.

I love you, and I hope you understand,
Jude
P.S. Tell little man I'll still come to his games when he joins the football team.

Folding the letter again, she stuffed it into the envelope. Kissing it gently, she placed it back in her purse. "I still love you, Jude," she whispered into the air. "I'll always love you, and I will never forget you." Deciding it was time she found her husband, she set off, thinking there was only one place that would keep him occupied so long: Anderson's room.

Tyree let out a boisterous laugh and pulled a chair next to Anderson's bedside. "Don't make me fuck you up." He was calm in his tone, but his demeanor was anything but. Richmond and Rock had been watching him cautiously, trying to make sure he didn't lose his cool, and so far he had been doing fine.

"Let's be real, Tyree. *Ty*," he snickered. "You can't do shit to me. You make one wrong move, those guards out there will arrest your ass. Daddy substitute numbers one and two won't be able to get you out of that. Your hands are tied."

Tyree lifted his hands and locked eyes with Anderson. "You're right, I can't touch you. As much as I would like to rip your dick off and burn it in front of you, I can't, but what I can do is let you in on a little secret."

"A secret, huh? You don't know one. It took you forever to figure out I was the one messing with you. You were so dumb you let me move into your house and spend time with your wife all because she thought I was this martyr. I bet it's still eating at you that you failed at protecting her. I took everything you had, and you were powerless to stop it."

"You may have taken it temporarily, but that woman is mine. Her heart, her body, her very soul belongs to me, and I will never lose that. She is the only reason you're still sitting here talking to me. If she weren't a factor, I would have killed you. I just wanted to look you in the eye and let you know that you lost. You may have caused a ripple and pitted us against each other for a brief period, but we are stronger than ever." He stood over him and looked down with such seriousness in his eyes that it startled the men behind him. "You don't win."

While Tyree stepped back into the comforting embrace of Rock, Richmond cleared his throat and looked over at Anderson, crossing his arms over his chest. When he started laughing, Rock and Tyree looked at him in confusion. "You did all this because of your wife. Angie, that sweet little thing, she was something. I remember her. Fondly, I might add."

Anderson's eyes went grim, and his lips curved into a hateful scowl. "Don't you talk about her. You and that bastard took her from me! She was perfect."

"Yeah, she was perfect. She was an angel. She loved you and only you," Richmond mocked.

"She was having my baby! It meant everything to us."

Rock and Tyree looked back and forth between the two guys. When Richmond slammed his hand down on Anderson's injured shoulder, he let out a loud scream. Richmond only laughed louder. "You meant nothing! You did all this, and you meant nothing. Do you want to know how we got her company and took her away from you? She gave it to us."

"You're lying! She would never do that."

"Oh, but she did. She signed it over to us willingly, and do you want to know why?"

"Shut up!"

"She was fucking John. She wanted to leave you for him, and here's the real kicker: that kid was his. She thought he was going to leave Karen, and when she figured out he wasn't going to, she stepped in front of that diesel. It was never about the company, and my family had nothing to do with your little grudge."

Anderson's face was filled with disbelief, and Richmond drove his point home. "What was she, like five months? That's what John said."

"You bastard! I'll kill you!" Anderson started rattling the handcuffs on the bars of the bed.

Richmond turned to Rock and Tyree, nodding toward the door. "Let's go. I think we're done here." Tyree and Rock walked out. Richmond turned back and reached for the pillow Anderson's head was resting on. He snatched it forward. He placed the pillow over his face, tucking it under his cuffed hands to make sure it couldn't be pushed aside, and walked out, stopping at the door. "Feel free to suffocate. I assure you no one will miss you."

With that, he walked out, looking at the guards. "Let him thrash around in there, boys. There will be an extra two hundred thousand in it for you if you do what needs to be done." Richmond winked at the guys, and they nodded, understanding exactly what he was asking. He wanted Anderson to take his last breath in that room. Prison was too good for him.

As Tyree rounded the corner, he found Mia leaning against the wall in tears. He reached for her, and it took her a minute to register that it was him. At first, he just thought she was still shaken by what happened to Whitney, but then he could tell there was more.

"Baby, it's okay." He wiped the tears away with his thumbs. "It's all over now."

"Tyree, you don't understand. Something happened. Something horrible, but I'm conflicted because it's also a blessing. I feel so guilty. Ty, I'm so . . ." She was rambling, and he stopped her, holding her face still.

"Calm down and breathe." He looked around and scanned the hall. "Where is Janelle? How is Chloe? Did she wake up?"

Her tears flowed freely, and he shook his head, thinking the worst. "No, baby. She's okay, right? I mean, she has to be. They said they were hopeful. The children made it, and she just has to be okay." When Mia shook her head, it was confirmed for him. "She's gone? What happened?"

"She woke up. We were laughing. She was thinking of the name for the baby girl, and just like that she was gone. She died right in front of us. She grabbed my hand right before the doctors rushed in, and she made me promise to take care of the kids, and she asked to never mention her to them. How can I not? How can I never mention her to them, and how am I supposed to be okay with knowing how we got those little blessings? It's my fault she died. I have to live with that every day."

He pulled her close and pressed her hard against him. "You loved that girl, we both did, but you will not blame yourself. She trusted you, and she was in danger long before she met you.

She knew this, and she still did all she could to protect the kids. We will do whatever it takes to give them a good life, and we will make sure they know her. If you want this, a life with the kids, we will have it. As long as it's what you want."

"I want it so bad, but is it fair to just take her kids and have all our dreams come true?"

"They will know her, we will tell them all about her, but someone has to be there for them. She wanted it to be us. The best way to honor her will be to take care of them." He felt her head nod against his chest, and without him trying, a smile formed on his lips. He knew he shouldn't be as happy as he was, but he couldn't help thinking that they now had the one thing he no longer thought was possible. Actually, they had two. "Baby, I know what would make you feel better."

"What?"

"Let's go see the kids. I need to introduce myself to them."

He started walking down the hall, but she stopped him, grabbing his hand. "Before you go, I know you already know the name for Tristen, but I named the girl."

"Without me? I'm hurt." He placed his hand on his chest jokingly. "What's her name?"

"Chloe." She smiled. "Chloe Janelle Johnston."

"I love it."

"I thought you would."

He turned to Rock and Richmond, signaling for them to follow. He saw the tension clouding Mia's face, and he kissed her gently. He knew things between her and Richmond were a work in progress, but she was still a little wary of him. He knew they would eventually work through it, and he hoped this would give them the extra push.

"Come on, guys. We need to introduce you to your new grandchildren, Mr. Tristen Tyree Johnston and Ms. Chloe Janelle Johnston."

The guys both fell in step, and Richmond walked up, brushing against Mia. Her breath caught in her chest, and Tyree pulled her hand to his lips. "Baby steps, kitten. Baby steps."

She turned and leaned in to press her lips softly against his. "Baby steps."

Chapter Twenty-eight

Mia was pacing the floor, and Rick was just watching her. Three weeks had passed since the day Chloe and Whitney died, and Mia and Rick had yet to talk to Richmond. They had talked in passing about little things, but they hadn't gotten into the serious discussion they needed to have. It had just been sidestepped. The repercussions of everything that happened that day had been keeping them occupied.

After the autopsy, they figured out that a blood clot that moved to the lungs killed Chloe. They also had been notified that Anderson died in the hospital under questionable causes, suffocation, and because of all the problems the two families had with him, it was anyone's guess who was responsible. As far as Mia was concerned, she was glad he was dead, and she also thought she knew who was behind it.

Not that she blamed him, but Tyree told her that Richmond was the last of them to see him when they visited, and she was sure he made the call if he hadn't done it himself. It gave her a small comfort, but it also made her uneasy because she knew what he could be capable of. Tyree had tried to explain to her the conversation they had, but she was still wary. She had other things on her mind.

The kids were doing great, and it was time for them to be able to come home, but it wasn't as easy as they thought it would be to take them. Even though Chloe had voiced her consent for them to raise her kids, they hadn't had anything in writing, and because they weren't blood relatives, things were difficult. The only person still living with a link to the children was Chloe and Renae's mother, and she hadn't come forward. They hoped she wouldn't. They had been with the kids every day and were completely in love with the little angels.

While Mia was still pacing the floor and Rick was watching her, Richmond walked in with Janelle. They were both smiling, laughing about something, and Mia felt a pang of jealousy in her chest. She wanted that with him. There was this sense of comfort and ease between them that she never had with her father. Taking a seat next to Rick, she grabbed his hand, giving it a squeeze. She saw the look on Janelle's face and instantly felt bad. She and Rick had grown so used to consoling each other over the years that they now had a connection no one else shared. Thinking of how she felt about Janelle's relationship with their father, she thought her sister may be feeling the same way.

Richmond had called them all there because he wanted them to finally sit down and hash out all the feelings they had for one another. Mia knew that Janelle was okay, but she also knew Richmond didn't really know how to talk to her and Rick without her. She was the buffer between them. She had been for the past few weeks.

Taking a seat, Richmond gestured for Janelle to sit as well. Once they were all settled, he began to talk. "I'm glad you're all here. I wanted to speak to you and get the air cleared. First of all, I wanted to let you know our family is in the clear with this Anderson mess. We are no longer under investigation, and his death has been ruled accidental."

Rick looked at Mia, and she saw that he couldn't hold his peace. "Come on now, what did you do? Buy a judge? We all know someone killed him. Not that I care that the bastard is dead, but whoever was responsible is someone in one of our two families. I actually think he is standing in this room."

Locking eyes with Rick, Richmond nodded. "You want to hear it, then fine. I don't give two shits about him being dead. The world is a better place because of it, and if I'd had the opportunity, I would have killed him myself just to see the life drain out of his face. I would have stood there until he took his last breath for what he has done to this family. He cost us years. I can admit that much, but I can't admit to killing him."

"Is that what you think?" Rick huffed. "He may have taken Mom and"—he paused, feeling his anger bubbling out of control—"manipulated my daughter, but he was only able to because you gave us a reason to stay away from you. Mother was afraid of you, and for good reason. You made her life hell. That's why I kept my daughter away, and she felt like we didn't love her because of it. I lost my only child." Tears were streaming down Rick's face. "For all the loss we've felt, you were responsible in some way."

"I deserve this. I deserve your hatred. I wish I could deny it all, but I'm to blame. Just know that I never meant to hurt any of you. I love you."

"I don't hate you," Rick snapped. "I wish I could hate you, but even with everything you've done, you still saved my baby sister. Having her here with us today means more to me than you will ever know. I've been holding on to this anger toward you for all these years, but looking at her"—he turned to Janelle—"makes me feel like I'm able to forgive you. My child is gone, and so is our mother. We don't have to lose what we have left."

Mia saw when Richmond was overcome with tears, and when he turned to her, she wasn't sure what to do. She was shocked and remained that way until Janelle slipped a hand on her shoulder. Mia looked up at her sister and saw the happiness in her eyes. She offered a sweet smile. Turning to face Richmond, she gathered all their attention as she began to speak. "Do you miss her?"

Without pause, he nodded. "Yes, every minute of every day. I messed up so bad, and I will never forgive myself for what happened to her. She was wonderful, and there is so much of her in you."

"Really? I sometimes can't remember what she was like before the drugs. I try really hard, but it's all hazy. I miss her the most when I try to remember a good time to share with Kyan and can't. I'm terrible for not remembering."

"Dancing."

"What?"

"You got your love of dancing from her. I know how Tyree hates to dance, but he does it because it's one of your favorite things. She was the same way. She used to force me on the dance floor during all those stuffy galas, and every time I see you dance, the way your smile lights up the room, I remember her. Just like at your wedding, the second one," he clarified. "The way you moved with Tyree, so in sync, so focused on him, I swear I've never seen you favor her more."

"You were there?"

"I wouldn't have missed it for the world." He turned to Janelle, and she nodded. "We were both there. My biggest regret was not being able to walk you down the aisle. You looked so beautiful. I've never been prouder."

Without saying another word, she crossed the room and threw her arms around him. "I missed you, Dad. I swear, I missed you so much."

"I missed you too, my beautiful girl, my sweet dove." Kissing the side of her face, he held her tightly. "I missed you more than you know."

Watching the scene must have triggered something in Rick, because soon he was standing with them, along with Janelle, and they all embraced. Mia had never known they would be this way again, that she would have her sister and father back, but now that she had them, she wasn't going to let go. She was now content with burying the past and moving forward.

When Mia and Janelle vacated the room, Rick stayed behind, closing the door behind them. He turned to Richmond and tossed him a cigar from his desk.

"Now, truth time, old man. You killed him, didn't you?"

"Maybe I did, maybe I didn't. Either way, he's handled, and our family is in the clear."

"Good. You know, I'll admit I have missed your cunning over the years. It was always something to rival."

"Well, get used to it, son. I'm not going anywhere, not anymore. If anyone dares try to touch this family again, it will be over my cold, dead corpse."

"I like the way you think. Welcome back."

"It's good to be back."

Chapter Twenty-nine

"Mommy, what if they don't like me? I never had cousins before."

Mia and Janelle shared a look, watching the nervous five-year-old. She was finally about to meet her cousins Meelah and Jonathan and her Aunt Asha and Uncle Terence. They had been taking some time out for Jenna to get adjusted to all the new family members, and they wanted her to develop a relationship with her father before they told her who he was. It was a failed attempt because the moment Miguel saw her he knew, and so did Jenna. Apparently, she had found a picture of him, and Richmond had explained who he was without telling Janelle.

"Sweetie, they are going to love you." Mia got down to her level and brushed her hand over the young girl's cheek. "Kyan loves you and they will too."

"I'm scared. Will you hold my hand?"

She smiled at Mia, and Mia felt her heart warm. She hadn't expected Jenna to accept her so quickly, but they had become fast friends. When Mia looked at Jenna, she thought so much about her little Chloe and how she hoped to have the chance to raise her and teach her things. She also wanted that chance with Tristen.

Even though the kids weren't her blood, she felt connected to them, and every time they saw her, they responded as if they knew who she was. She just hoped they could get the issues with their custody worked out, because she was ready to bring them home. They already had a room made up for them, pink on one side and blue on the other with the sky painted at the top.

Kyan had been a big help with getting the room together, and he seemed okay with the idea of having a new brother and sister, but Mia wanted to make sure. He was usually on board with anything she asked, and she was grateful for that. She could have never imagined having a better kid. She knew she was lucky in that sense.

Grabbing Jenna's free hand that did not contain her favorite doll, Mia walked her into Asha's living room. Meelah looked over, stopping what she was doing. Jonathan was with Kyan. He also stopped playing and ran in their direction as fast as his little legs would carry him. Reaching out a little, chubby arm, Jonathan studied the girl while chewing on his finger. "Aunt Mia, who dis?" He touched Jenna's face, and she let out a cute giggle. He started laughing too, and Mia felt Jenna release her hand to touch his cheek.

"Hey. This is Jenna, your cousin."

Jonathan's face scrunched, and he tilted his head to the side. "Cosen? Wut dat?"

Mia laughed quietly. "She's your cousin like Kyan is. She is your Uncle Miguel's daughter."

"Like Kyem?" He turned back to Jenna and pointed. "You do airpane too? I like airpane. Kyem do dat. Uncle Gel do it too."

Jenna looked at Mia with a confused look on her face, and Mia stepped in. "Kyan does the airplane with him. It's their thing. Kyan, baby, can you come do the airplane with Jonathan?"

When Kyan approached, Jonathan walked away but turned back to call out to his aunt. "She pretty, Aunt Mia. I pay wift her later." Jenna let her gorgeous smile show and let it drop when she saw Meelah approaching. Extending her hand, Jenna waited for Meelah to be introduced. Instead of taking her hand, Meelah looked at it and crossed her arms over her chest.

"Do you like *Frozen?*" Meelah asked bluntly. Jenna nodded and held up the Elsa doll she'd brought in with her. Meelah's eyes lit up. "She's my favorite," Meelah squealed. "Let's go play in my room. I have all the other dolls, too!"

The girls ran off. Janelle let out the breath she had been holding in and laughed at herself. "I swear I was nervous for her. She hasn't been around many kids, and I just hoped they all got along. They missed out on so many times together."

"I knew she would be fine. This is a good bunch of kids. We really got lucky." Mia's head turned toward the door, and when she turned back, she saw Janelle looking at her. "I'm sorry."

"For what? I know you're worried, but it will be okay. You will have those beautiful babies in that gorgeous room in no time. Sweetie, you're already an excellent mother. They're going to be so happy."

"I really hope so." Mia lowered her head and looked up to see her sister's nervous expression. "I'm so selfish. With everything going on, I forgot to ask how things went with Miguel. Have you guys made any headway?" Janelle's expression went from nervous to giddy, and Mia had to know. "Spill," Mia prodded and pulled her down on the couch. As Janelle began her story, Mia sat back with her hand on her cheek.

Arriving at Karen's house, Janelle wasn't sure what to expect. She had called and spoken to Karen, and Karen informed her that Miguel was on his way over. Apparently, he had received a call from Mia, telling him to head straight over to Karen's. When Janelle pulled up, she noticed that his car wasn't there. She felt her racing nerves calming down.

When she stepped in, she was greeted by the housekeeper and rounded the corner to find her little girl sitting on her grandmother's lap, telling her a story. Karen was completely entranced by the doe-eyed child and hung on her every word.

"And that really happened," she heard Jenna's enthusiastic voice say. Janelle let out a laugh, drawing their attention.

When Jenna saw her, she jumped up and raced over, hugging Janelle around the legs. "Mommy, you have to meet Mrs. Karen. She's nice."

Janelle looked at Karen nervously and said, "We've already met. I've known her for quite some time."

Jenna looked between the two women and sighed. "Does she know my daddy?"

"Your daddy? What about him?"

"Daddy's picture is here. I saw him."

Janelle was confused. They had never discussed Jenna's father, and as far as she knew, she didn't know a thing about him. "Baby, what are you talking about? How do you know what your daddy looks like?"

"Papa showed me his picture. I asked him if he was my daddy and he said no, that he was just Mommy's daddy, and he showed me his picture. Papa says I have his eyes."

Janelle felt the wind leaving her. She had no idea they had had these talks. She was stunned, but a part of her was happy she didn't have to explain it to her daughter. She was glad that part was already covered. Now she just had to break it to Miguel. Looking up at Karen, she saw that she also had questions. As if sensing the tension in the room, Karen called out to Jenna.

"Sweetheart, do you think you can run upstairs and check on Mrs. Kiyoko? See if she wants to show you more pictures of your daddy."

"Okay, Mrs. Karen." Jenna got as far as the foyer when they heard her little voice yell, "Daddy!"

Janelle rushed around the corner, and the look on Miguel's face was priceless. He looked down at the little girl and then back at Janelle. Karen rounded the corner, catching everything. "Jenna, sweetheart," she called out, "how about *you let your mommy and daddy talk? They need a minute."*

Janelle watched as Jenna placed her hand in Karen's and followed her to the stairs. Once they were out of view, Janelle stepped forward, reaching out to touch him. She knew he was blown away. He had left the party early and missed everything, including her reemergence into their lives. Touching him, she felt him shiver, and he closed his eyes, pulling her hand to his lips. He had yet to speak, and she just studied him, taking in all the changes to his body over the years. He was way more fit than she remembered. His face hadn't aged a bit. He was still the total package, and when he opened those eyes, those deep brown eyes, she felt her head leaning toward his.

When their lips touched, she felt like she was home. The kiss was hesitant, and it took him a minute to respond, but when he did, everything that had been bottled up erupted, and he grabbed her, pressing her hard against him. They stayed like this for what seemed like an eternity, and when he pulled back, he ran his hand down her face and placed his hand on the back of her neck.

"Where did you come from? How are you here? This has to be one of my crazy dreams. I

swear there is no way you are standing here and I have a child upstairs. This shit is not funny."

"I'm here, Miguel." She touched him, and he jumped back. "I wanted to see you, to tell you about her, but we had to get things settled, and I wasn't sure if you wanted this. I know it's a lot to spring on you, and if you don't want to know her, I understand. I didn't tell her about you. Dad did. I was just as shocked as you were that she knew you. I'm sorry—"

"What's her name?" he said, cutting her off.

She was caught off guard by his calm demeanor. He actually seemed almost excited. "Jenna."

"She's five, almost six," she heard him mumble. "Damn, I've missed five years of my baby's life. I can't believe I have a kid. Does she know . . . does she know why I wasn't around?"

"Honestly, I'm not sure what she knows or what he's told her about you. Up until about five minutes ago, I had no clue she knew anything. She seemed so happy to see you, so I assume everything he said was good. She was so excited to meet you."

"J, I'm nervous. I've never done this before. I don't know how to talk to a kid who's mine. What do I say to her? What does she like?"

She smiled at his cute rambling and felt her heart flutter. She thought he would be freaking out, and he was, but it was for a completely different reason. "She's your daughter, Miguel. She's gonna love you."

Miguel let a smile tug at his lips and caressed her hand. "I can't believe you're here. You're here, and you have my baby. This is crazy, but I'm excited. Can I meet her?"

Janelle stood silent, swearing that if there had been a gust of wind, it would blow her over. She had anticipated this moment.

"J?"

"Of course you can."

"I want her to love me. I want to be a big part of her life, J. Yours too."

She swore that was the sweetest thing he ever said, and she searched his eyes for sincerity and concluded that he was serious. He had never said anything about being anything more than what they were before, and she wanted to believe him, but her heart had been broken by him once before. She had to be cautious.

"Jenna is the most important thing in the world to me, Miguel. Just promise me you won't hurt her."

"Janelle, now that I know I have her, nothing in this world means more. I love her already."

She gave him a subtle nod and put her hand in his, and they walked up the stairs.

At first, she wasn't sure what room to start with, but Miguel seemed to know exactly where to go. He led her down to a room, and when he opened the door, he saw Jenna with his mother and grandmother and gave Janelle's hand a light kiss.

Looking down at their little girl, he leaned to her ear and whispered, "Marry me, J. Let me be her dad, but let me be your husband, too. I need you."

She looked at him with tears in her eyes, but before she could answer, Jenna interrupted. "Mommy, Daddy, come sit with us. Mrs. Karen showed me pictures of you when you were young."

Miguel let Jenna lead him down to the floor, and he gathered her in his arms, kissing the top of her head. "Actually, baby girl, that's Grandma Karen. She's my mommy."

"Really?" Jenna lit up. "I've never had a grandma before."

"Well, now you have two." Miguel smiled. "You have Grandma Karen and Kiyoko, and you have Daddy." He turned to look at Janelle. "Hopefully I will have you and Mommy too." He leaned to whisper in her ear, "Are you going to help me with that?"

"Yes, Daddy!" she squealed. "Just like in my dream."

"It's my dream too, baby. I want you to know I love you, baby girl."

"I love you too, Daddy."

"Wow." Mia elbowed Janelle in the side. They looked over to see Asha making her way into the room, and they stood to greet her. The girls all sat down, and the room was quiet until Asha broke the ice. She looked them both over, and they knew she was wondering what they were keeping from her.

"If you're discussing my brothers, you can talk in front of me unless it's about sex," she laughed. "If it's that, I don't want to hear it."

"Girl, please," Janelle sighed. "Sex is the last thing on my mind. I haven't had sex in a long time. I'm just trying to figure your brother out. Mimi says he's different, and I can admit when I see him with Jenna, he is the sweetest guy. I just don't want this to be a fleeting feeling. I'm afraid he's excited because we're here and that it will wear off after a while. I don't want to get my hopes up."

"He proposed to you," Mia blurted and slapped her hand over her mouth when Asha's eyes widened. "Sorry."

"My brother proposed? Wow."

"That's what I said," Mia laughed.

"Not funny, you guys. You know how I feel about him. I want to raise our daughter together, but I'm afraid. I don't want to get too close to him and have him back out again."

"J, he has grown so much." Asha rubbed her hand. "I wouldn't tell you this if it weren't true. I had a talk with him before all of this, and he was saying how much he wanted a family, how much he wanted to get married, and how he had missed his chance. He was talking about you."

"I hear you, and I get what you both have to say, but I need a little more time."

"How long are you going to keep him waiting?" Mia questioned.

"I don't know. I guess I'll know when it feels right."

They were still talking when they heard the voices of the guys. They didn't seem to get distracted until Mia heard the faint sounds of a baby crying. She shook it off until it got louder, and when she looked up to see Tyree holding baby Tristen, she stopped in midsentence and stood, walking over to him quickly. Miguel followed him, holding little Chloe, and Mia was overwhelmed. She wasn't sure what was going on. When she reached out to touch the tiny baby, he cooed, and she took him from Tyree's arms.

"What's going on, Ty? I thought they wouldn't let us bring them home until all the issues were settled. They said it could take months."

"That would have been true if Richmond hadn't found Chloe's mother. He tracked her down, and she signed away any rights to the kids. We're the only ones putting up a fight for them, and they couldn't stay in the hospital forever, so Terence pulled some strings. The adoption is still processing, but until then they're with us."

"Oh, God, Ty. I'm so happy."

"Good." He ran his hand through her hair. "Where is the boy? I want him to meet them."

"Ky, baby, come in here," Mia called out. "Come and meet your new brother and sister."

Kyan walked from the back and came up to his mother, looking at the baby in her arms. Tristen was half asleep, but when Kyan touched him, he moved. "He's so little." Kyan smiled.

"You want to hold him?"

"Can I?" When Mia nodded, Kyan reached his arms out and took the baby. Mia walked him to the couch and helped him get settled. He looked down at the small baby.

Running her hand over Kyan's shoulder, she sat down next to him, wanting to get her conversation with him out of the way. "So, how do you feel about the babies? Are you okay with all this? I know it's more than what you thought it would be."

"You wanted them, Mama."

"I know, but I want you to be okay with sharing your parents. I promise you, we will still be there for you. Now we just have a bigger family to love."

"I know that. I know you've been sad because you wanted a new baby, and now you have two. I wanted to be a big brother, and now I am. It's kind of cool."

"I'm glad you're happy, baby. I just wanted to make sure."

"Well, it's kind of late for that, but maybe they can help me out with something."

"Something like what?"

"Maybe now that you have actual babies, I can get you to stop calling me that," he laughed. "I'm ten, Mama."

"Fat chance. You're my first, and no matter how old you get, you're always my baby. Get used to it."

While Mia and Kyan cooed over the baby, Janelle walked over to Miguel and touched little Chloe. She was wide awake, clinging to his finger as he talked to her. He looked so at home with the baby in his arms that she couldn't help but smile. "I think she likes you."

"Yeah," Miguel said without looking up from the baby. "I kind of like her too. She's adorable. I just hate that I missed this with Jen."

"I'm sorry. I know you missed a lot and I really feel bad. But we couldn't be here."

He stepped forward. "J, I don't blame you. I know you had a hard decision to make, but you made the right one. I wasn't right back then, and I did a lot to hurt you, but I'm glad you had her. You've done an incredible job. I can't thank you enough."

"Miguel, having her was the best thing to happen in my life. I wouldn't trade one minute. I just wish she could have had us both. Seeing you like this, I know that you're not the same man I knew before. God, Miguel, I love you. I'm in love with you."

"I love you, J." He had never said it before, and it felt good to finally hear. She wasn't really sure what to say or do.

"I thought about you all the time. Looking at our daughter made me miss you so much."

"I didn't know how to handle losing you. I was pretty ridiculous for a while."

"I know." She smiled. "It's okay that you had your little whore stage. I just hope it's out of your system because your daughter and I might need a place to crash. You know, Rick's place is awesome, but it's missing something."

"What's that?"

"You."

"Me?" He grinned.

"I've lived without you for six years, and now that you know you want us, I want it too."

"I love you and Jenna so much. She's perfect. She's the best thing I ever did. I promise you I won't screw this up."

"We're gonna screw up sometimes, but at least we will have each other to pick up the pieces."

"So, my proposal, have you thought it over?"

"I have."

"And?"

"I can't make that kind of decision right now. We have to figure out if we're the same two people who fell in love. You have this trumped-up image of me, and maybe I'm not the same woman you remember."

"You're so much better than I remember, J. We were so young then, and I was a mess, but being with you these past few weeks has shown me that I could love you forever. I've spent a lot of time trying to find someone half as good as you, and now that I have the real thing, I'm not letting that go." Leaning in, she latched her lips on his, and they kissed for a few seconds before she pulled back. "What was that for?"

"I just love you, that's all. If you're serious and you want to try this thing out, then I'm all in. But I want you to be sure about all this."

After walking over and placing Chloe in Tyree's arms, he came back, fishing around in his pocket. When he pulled out a fresh set of keys, she looked at him curiously. "Here." He reached them to her. "They're yours."

"What is this for?"

"Our house. I was going to ask you and Jenna to move in before you mentioned it. I think it should be the next step for us."

Giving Miguel a shy grin, Janelle wrapped her arms around him. "In that case, yes. We will move in, and we'll see where it goes."

With a silly grin on his face, Miguel tugged her hand to his lips and kissed it. "I'm not trying to be funny, but I need a little something from you." As he roamed his eyes over her body, she knew what he was hinting at and gripped his hand tighter.

"Okay." She smiled. "I can agree to that, but you have to promise me something."

"Anything," he agreed before she even got her request out.

"I don't want this to change us because I think we're in a pretty good place."

Giving her a light kiss, he ran his hands down to grip her hips. "The only thing this will change is your mind. After I show you what really loving me is all about, I know you're going to marry me. You're not gonna want another woman getting all this good action."

Swatting at him playfully, she looked into his eyes and saw her future. Whether she admitted it out loud or not, she had already accepted the minute she saw him walk through the door. The thought of getting back to him was what had kept her sane over the years.

Wrapping her arms around his neck and breathing him in, she let out a joyous laugh. "Take me home?"

"Home?"

"Yes, to our home. I want to lock myself in with you, and I don't want to come out until the sun rises tomorrow. See if Jenna can stay the night here."

"Already covered." He smiled. "I asked Terence on the way here, and he said it was cool. I wanted tonight to just be you and me."

"Well, you got me. Let's go."

"Let's." He grinned, running his hand down her face.

Tyree grinned after watching his brother and Janelle make their speedy exit. "Looks like things are picking back up there."

"Yeah. I guess I got my answer." Mia beamed.

"About what?"

"They're getting married. He proposed."

"Miguel, my brother? Miguel proposed to someone?"

"Not just someone, baby. The one. She's the one for him."

"Yeah, she's the one who can rein his crazy ass in."

"You're silly." Mia pushed his head away in time to look up and see Jonathan standing in front of her. "Hey, baby boy, what's going on?"

"Mama call Daddy silly too. Wut dat?"

"Um . . ." Mia looked around the room, and they all laughed. "You guys are no help," she hissed.

"You have to start getting ready for questions like this, kitten. We have three little ones to answer to now."

"Three? Those two are going to be a while," Asha pointed out.

"It should be way more than three," Kyan quipped. "They're always—"

"Kyan," Tyree interjected.

"What, Dad? You are. Everyone jokes about it."

"They do?" Mia scanned the room and looked at Terence and Asha acting like they weren't listening.

"Well, son, I love your mama so much I can't help it. She's beautiful."

"Dad, that's gross."

"Son, it's life. How do you think you got here?"

"I try not to think about it," he laughed, standing up with Tristen. "Come on, little brother, let's get out of here before Mama and Daddy corrupt you before you can talk." He looked over at Chloe and shrugged his shoulders. "I'm sorry, little sis, I only have two hands. I'll come back for you."

Tyree looked to Mia and then back at Chloe. "Kitten, our son is crazy, but I'm glad he loves them already."

"Things are really working out, huh?"

"Just like I promised you they would. I told you, I got this, baby."

"That you do." She grinned, pulling his head to hers. "You always take care of me."

"I always will."

Chapter Thirty

Mia and Tyree had finally gotten the kids home, and while putting them to bed, she leaned over, looking down into their cribs. While she did this, Tyree stood back, watching her for a second, in awe of the woman he loved. Staring at her, he couldn't believe they were in this place. Any other time, he would be freaked out by the situation, but with everything that happened, all the obstacles they overcame, he was just happy. It was special, she was special, and now they were going to have three children to love. He had never felt more blessed.

Wrapping his arms around her small frame, he placed a light kiss on her neck, causing her to turn around in his arms. When her arms found refuge around his neck, he leaned in to claim a sweet kiss. Feeling her pulse racing, he scooped her into his arms and wrapped her legs around his waist.

Exploring her mouth, being careful not to drop her, he walked to their room and placed her on the bed. He had never been more ready for her, but before he could fully enjoy her, he had to shrug this feeling he had. His paternal instincts had kicked in, and he needed to be sure everything was fine. After excusing himself and creeping quietly down the hall, he walked toward the nursery and heard the cooing of baby Chloe. He stopped suddenly when he heard Kyan's voice and leaned against the wall.

"It's okay, little sis. I'm here. I know we don't know each other well, but we're going to be good friends, and you're going to love being with Mama and Dad. They're crazy and sometimes gross, but they are the best parents. I didn't always live with both of them, and it was a pretty rough time, but you don't have to worry about that. Now they're back together, and I don't think they will ever break up again. They figured out what Aunt Asha said everyone always knew, that they're crazy about each other. One day when you're older, we'll talk about so many things. I can't wait. Just know that we're lucky, little sis. Our mom and dad are amazing."

Without saying a word, Tyree walked back down to their room and closed the door quietly. Mia was already undressed, waiting for him on the bed. Without the usual urgency, he pulled his clothes off slowly, savoring the moment. Watching her watch him, he enjoyed the pleasure in her eyes. She was beautiful. She was always beautiful.

When he approached the bed in all his naked glory, she sat up, running her hands down his toned abs. "What happened? The kids okay?"

"The kids are fine." He pushed her back, hovering over her warm, naked body. "How did you know that's where I went?"

"You had your 'I'm worried about the kids' face on and then you jumped up and ran out," she chuckled. "So is everyone sleeping?"

He began to kiss her neck. He loved the soft moans escaping her. "No. Chloe woke up, but her big brother has her. He's going to be so good at this."

"I know."

"You showed him how to be kind and compassionate."

She grabbed the back of his neck and forced their lips together. "And you showed him how to be a real man and taught him about respect. The combination of us made him what he is. We make an excellent team, and now he will be a part of that team with the younger kids."

His eyes searched her body, and he saw her smile widen. "It's really happening, isn't it?"

"Yeah." She pulled him down, and his hands went all over her body. "It's unreal."

"I don't want to talk about the kids right now. I just want you." He ran his hand up her thigh.

"Uhh . . ." Mia's head rolled back, and Tyree sucked on her bottom lip. Rolling his hips against hers, his hand slid down her arms and gripped around her wrist as her body arched into his. Sliding his body against her, he moaned at the fire building between them. Every time he grazed over her she quivered. "Tyree." Her head twisted to the side, and she pressed a kiss to his earlobe that made him shiver. "Baby," she panted, wrapping her arm around his neck. "Make love to me, please."

"I can do that."

"I know you can," she giggled, bringing him back down for a rough kiss. She nipped his lip. He let out a growl, rolled his hips against hers, and made her body start to tremble. Sucking on his lip when he moved his hips and slid into her, he watched as Mia's mouth slammed shut just to open again.

"Uhh, that feels good." Her eyes fluttered shut, and her head dropped back into the pillow. He smiled looking down at her. She was the sexiest sight he had seen with her legs spread around him and her hands gripping his hips. Pushing harder into her, he felt her nails digging into his sides.

"You feel good." He smirked, running his hand down her side and gripping her thigh. "You feel so damn good," he hissed across her lips before running his kisses along her jaw and back to her neck.

"Tyree." She tilted her head to the side, and he buried himself in her neck. "Baby. God." She slammed her eyes shut when he gripped her hair, tugging her head and exposing her sweet neck. He moaned against it when he felt her warm, wet walls bathing him in her sweet juices. He loved how wet she got. He loved the way her body felt when he plunged himself inside.

He loved this. He loved smacking against her, tasting the screams, hearing the raspy exclamations of sheer pleasure. He couldn't get enough of the feeling he got when her nails dug into his back and the way his lips tingled from her kisses. It felt so good to have his hands on her. The burning in his lungs and the ache between his legs let him know his want for her had grown to an almost unhealthy high. This was his wife, his love, his everything, and nothing would ever curb the desire he had for her. Nothing would ever satisfy his hunger. Raking his teeth along her neck, he bit down on her collarbone and made her body arch toward him. Sinking farther into her, he buried his hands in her hair.

"I love you." He grabbed her face, slamming his lips back against hers. He flipped them over, his body never once leaving hers. Her hands held on to his face as she swiveled her hips against his. His hands instantly found her hips and guided her into their special rhythm as she rose to slam back into him.

"Mia," he moaned against her mouth, sliding his hands down her arched back. She gripped the back of his neck. He growled when her nails dug into his neck, leaving a stinging feeling that made him harder. Almost not able to contain himself, his hand slid up, tangling in her hair as she nibbled on his bottom lip before slipping her tongue back into his mouth.

"Don't stop. Please don't," he begged, hoping the feelings taking over his body lasted forever. Relaxing back into the heat and shivers and chills, he kissed her harder. Throwing her head back as his mouth bit down on her neck, he flipped her on her back, his pace quickening inside her.

Closing his eyes, taking in the moment, he realized how lucky he truly was. Having her and having their children was everything. He couldn't have asked for a better life, and here she was living it with him, sharing the best part of herself. He knew they had it rough growing up. Even with all the money and fame they still had their share of problems, but they overcame so much to get to where they were.

His speed started to increase, and each thrust became harder with all the thoughts filling his head. His mouth sucked hard on that pulse point in her neck because he knew he was almost there. He wanted her to hear what she did to him, but he also wanted to keep it down and not disturb the children. Sucking on her neck while still driving into her caused a domino effect. Joining him in his erratic thrusts, she moved beneath him, taking it to a new level of intensity.

"Tyree, faster," she begged, sliding her hips back and forth as he increased his speed. "Mmm, Tyree." She dug her nails into his back and made him groan into her neck. "God, you feel so, uhh, more . . . I want to feel . . . Tyree!"

"Shh, kitten. The kids." He bit down on her lip. "You can't do that because then I'll want to get loud and we will wake up not only the kids, but the whole damn street." His speed increased, and he pushed in deeper, hitting a spot he never touched before.

"Our closest neighbor is a mile away."

"That's how loud you make me want to get. Just, uumm, just keep it down. Please?"

"Mmhmm," she moaned against his lips, trying desperately to catch her breath, but he could tell it was nearly impossible with him hitting the same spot over and over again. He felt it, he could feel it building up in him, and by the way she was thrashing around, he knew it was building in her too.

"Mia," he whispered, knowing that if he hit that spot one more time, she was done for, and as soon as she exploded, he wouldn't be far behind. He made the move he knew would end it all, and her back arched, bringing her breasts in perfect alignment with his mouth. Feeling the shudders of her body, he popped her breast in his mouth to quiet the screams. He had never screamed before, but this time he let it out against her breast. While he sucked, she dug her nails into his back, screaming into his shoulder as her walls clenched around him. The hot tingles washed over both their bodies, and the only sound left was the loud panting they both tried to regulate.

"That was pretty awesome," she spoke, finally catching her breath.

"We're pretty awesome and apparently gross."

"Huh?"

"I heard Kyan telling Chloe we were great parents, but we're gross. Do we really have that much sex?"

Mia laughed, and he sat up skeptically. "Are you serious? We have three kids. We have more sex than anyone I know."

"Hey now, two of those we didn't have naturally." He saw the look on her face, and he made her face him. "What's wrong?"

"Are they gonna grow up one day and not be happy because they're stuck with us, because their mother is dead? What if we're not enough?"

He pulled her closer and kissed her forehead. "Baby, stop that. We discussed this, and I don't want you thinking that way. This family only works because of you. Those kids already love you, and when they are older, we are going to sit them down and tell them about Chloe. But they will never want for anything. Those kids are going to have a great life, and we will make it possible. Just because you didn't have them doesn't make them any less ours than Kyan."

"Why did she tell me not to mention her to them?"

"She didn't want you to have to explain that you aren't their birth mother. She wanted it to be easier for us."

"Why us?"

"Why not us? We love them, and we loved her. Don't worry. You will be great. You're already great, and I couldn't ask for a better partner."

"How did I get you? How do I deserve a man as wonderful as you?"

"You don't." He shrugged. "But you got me anyways," he laughed.

She sat up, pulling his lips to hers. "You're such a great man. Damn, I love you."

"I love you too, kitten."

She smiled and lay down, closing her eyes. Suddenly they popped back open. "I never figured it out."

"Figured what out?"

"Why you call me that."

"You really have to ask?" He flipped over and ran her hand down his back, and she chuckled.

"Guess I do go a little overboard. Does it hurt?"

"No." He kissed her, laying her on her back. "Lets me know I'm doing it right."

"I thought the screaming did that."

"The screaming helps, but the scratching got you your name." He ran his hand over her chest and stopped near her heart. "And this got you me."

"How long can I keep you?"

"Forever. You're not getting rid of me."

"You promise?"

"Yes, baby. It's always going to be you and me and our kids. I will love you for the rest of my life."